Praise for *Farnsworth's Secret War*

"It is one thing to be informed or entertained by what you read, but this author transports the reader into the nightmares of combat and the bed of lovers with equal emotion and intensity. If you have served in the military or remember the Vietnam War, you immediately grasp the fear and vulnerability of soldiers on the battlefield.

"The trauma of war and the complexities of human relationships come alive both artistically and boldly. The mysteries and intricacies of special military operations drive the reader page by page and leave you wanting more.

"*Farnsworth's Secret War* achieves all of this in a must-read novel. The story mesmerizes the reader with the author's depth of insight into the human condition and the conflicting pursuits of peace, love, and war."

—Priscilla Berry, PhD

"*Farnsworth's Secret War* reflects on the human tragedy of war and how it affects the soldier on a very personal level. The postwar romantic interludes are exquisitely presented and add to the intrigue of the storyline.

"The author makes you a fan of the main character, Farnsworth, and you as a reader want him to win his battles in war as well as in his personal life. It is a satisfying reading experience."

—Sandy Livingston, Pastry Chef

"With my having spent time in Southeast Asia, I find *Farnworth's Secret War* brings back memories: It was a long year. Ron has such a perceptive way of describing the terrible conditions of war, that his detailed writing encourages you to keep reading ... enjoyably."

—Phillip H. Parsons, CEO

FARNSWORTH'S SECRET WAR

FROM WEST POINT TO LOVE AND WAR

RON AUTREY

Book design by Sagaponack Books & Design
Cover design by Kerry Jesberger at Aero Gallerie

ISBNs
979-8-9881881-3-1 (softcover)
979-8-9881881-4-8 (hardcover)
979-8-9881881-5-5 (e-book)

Library of Congress Control Number: 2025901117

Summary:
Farnsworth's Secret War is a novel based on the life of a US Army intelligence officer and his secret missions during the Vietnam War and afterward, in Turkey, Germany, and Alaska, while juggling love affairs back in the USA.

FIC032000 Fiction / War & Military
FIC027220 Fiction / Romance / Military
FIC002000 Fiction / Action & Adventure

RonAutrey.com

JSA Publishing
Ponte Vedra Beach, Florida

Printed and bound in the United States of America
First Edition

Acknowledgments

I could not have accomplished the work required to complete this book without the professional assistance provided by copyeditor Beth Mansbridge and publishing consultant Frances Keiser. My endless thanks go to my friends and family who provided the encouragement I needed to pursue my dream of becoming a published author.

*Never think that war, no matter how necessary,
nor how justified, is not a crime.*

—Ernest Hemingway

Contents

Chapter 1

The Pentagon

aj. Richard Thomas Farnsworth arrived in Washington, DC, on December 7, 1972. A black Department of Defense sedan transported him to the century-old Willard Hotel at 1401 Pennsylvania Avenue NW. He did not need to check in. The Department of the Army kept two adjoining suites for use by the United States Army chief of staff and other staff officers. Three-star Gen. Thaddeus Broughton was vice chief of staff of the army and a close friend of Army Chief of Staff Gen. Creighton W. Abrams. General Broughton was also the father of the woman Richard Farnsworth was intimately involved with. High-ranking military officers visiting the Pentagon frequently stayed at the Willard Hotel prior to White House briefings and House Intelligence Committee meetings. Foreign diplomats and Defense Department officials were also frequent guests at the Willard. For this trip, General Broughton's staff had made Major Farnsworth's arrangements for travel and accommodation.

Richard skipped dinner and went directly to the hotel's famous Round Robin Bar for a Hayman's Gin martini straight up. The scene could have been a stage set for the next James Bond movie. The rich, century-old wood paneling and dense marble bar had seen the likes of President Abraham Lincoln, Mark Twain, Walt Whitman, and hundreds of foreign heads of state. In 1963, Dr. Martin Luther King Jr. visited the Willard bar and worked on his iconic "I Have a Dream" speech in the lobby outside the Round Robin.

Relaxing on a plush leather banquette, Richard savored his martini while thinking about the last few years and the upheaval his life had seen since returning from the war in Vietnam. In the war, he'd lived in a tragic and highly focused compartment defined by a sense of duty and an obligation to his troops. The drumbeat of battle and life in the bush pushed aside thoughts of the outside world. The realm of normalcy he had crafted from months of deadly incursions into enemy territory had hardened his emotional responses to the events and people outside the arena of battle in Vietnam.

While politicians and clueless civilians contemplated the victorious claims made through the course of the war by Commanding General Westmoreland, Richard still saw only visions of death and bloodshed. The Tet Offensive was five years ago, yet remained a fresh memory. Still, he knew he had to transition—remake his persona and the way he interacted with his family and friends.

In the war, Richard had served in the Army Security Agency's 405th Radio Research Battalion. Their secret mission was to provide electronic surveillance and collect intelligence on the enemy's locations and troop numbers. ASA companies were positioned with the Fifth Special Forces Group near and sometimes behind enemy lines. They were also attached to army infantry and armored cavalry units that provided firepower for the ASA specialists as they set up radio direction-finding equipment to triangulate the location of intercepted enemy radio transmissions.

The first casualty in Vietnam was an ASA infantry soldier stationed at Tan Son Nhut Air Base on the outskirts of Saigon. On December 22, 1961, 25-year-old Specialist 4 James "Tom" Davis was wounded in an ambush and shot in the head by the Viet Cong while he was attempting to pull his Army of the Republic of Vietnam driver from the wreckage of their vehicle. The next morning at 0630 hours, Maj. Richard Farnsworth stepped out of the Willard Hotel dressed in his Class A uniform adorned with gold oak clusters on his collar, along with four rows of service and combat medals, and his combat infantry and paratrooper badges. The Army Security Agency patch—a hand clutching two lightning bolts—was prominently displayed on his left shoulder. He was the perfect image of the ideal army officer: six feet of hardened good looks, with military-style cropped black hair and penetrating blue eyes that commanded immediate attention from anyone he encountered.

A driver in a black sedan was waiting for Richard at the hotel entrance loop for the ten-minute drive to Pentagon City in Arlington County, Virginia. "Good morning, Major. You're getting an early start. The traffic will be light. You will find bottled water in the armrest. We can stop for a coffee if you like."

Richard replied, "No, thank you, I'm fine."

After the driver was in the flow of traffic, he said, "Yesterday was a mess. The war protestors had Pennsylvania Avenue completely shut down. It took an hour for the Capitol Police to clear them out."

Richard was thinking about the soldiers in his company who had died in battle. *Their wives and mothers and fathers could rightfully protest, but they do not. Most of them honor the memory of their loved ones and put up a façade of noble patriotism.* He knew that deep in their thoughts they were screaming at everyone and asking, *"Why my son? Why did he have to die!"* The student protestors had good intentions, Richard assumed, though their methods were often disruptive and lacking real substance. Their only impact came from the large number of chanting and flag-burning activists they were able to assemble.

The driver pulled on to the loop road in front of the Pentagon, and Richard said, "Pull around to the river entrance if you can, please."

The driver did as instructed. "Have a blessed day, Major. Perhaps I'll see you for a pickup later."

Richard thanked the driver and got out of the vehicle.

Three-star Gen. Thaddeus Broughton had an office in the National Military Command Center. Richard had been to the six-million-square-foot octagonal military complex many times before. After returning from his last deployment in Vietnam, in 1970, Richard, an ASA army captain at the time, was debriefed by General Broughton's staff officers. Also during his assignment at Fort McNair Army Base in DC, he had developed and presented intelligence briefings to the task forces and staff departments based in the Pentagon.

Richard was casually chatting with General Broughton's personal assistant when the general abruptly walked by and said, "Stand by, I will be with you in five minutes."

The general entered his office and closed the door. Richard could hear the general's loud but muffled voice shouting at whoever was on the other end of the phone line. After two minutes of the heated exchange, Richard clearly heard the phone slamming down on the receiver, followed by what sounded like "That stupid bastard!"

The phone on the assistant's desk beeped once and she answered it, nodded, and turned toward Richard, saying, "The general will see you now."

As Richard entered the office and before he could raise his arm to salute, General Broughton stood behind his desk and said, "Come in, Major, and have a seat. This may take a while."

Chapter 2

A Time for War

In the spring of 1967, 24-year-old 2nd Lt. Richard Farnsworth received orders assigning him and others in his company to a support group attached to the US Special Forces border outpost at Loc Ninh in the Bình Long province of Vietnam. Richard would join 400,000 other army soldiers and 80,000 marines locked in a guerilla war with over 430,000 battle-hardened Viet Cong guerrillas. It was a war which half of the people back home thought was a mistake. Families and friends of soldiers fighting the war in Vietnam were tired of measuring success by body counts and kill ratios. Potential draftees and college students joined forces to protest the war. Some young men left the country to avoid being drafted into the US military. The messaging from Gen. William C. Westmoreland and President Lyndon B. Johnson that we were winning the war appeared to be more of a political effort to counter the protests and criticism of the war in Vietnam.

Richard's undergraduate degree at West Point was in engineering management. He was not a pilot and his training was like other ground operations units. He did not pilot aircraft, yet he was proficient at jumping out of them. In Vietnam, Army Security Agency personnel supported Military

Assistance Command Vietnam and were attached to army infantry and cavalry units. Some ASA Special Operations teams were assigned to Army Special Forces companies. While the ASA mission included studying, listening, and intelligence gathering, the assignments were not without danger and exposure to enemy fire.

After joining the 509th Radio Research Unit, Richard was deployed to Vietnam. As platoon leader, Richard led his ASA team on weeklong missions to locate and mark future radio tower sites on and around the hills outside of the Khe Sanh Combat Base camp. They were accompanied by three infantry platoons from the Fifth Special Forces group. They provided a protective perimeter and enough firepower to combat and repel the VC forces patrolling the area. The ASA's airborne battalion provided single-engine De Havilland RU-6 Beaver aircraft, flying at 160 mph at low altitudes, to plot enemy locations using landmarks and crude radio signal detection methods. The slow-moving planes were easy targets for enemy ground fire. When army platoons were located by the enemy, they were readily exposed to sniper fire. Richard's physical height and stature made him a first-choice target for Vietnamese guerilla soldiers. After three months and the completion of a dozen radio towers—or elephant cages, as the infantry soldiers called them—Richard and his ASA team returned to the remote combat base camp at Khe Sanh. Khe Sanh Combat Base—KSCB—would soon become ground zero for some of the deadliest combat operations.

At Khe Sanh, Richard's Army Security Agency platoon had a new mission: to locate and monitor enemy radio transmitters. This required stealthy squad movements to suspected enemy signal detection points. The intercepted intelligence would be analyzed by ASA signal security specialists and shared with the commanders of the Second Brigade of the First Infantry

Division. Death came to the very first patrol when Signal Supply Specialist Carlos "Sonny" Button was killed after stepping on a mud mine crafted from a recovered US M26 grenade. The dried mud cracked open, detonating the grenade when it was stepped on. First Platoon's S.Sgt. Donald Blake was also seriously injured in the explosion.

Richard's team lost a dozen more men over the following three months. Injury and death came indiscriminately to voice interceptors, teletype operators, linguists, and radio repairmen. The Special Forces soldiers were regularly targeted by sniper fire and enemy ambushes. The sound of mortar fire was a constant background noise in the Vietnamese jungle outside of Khe Sanh. Those who avoided injury from gunfire or mortars suffered from exhaustion and mental fatigue that robbed good soldiers of the will to engage the enemy.

Chapter 3

1968 – Tet Offensive

The Tet Offensive in January of 1968 was well planned by the Viet Cong and caught US forces by surprise, when 85,000 Viet Cong soldiers staged simultaneous attacks on five major Vietnamese cities and dozens of military bases over a two-month period. Richard lost 17 men, and over 100 more were wounded during the offensive. Not only was the Army Security Agency caught off guard. The entire US Command suffered significant casualties in the surprise attacks.

Richard's commanding officer had been in the country for 13 months and was starting his second tour. He had troops spread out and posted with cavalry and infantry platoons in a dozen outposts near Saigon's provincial capitals. Patrols endured days of boredom punctuated by ambushes that sent young men home in wheelchairs and body bags. ASA specialists were working with army engineers and marine platoons in the construction of radio towers and placement of listening devices near and sometimes behind enemy lines. The activity invited attacks from North Vietnamese Army (NVA) sappers (experts in demolitions, booby traps, and ambushes) and snipers. The antenna towers provided an essential component in the process of triangulating intercepted enemy radio signals. ASA teams provided combat troops with coordinates to locate and attack enemy forces.

The Second and Third Battalions of the Third Marine Regiment were on the ground engaging the enemy controlling Hills 861 and 881 north and south. The hills surrounding the base at Khe Sanh provided the enemy visual observation of the base and a platform for their artillery pieces and rocket launchers. Army and marine outposts near Khe Sanh Combat Base were under constant artillery assault and mortar fire from the People's Army of Vietnam. The longer range of the PAVN's 130mm and 152mm artillery overmatched the marine firepower, making it difficult to drive the PAVN forces out of the area around KSCB.

The role of Richard's radio research team was essential to the survival of the base camp at Khe Sanh. The ASA's 224th Aviation Battalion was armed with a newer fleet of aircraft which supported Richard's squads. The airborne missions were flown in twin-engine Beechcraft King Air RU-21 planes equipped with onboard radio direction finders and Doppler inertial navigation systems which provided 360-degree direction-finding coverage. Military Assistance Command, Vietnam, flew 13-hour missions from Cam Ranh Air Base over the base and outposts at Khe Sanh. RU-21 and RP-2E aircraft flew "ferret" missions with the call sign "Crazy Cat," and intercepted enemy voice and Morse code signals that the ASA radio research specialists would interpret to provide real-time intelligence for US combat forces.

The intelligence gathered by Richard's team and the other ASA companies, coupled with the USAF and marine combat missions, held back three divisions of the People's Army of Vietnam forces converging on Khe Sanh. Observation flights showed the locations of the enemy assembled in large numbers within striking distance of the base. While some in the US Command Center believed the battles around Khe Sanh were meant to be a distraction to the planned Tet Offensive, General Westmoreland saw the situation as an opportunity to effectively engage and kill the enemy in a remote, unpopulated area.

On January 20, 1968, Lt. Gen. Robert E. Wakefield learned from an enemy defector that an attack was planned for Hills 881 and 861, and the main base at Khe Sanh. The Second Battalion, 26th Marines prepared for battle. Shortly after midnight on January 21, 300 PAVN troops attacked Hill 861. They were supported by bracketed artillery fire and managed to penetrate the perimeter, but were driven back after engaging in close combat with the marines.

The main base at Khe Sanh was severely damaged by a barrage of hundreds of mortar rounds and rockets. Buildings were leveled and the ammunitions dump destroyed. Tear gas cannisters and mortar rounds from the dump were blown into the air and exploded on impact. During the attack on KSCB, 3 kilometers to the south, Khe Sanh village was attacked by a battalion-strength PAVN force. Rescue attempts by the marines and an ARVN regional force company in nine UH-1 helicopters were repelled and abandoned the fight after five marines and many of the ARVN troops were killed. The deputy advisor to the Quảng Trị Province Lt. Gen. Joseph Seymore was killed in the attack. The next morning the remaining Americans were evacuated from the village by helicopter.

The surviving local ARVN fighters were escorted to the base at Khe Sanh. On January 22, 1968, General Westmoreland ordered the most concentrated aerial bombing campaign in the history of warfare. The USAF launched a campaign to suppress the enemy attacks. Over a three-month period, Operation Niagara flew daily missions in 350 tactical fighter-bombers and 60 B-52s, dropping over 14,000 tons of bombs. The US Marine Corps and US Navy aviators dropped another 17,000 tons. Bravo Company from Marine First Battalion, Ninth Marine Regiment, fired nearly 200,000 artillery rounds in defense of the base. Enemy forces suffered over a thousand casualties in a bloody three-day battle that took the lives of 155 US Marines and wounded 425 more. The fighting continued in and around the base at Khe Sanh, but not for Richard and his men. Ten went home in body bags, along with a dozen more severely wounded Army Security Agency soldiers, including Lt. Richard Farnsworth. Richard was severely injured by shrapnel in the rocket barrage on Khe Sanh. On the night of the initial attack on KSCB, Richard was in the control center trying to protect some of the sensitive electronic surveillance equipment when a rocket exploded just outside the hut. The explosion was louder than anything he had ever experienced … and then, nothing.

No sound. No light. Only darkness and searing pain.

A white-hot shard of steel had pierced the upper right side of his chest and upper lobe of his right lung. Blood was gushing and spurting, and he soon lost consciousness.

After medics rushed in and revived him, they treated his excruciating pain with an aggressive 15 mg shot of morphine. They cleaned the wound and placed a pressure bandage on his chest. The greatest concern for Richard's injury was the risk of infection. Gunshot and shrapnel wounds are much more likely to become infected. The prompt attention by medics at Khe Sanh was key to avoiding what could have been a death sentence from the loss of blood and toxic shock.

In less than an hour, Richard was transported by a Huey UH-1 "dustoff" helicopter to Camp Evans field hospital in the Quảng Trị Provence. After evaluation and treatment of the shrapnel wound, and a night of drug-induced rest, Richard was transported by helicopter to the 45th Surgical Hospital at Tay Ninh. It lacked the medical capabilities for treatment of his damaged lung, so arrangements were made to transport him to Clark Air Force Base in the Philippines. Two weeks later, Lt. Richard Farnsworth was resting in a hospital bed in Washington, DC, at Walter Reed Army Medical Center.

Richard recovered from his wounds, but like many patriots who had served in combat, his only desire was to return to Vietnam and rejoin his ASA company and the soldiers he had so closely bonded with on the battlefield.

While recovering at Walter Reed, Richard had been visited by Gen. Jack V. Mackmull and his aide, Maj. Don Clemmons. As commander of the 164th Combat Aviation Group in Vietnam, Mackmull was aware of Richard's ASA missions and battlefield valor. He promoted Richard to 1st lieutenant and awarded him a Purple Heart and a Bronze Star, along with other Vietnam service medals and unit citations. The medals and commendations did very little to alleviate Richard's feelings of remorse over the deaths of his men. As a result of his extended hospitalization, the army provided him with 30 days of leave time and commercial transportation home.

Home was an uncomfortable word for Richard. His memories of their home in Santaquin, Utah, were not pleasant. His mother, Eloise, was his savior and the only reason he had survived his younger years growing up on the north shore of Lake Utah. His father, Gardner Farnsworth, was an eccentric genius who had made and lost a million dollars by the time he was 40 years old. He invented the first electronic television, along with over a hundred other notable electronic inventions.

When Richard was leaving for Vietnam in 1967, his father was busy with fusion research at Brigham Young University. Except for a lack of funding, he would have likely succeeded in that endeavor. While Richard was struggling with adolescence and the issues of teenage life in the sixties, Gardner Farnsworth was working on electron microscopy and infrared night vision. When his father was not in the lab, he was home experimenting with the effects of excessive alcohol consumption.

Chapter 4

Back to Vietnam

In April of 1968, three brigades of the US Army's First Cavalry and the 101st Airborne Divisions ended the siege of the Khe Sanh Combat Base with a massive airmobile operation. The vulnerable base was abandoned after the Tet Offensive wound down in July of 1968. The bloody six-month-long Battle of Khe Sanh cost the lives of 1,000 US soldiers and more than 5,000 enemy combatants. The mission of the Army Security Agency in Vietnam was ongoing, and much of the surveillance and signal intercept tasks were now performed by the ASA's 224th Aviation Battalion in Da Nang, Nha Trang, and Saigon. ASA techs were packed into RU-21 twin-engine airplanes equipped with 360-degree direction-finding capability. The signal intercept technology and the intelligence gathered provided a map for the US bombing campaigns which would continue into the next decade.

In November of 1968, Richard returned to Vietnam and was assigned the title of executive officer—XO—to the 371st ASA Company attached to the First Army Cavalry Division. The complexities and logistics of the ASA airborne missions kept him busy, distracting his mind from his men who had died at Khe Sanh. The 371st was successful by all measures of wartime metrics, but planes and men's lives were still lost. Richard had the job of notifying families back home that their husbands, sons, or fathers would be coming home in a flag-draped casket. The loss of his men put Richard in a mental state which robbed him of any open emotions. He carried on performing his duties; however, most of the time his face had a 1,000-yard stare which revealed nothing—not hate, not compassion—just a pale, cold, expressionless portrait. The feelings of loss, fear, and anxiety were suppressed into a part of his brain which did not speak to the outside world.

The 371st ASA Company served well, and received two Presidential Unit Citations, four Meritorious Unit Commendations, and a Valorous Unit Award. In the last days of his 12-month second tour, Richard's excursions into the combat zone were 5,000 feet above the jungle in a Bell OH-58 observation helicopter. The effectiveness of the listening and locator network installed by the ASA provided precise locations of enemy radio transmissions which were quickly targeted by machine gun suppression fire and 2.75-inch air-to-ground missile fire from H-34 Choctaw gunships.

***

Richard had only two weeks left in his second tour in Vietnam. There were 6,000 ASA troops in Vietnam. He would be replaced and the war would continue. On this day the war ended for four of his men when their EH-1H Bell Huey was shot down in Phuoc Long Province. They were on an airborne intercept and locate mission when they received enemy ground fire and crashed, killing everyone on board. The downed aircraft was later destroyed by US airstrikes to keep the enemy from recovering the onboard mission equipment. Four ASA soldiers were going home in body bags: CW2 Jack Knepp (California), WO1 Dennis Bogle (Oklahoma), SP4 Henry

Heide II (Florida), and SP4 James Smith (Oklahoma)—all killed in action.

For Richard the war would play on in his head. He would refight every battle and remember every lost friend in arms. He was determined to avoid the debilitating depression and anxiety so many of his fellow soldiers experienced after their combat tours. Alcohol and drugs took the lives of far too many soldiers after their return home. He knew this firsthand, from memories of his father wallowing in a sea of self-pity after drinking himself into a state of semiconsciousness. There had to be more to life than sadness.

Chapter 5

1970 – Fort Devens, Massachusetts

After two back-to-back tours in Vietnam, Richard flew from Saigon to Honolulu for the army's prescribed 12-day R&R. He had previously done the stroll down Kalakaua Avenue with a few of his men, after the first tour. The lucky soldiers who survived the war dubbed it the I&I, or intoxication and intercourse tour. He missed his mother, and as an only child he didn't have any other family to visit when he returned to his home in Utah. Richard was halfway through his planned 10-year military career and he often wondered if it was worth it. With his Army Security Agency training, he could easily lean on his father's old associates at RCA for a meaningful job. For now, after what he had been through, it wasn't enough.

After taking some accrued leave time and visiting his mother in Provo, Utah, Richard reported for duty at the ASA Command Headquarters at Fort Devens in Lancaster, Massachusetts. It was a good time to mentally recuperate and figure out what his future should be: in or out of the army. Richard fit in well with Fort Devens's cadre in Charlie Company. To friends and senior staff, he was known as "LT Rick" or just "LT." Richard had pushed aside the mental anguish that followed him home from the war zone. It may have been a bogus defense mechanism, but it worked. His men saw him as smart and quick-witted, with an endless supply of dry humor and anything-goes behavioral antics. Despite LT's easy demeanor, no one questioned his authority or leadership in the ASA's 405th Battalion.

Life on the base was safe and pleasant, with ample time to reflect on and heal the wounds of war. Looking back on the past five years, Richard thought about his journey from four years at the United States Military Academy at West Point and his army commission as a 2nd lieutenant in 1965, to a war still raging on with young men and women dying for a cause now obscured by issues of morality and politically driven agendas.

It was day two on base. After a rigorous workout and a two-mile run, Richard showered and dressed in the winter uniform, and visited the officers mess hall for breakfast. He was scheduled to meet with the company commanding officer (CO) at 0900 hours.

As Richard entered the food line, he heard a voice call out farther down the line: "All you fresh lieutenants look alike. You look like you just got off the bus from Utah!"

Richard stared down the line to spot his S.Sgt. Buster Browning from the 371st, grinning from ear to ear. Buster and Richard had become close friends during the last combat tour.

"Buster," Richard yelled back, "I can't believe it's you! Here, of all places."

Buster replied, "I have a break at 0830. Let's talk then."

Richard and Buster met outside the mess hall and walked along the wide promenade separating the parade field from the administration building and barracks.

"I am damn happy to see you, Buster. How did you end up with orders to Devens?"

In Vietnam, Buster was a transplant from the Fifth Special Forces. He washed out after a knee injury took him off the front lines.

"Rick, I had the opportunity to pick up an electronics intercept MOS and be reassigned to the ASA."

Richard replied, "That's wonderful. What platoon?"

Buster replied, "F Troop."

The electronics radio repair and operations support positions were assigned to F-Platoon. It was a catchall group for soldiers in a holding pattern for the army's Officer Candidate School at Fort Moore, near Columbus, Georgia. Richard's platoons included traffic decoders, intelligence analysts, and interrogation specialists.

"So, Buster, what's with the three chevrons? You were a sergeant first class when I left you in Khe Sanh."

In a low voice he replied, "You know some of the Fifth Special Forces squads got relocated to Devens. When I was at the airport preparing to fly here from Bragg, this long-haired hippie dipshit got in my face. I gave him the old *De oppresso liber* salute ("To Free the Oppressed"), throat-punched him, and broke his nose. He went to the ER, and the airport police turned me over to army CID."

For the next minute or two, Richard and Buster strolled without speaking.

Buster spoke first. "I kept my clearance, but DOD pulled my special intelligence access. So I'm on the front line—the chow line."

Richard remarked, "You're a cook?"

"No, Einstein, I'm a gourmet chef in the potato-peeling department. Yeah, I'm a cook!"

The Army Security Agency operated at Top Secret levels. MPs, cooks, and radio operators had to maintain a posture and behavior that complied with Defense Department regulations for Top Secret Clearances and access to special intelligence. Drunkenness, adultery, or other crimes and misdemeanors could end careers in the ASA.

After a glance at his watch, he said, "Hey, LT, I have to get back to the mess hall. Let's catch up over a beer later."

"Count on it, Buster!" Richard kept walking toward the Command Headquarters Building for his introduction to the C Company commanding officer.

He was looking down at the cracks in the pavement when the distinct sound of rapid footfalls clicking toward him got his attention. He raised his head in time to see one of the most beautiful women he had ever encountered in the army. Her blonde hair was neatly tucked under a tilted army-green garrison cap. Her knee-length skirt did not hide the curves of her perfectly proportioned physique.

Approaching him, she said, "Good morning, Lieutenant."

Richard replied, "And a very good morning to you, ma'am."

She passed him with the same short, unbroken stride.

Richard thought, *Yes, a very good morning indeed.*

Army Security Agency Capt. Gene Mason from Springfield, Tennessee, was a third-generation legacy in the US Army. He'd fought in some of the same battles as Richard in the 303rd, and also in the 409th Radio Research Unit attached to the Eleventh Armored Cavalry during the Tet Offensive. Captain Mason was smaller in stature than Richard and his demeanor was clear-eyed, seasoned, and army tough.

Richard entered Mason's office and stood at attention. "Lt. Richard Farnsworth reporting for duty, sir."

"At ease, Lieutenant, have a seat."

Richard had been in the army long enough to make quick assessments of most people he encountered. As to Captain Mason, he had a good feeling. They shared the same experiences and troubled recollections of the war in Vietnam.

At lunch, Richard skipped the chow line. He sat alone with a cup of coffee and stared blankly across the officers mess hall. Sensing a presence, he turned to face the same woman he had encountered that morning on the promenade.

"Permission to sit, Lieutenant?"

Richard immediately stood and pulled out the chair adjacent to his.

She set her tray down and put out her hand. "I'm Stacie Shatner, Alpha Company, 04 Bravo and 96-Bravo."

Richard knew that meant she was an expert language interpreter with intelligence training. "In that case, Lieutenant Shatner, please join me."

Relationships developed quickly on the base. The uncertainty of what the future held cut away pretense and unnecessary social protocol. Richard was as handsome as Stacie was beautiful. Together they presented an enviable and obvious made-for-each-other image.

Stacie and Richard soon became inseparable. They had to remain discreet and keep their personal feelings and their time together obscured from daily army life. Both of their army careers depended on their security clearances and access levels. As an ASA linguist, Stacie was fluent in Russian, Chinese, Arabic, and Vietnamese. The army had listening posts around the world, and the intercepted traffic was fed to expansive computer banks for analysis by ASA officers and noncommissioned soldiers with special analytic skills. Her skills proved her to be invaluable in the analysis of Vietnamese and Russian radio traffic during the Vietnam War.

The historically famous Walden Pond lies 18 miles from Fort Devens. It was the first choice for weekend leave time. Stacie and Rick spent many Saturday afternoons on the shore of Walden Pond, sipping wine and enjoying the picturesque lakeside scenes. Occasionally they made the 40-mile drive to downtown Boston and stayed in a quaint boutique inn on the Boston Commons.

Their love affair stayed on the periphery of what could easily become a deeper, more meaningful relationship. The intensity of their feelings caused more concern than satisfaction. They knew they could be reassigned for duty at some remote overseas post. Orders to Alaska, Turkey, Japan, or back to Vietnam could come at any time. While other soldiers returning from the war often found duty stations stateside or at desirable bases in Germany and Thailand, the ASA listening posts were in remote locations such as Shemya, Alaska, and Sinop, Turkey. Richard was at a low risk for such an assignment. Stacie was a prime target.

Richard's duty schedule kept him busy during the day, and he had evening conferences with his men. They reviewed the soft topics of army life. As the company XO, he was expected to enlighten the troops on the topics of racism and protocol for off-base behavior. He offered his counseling services to soldiers experiencing psychological stress or family problems back home. He also dealt with disciplinary matters when required.

After a lengthy morning of performance reviews and training module evaluations, Richard left his office and headed to the mess hall for fresh coffee.

Along the way a voice called out: "LT! You've been avoiding me."

Richard replied, "No, Buster, you know I've been busy getting oriented and setting up new training modules for Charlie Company."

That was partly true. Buster knew Richard was also waist-deep in an affair with the beautiful Stacie Shatner. Everyone knew it.

"You need a diversion," Buster said, "and I know just the place. We can't fraternize on base, but the Mouse Trap on the Commons is the demilitarized zone."

The Mouse Trap was a gentlemen's club situated next to the more famous Playboy Club in Boston. The Playboy Club was off-limits and known as a platform for compromising ASA troops with beautiful escorts run by Russian operatives. So far, the Mouse Trap had produced no such entrapments. While the Playboy Club was more of a corporate entity, the Mouse Trap was rumored to be owned and operated by an organized crime family in New Jersey. Others said it was owned by a wealthy Russian playboy.

"I'm sorry, Buster. I just can't do it," Richard said, shaking his head and trying to appear regretful. "You go and have a good time. Maybe we can pop a few at the pond this weekend. I'll introduce you to a new friend of mine. You'll like her more than you probably should."

Richard knew the clubs were nothing but trouble. Captain Mason had explicitly warned him about the potential harm any suspicion could bring to his future at Fort Devens and the Army Security Agency. When Richard chose the ASA for his preferred duty assignment, he had his sights on embassy duty and possibly recruitment by the National Security Agency.

Stacie did not want to wait for the weekend to see Richard. She was the aggressor when it came to their more intimate encounters. She called Richard's desk in the office area attached to Charlie Company's platoon barracks. Though Richard lived in the officers' quarters on base, his duties as company XO required him to be near his men daily.

He answered the phone on the first ring. "C Company, Lieutenant Farnsworth here."

"Richard, it's me. Tonight, please, let's go somewhere on base. I want to see you."

He thought for a moment. *Where can we go and have the privacy we both want?* "Meet me at the carpool lot. My personal vehicle is there."

Stacie asked, "Where are we going?"

He coyly answered, "We need a little practice on the firing range."

The firing range was remote, and they ended up at a grassy knoll overlooking the hand grenade pits. Richard had brought a blanket. Not for the cold so much as the mosquitoes. He placed the blanket on the ground, and they sat and held each other in a passionate embrace. After an exchange of kisses and frantic groping, they partially undressed.

He could feel the bugs attacking his exposed skin.

Stacie said, "You should have brought two blankets."

They shifted their bodies and pulled the army-issue bedcover over Richard's backside. The ground was cold and hard under Stacie's bare back. She groaned, not from pleasure, but from the misery of their uncomfortable setting. The mission was accomplished, and they swore never to use the same coordinates or tactics in future engagements.

The months crept by, and Richard's training squads had completed their courses and were ready for their next assignments. Most of the men and women would go on to Fort Huachuca in Arizona for advanced individual training. The post provided advanced training for military intelligence systems integrators, imagery analysts, and intelligence analysts. ASA defense language specialists attended the Army Defense Language Institute in Monterey, California. Arabic, Farsi, Iraqi, Russian, Vietnamese, and Chinese languages were all taught at the institute. After AIT, most ASA troops received orders for operations in Germany, Thailand, Vietnam, and remote listening posts around the European theater, for signal and imagery intelligence interception and analysis.

Richard and Stacie made the one-hour drive to downtown Boston and checked in to the historic Godfrey Hotel Boston as Mr. and Mrs. Richard Farnsworth. As free as the early seventies may have been, unmarried couples and other assorted groups of young adventurous adults were still frowned upon by the conservative hotel management at the Godfrey. Their room was in keeping with the salaries of army officers: not a luxury suite, yet premium quarters with the finest hotel amenities.

After an hour of catching up on their close-quarter hand-to-hand carnal needs, they showered together and dressed in their Class A uniforms. There was a low-level risk the uniforms would draw unwanted attention from unruly students protesting the Vietnam War, but neither of them had any upscale civilian clothes readily available. After a drink in the lobby bar, Richard and Stacie took an easy stroll across the North Washington Street Bridge to the historic Warren Tavern. It was named after Maj. Gen. Joseph Warren 190 years earlier, in 1780. The restaurant's clientele then included notable patriots such as George Washington and Paul Revere. Richard and Stacie opted for a carriage ride for the return trip to the hotel.

Holding open the heavy bronze door, Richard suggested they have a nightcap at the hotel's lobby bar.

Stacie declined, saying, "I have a better idea. How about a bottle of French red Bordeaux from room service, and a couple of hours of horizontal calisthenics?"

"That's what I love about you," Richard said. "You always have my physical health in mind. You're on. To the room we go."

In the elevator, Stacie asked, "What else do you love about me?"

Richard paused and turned toward her. "Everything! I love everything about you."

At 29 and only two months short of 30, Stacie was 18 months older than Richard. When he finished West Point, she was graduating from George Washington University with a master's degree in foreign languages and linguistics. With her fluency in Russian and Vietnamese, she was eagerly recruited by the army recruiting station in Washington, DC. The university's student affairs director had contacted the recruitment office and alerted them that she was available and overqualified for service. Stacie had family back in Coral Gables, Florida, but she was not close to her mother and stepfather. Her biological dad had been killed in an automobile accident when she was eight years old. His death subdued her personality; she became a tranquil yet not timid introvert through her teenage years in South Florida. Her proficiency in foreign languages had given her a stronger voice. The army gave her a purpose and a reason to use it.

Room service delivered a very fine red wine and two elegant Riedel glasses. A cheese and fruit tray accompanied the order. They enjoyed the wine in the sitting area of their cozy, tastefully decorated room. Richard massaged Stacie's feet.

"Well, Richard, what would you like for dessert? I'll order it."

His hands moved to her legs. "I want you for dessert," he said.

Stacie pulled her knees to her chest and said, "I guess we should take advantage of our time here."

Richard reached over to Stacie and began unbuttoning her shirt. She loosened her tightly wound hair bun and the long strands flowed to her shoulders in beautiful blonde waves.

The bedcovers at the Godfrey Hotel were something that neither Richard nor Stacie had ever experienced. The 1,000-thread-count wool and Egyptian cotton sheets and pillowcases were an aphrodisiac. The silk comforter was an invitation to what would be a surreal night of lovemaking they would never forget.

After a full-length embrace of their bodies, Stacie positioned herself over Richard, straddling him in a saddle-like posture. Her luscious breasts were pillows of soft, warm flesh, and he pressed his face to them. The scent of lilac from the sheets mixed with a hint of Stacie's perfume set the stage for an evening of intense sexual and romantic passion.

Sunday morning at 0900 hours, Stacie and Richard lay pleasantly under the silk comforter. The sheets were twisted and buried somewhere around their feet.

"You didn't allow me much sleep last night," Stacie said with a sigh.

Richard took her hand and looked into her eyes. "I'm sorry. No, that's a lie. I am not sorry at all." He pulled her to him and lightly kissed her face. Richard sat up in bed and said, "I have to be on base by 1300 hours. We have a security briefing scheduled with some brass from brigade headquarters."

Stacie replied, "On a Sunday? What's up with that?"

Richard was purposefully vague, yet responded, "Something's going on with Turkey."

The rumors about a possible confrontation with Turkey had been quietly circulating all week. The real concern centered around Turkey's desire to develop nuclear weapons capability and join other NATO countries in the alliance. A worse scenario would be for Turkey to take control of the US air bases in Turkey and the US nuclear arsenal stored there.

While making the drive back to base from Boston, Stacie turned toward Richard and said, "I love you, Richard."

"I love you too, St—"

"Richard," she said, "do you love me like Playboy Bunny love, or the 'I want to spend the rest of my life with you kind of love'?"

After an awkward pause, Richard said, "Stacie, I don't know what our future holds. Hell, last year I didn't know if I even had a future. Stay with me. Let's see where we are after the holidays. Okay?"

She stared out the windshield and said nothing. They drove on without conversation as Simon and Garfunkel's "Bridge over Troubled Water" played on the radio.

Chapter 6

December 7, 1970 – ASA Battalion Briefing

Col. Samuel Blaise, commander of the 311th ASA Military Intelligence Battalion, strode into the conference room located just off the lineup of other brigade-level offices in the Administration Complex.

Before Richard and Captain Mason could stand, Colonel Blaise said, "At ease, gentlemen. Let's get right to it. We have a situation in Turkey. You know we have air bases in Istanbul and Incirlik, Turkey. Communications Reconnaissance has intercepted traffic that Turkey may be planning to close our bases and possibly attempt to gain control of our nuclear weapons stored there. I need to know if Charlie Company is in a position of readiness. Can you be ready to deploy the first of January? We need real-time access to all of Turkey's government and military radio signal and voice communications. The secondhand crap we are getting is filtered through too many layers at the State Department and the European Command Center."

Captain Mason turned his attention to Richard and saw what he hoped was a nod.

"Colonel," Richard replied, "we can have all five platoons of C Company ready and standing by for orders in three weeks. Alpha and Bravo Platoons are ready right now."

Colonel Blaise reminded them to keep a lid on this development and added, "Get me your rosters and comm hardware requirements ASAP. That is all."

Richard was stunned. He was thinking, *Can I really be in Turkey in January?* His Fort Devens assignment was originally a 36-month tour. After which he thought he might be assigned to embassy duty, or even resign. *Now,* he thought, *this changes everything and it sure as hell isn't DC embassy duty.* It wasn't Richard's place to ask; still, he also wondered what other Army Security Agency companies would be mobilized. Certainly, they would need language support in both Russian and Turkish. In Turkey there were multiple languages spoken, including Bulgarian, Syriac, Georgian, and others. He wondered if Stacie knew she might be deployed. Surely the army and air force already had adequate interpreter support at the air bases and radar stations in Turkey. He didn't call Stacie that evening. He needed some time to think, and to make up for the lost sleep in Boston.

US bases in Turkey were opened in the early 1950s. Marines, army, and air force squadrons were there to defend NATO's southern flank by projecting a cohesive show of combat support and Allied strength. The army radar station in Kurecik, Turkey, was a missile detection site. Turkey partnered with the US Navy and Air Force to protect NATO Allies and keep them safe from missile attacks and nuclear threats. Unknown to the civilian world, US forces had more than 7,000 nuclear weapons stored throughout the European theater.

In the late 1960s, Turkey began showing interest in uranium exploration and the development of a large nuclear reactor. This raised many concerns with US Ambassador Parker T. Hart, and was the topic of discussions in Geneva, where the Nuclear Non-Proliferation Treaty negotiations were underway in 1969. Turkey made it no secret that they wanted the bomb. While Ambassador Hart was not overly concerned,

NATO planners were busy reviewing the possibility of the use of nuclear weaponry in Europe.

NATO was developing plans for the deployment of atomic demolition munitions in Turkey. ADMs had the advantage of power and portability over more conventional weapons. With their backpack size and weighing in at 50 pounds, they were relatively small and lightweight. Like landmines, they could be placed by Special Forces or army engineers and detonated by timers or on command. The explosions could create massive terrain obstructions to enemy troop movements and the deployment of tanks and artillery. The closure of mountain passes and the destruction of bridges, coupled with the obstacles imposed by radioactive contamination, created a new way to stop and kill the enemy.

The post–World War II strategy for Europe's NATO countries was to be ready to react and defend against any aggression from their expansionist Russian neighbors. After warnings from the Soviet ambassador to the United States, Anatoly Dobrynin, US President Richard Nixon addressed the tensions and ordered Secretary of State William P. Rogers to defuse the situation and cease all NATO planning for the use and production of tactical nuclear weapons, or ADMs. Any deployment or use by US forces must be authorized only by the president. Germany resisted being controlled by the United States, and Turkey's compliance with directives from the United States came with great reluctance.

Richard knew Turkey was a smoldering hotbed of potential conflicts. Europe needed a strong and visible coalition to deflect any Russian plans for further annexation of its bordering countries. The presence of US air bases and army and marine posts were essential to the strategy of deterrence. The timely interception and analysis of communications to and from Russia and between our NATO Allies were also essential to the maintenance and development of diplomatic and US military strategy. It was what Richard and his men were trained for.

While at lunch with Stacie, Richard planned to open the discussion of their latest assignments.

Before he could begin, Stacie gripped his arm and said in a low voice, "I know about Turkey."

He said, "What do you know?"

Stacie replied, "Just that you and your platoons may be sent there soon."

Richard answered, "How the hell do you know about my orders? This is not public information."

Rumors were always circulating—and embellished—around most military bases. It happened in this case to be true.

Richard frowned and said, "Let's not talk about this here. People with big ears also have big mouths."

Sitting on a bench near the physical training field, Richard asked again, "What do you know?"

Stacie replied, "I know you got orders to take all or part of your team to one of the US air bases in Turkey, and maybe even that tiny shithole in Sinop."

"You heard wrong," he replied. "I do not have any orders to go anywhere."

"Then why don't you tell me what the hell is going on?"

Richard sighed and said, "You know I can't. I can tell you that deployment to Turkey is a possibility. What about you? You're just as likely to get the same invitation."

They walked toward Richard's office in the C Company barracks building.

Richard stopped and turned toward Stacie. "If I do have to go, it would only be a single 12-month tour of duty."

Stacie snapped back, "Yeah, sure, unless some idiot drops a bomb or attacks one of the bases. Then the shit hits the fan and you're back in the war zone."

"The probability of a war in Europe is pretty low," he said. "A skirmish could develop in Poland or maybe Czechoslovakia, but would likely be put down relatively quickly."

As a student of world history, Richard knew the entire European continent was less than stable. In addition, any military excursions initiated or sponsored by the Soviet Union would promptly pit the forces of NATO, including the United States, against the "Soviet empire" led by General Secretary Leonid Brezhnev. The Warsaw Pact countries of Albania, Bulgaria, Czechoslovakia, East Germany, Hungary, Poland, and Romania were hotbeds of political and cultural unrest. The underlying desire of the people was to be independent and away from the dominance of the Russian Empire.

Concerns about Poland and Czechoslovakia were not without basis. Czechoslovakia had a troubled Communist past. As recently as 1968, the Russian army invaded the country and took their political leaders hostage. Despite efforts by Czech President Svoboda's appeals to Moscow and the return of their leaders to Prague, Soviet troops remained in Czechoslovakia and imposed strict political and cultural controls on the population. The country became the Czech Socialist Republic and a member of the Warsaw Pact, adhering to the Brezhnev Doctrine.

In 1970, Czech Communist Party Secretary Alexander Dubček was fired and a Slovakian undersecretary by the name of Gustáv Husák became the general secretary of the Czechoslovakian Communist Party. Husák reformed the party and focused on the normalization of Czechoslovakia while maintaining strict adherence to the Communist doctrine. The Czech Republic shifted their attention to the repair of the country's economy and away from past difficulties with Communist Russia. The Soviet Union continued to impose its control of the party in the Czech Republic.

In Poland the conflicts were not politically motivated. They were based on economic failure and hunger. The people were revolting against government-imposed food and dairy price increases. Striking workers and students were met with deadly violence and were repelled by armored troop carriers and tanks. More than 1,000 men, women, and children were injured, and over 50 were killed in battles with the police and military. The riots and mayhem ended only after Soviet President Leonid Brezhnev forced the resignation of political leaders and ministers in Gdansk, Gdynia, Elbląg, and Szczecin.

"Stacie, the bottom line is I do not have firm orders for deployment to Turkey. However, it is possible, if not likely, that any day now I will be ordered to Incirlik Air Base in Turkey, along with all five of Charlie Company's platoons. My concern is not my situation, but yours. The mission requires intercept and analysis capabilities. I don't speak Russian or any of the Turkish languages. You do."

Stacie gripped Richard's arm and replied, "My skills include the interpretation and use of foreign languages, but I've been told by high-ranking and reliable sources that my most likely assignment will be as an instructor at the army's language school in Monterey, California, or possibly the Defense Language Institute at Fort Bliss, Texas."

The demand for military interpreters in Europe was not for one or two or even a dozen specialists. The ongoing threat throughout Europe demanded the availability of hundreds of language specialists in dozens of languages and dialects. For Stacie, her highest and best use, according to the ASA, was to teach and refine the language skills of our army soldiers, as well as the air force and marines.

Though Richard might not see it, she was far more than his limited image of the voluptuously beautiful Stacie Shatner from Coral Gables.

Chapter 7

WAC Barracks

"Hello, Richard! Where did your mind go? I was talking. Did you hear anything I said?"

After accepting his apology, Stacie said, "Enough of the doom and gloom. Tonight after chow, you're coming to my quarters."

His eyebrows shot up a second in surprise. "Stacie, that's not allowed and you know it."

She laughed out loud. "There are so many Green Berets and Army Garrison Caps roaming the hallways of the WAC barracks, you'd think the Women's Army Corps lived in a coed college dormitory. Come to the double doors at the north end of the barracks at 2100 hours. They'll be unlocked. Take the pink stairwell, go up one floor, and enter the hallway. Proceed to and open the third door on your left. You will not regret it, I promise."

Richard was astonished, and replied sheepishly, "Hooah, LT. I will report as commanded."

That night after retreat, Richard met with his friend Sgt. Buster Browning at the lounge located in the entry area of the PX. They shared a six-pack of Schmidt's beer. At 25 cents per can, it was a popular brand at military post exchanges. Richard and Buster shared stories from their time in Vietnam. They chided a couple of Special Ops soldiers seated at the end of the long plastic table, and asked if they were in the post's choir. It was in jest. They were all in the brotherhood of warriors who had been to the "Valley"—the Valley of Death. Serving and surviving combat tours in Vietnam stripped men of any pettiness or sensitivity to friendly sarcasm.

One of the Rangers at the shared table replied to Richard. "LT, why are you hanging with that shoeshine boy? Slide on down and have a beer with the Night Stalkers."

Richard chuckled and said, "Nah, boys, thank you. Buster here is a real sensitive type and I don't want to hurt his feelings."

In a mock show of being offended, Buster abruptly stood up, clenching his fists, and glared at the others.

Richard grabbed him and pulled him down. "Now there, Buster, you can't kill them. They are on our side."

After another round, Buster and Richard got up and, on their way to the exit, stopped to put up a handshake with the two Rangers. They exchanged names and pleasantries and promised to buy each other a beer next time they hit the PX.

In his quarters, Richard changed into his winter workout sweatpants and running shoes. He pulled on a long-sleeved T-shirt and an olive-green wool sweater.

When he reached the WAC barracks and tried the double doors, they did not open. Puzzled, he pushed inward and could tell the vertical lock posts were not engaged, so he carefully pulled on the steel doors until they opened. He entered the stairwell and saw the framed portraits of senior female army officers on the painted pink block walls. As instructed, he walked up one level, entered the hallway … and immediately saw a cluster of women at the opposite end of the corridor.

One of them yelled out, "Man on the floor!"

This was not a call to the Officer of the Watch. It alerted the other ladies not to come out without a towel or some level of clothing on.

Entering Stacie's room, Richard could see it was set up with a sitting area and two bunks individually shielded with a floor-to-ceiling room divider. The en suite bathroom had a shower room with two stalls shared with the adjacent suite. Stacie was sitting up in bed with a Condé Nast *Glamour* magazine held in both hands.

"Hello, handsome," she said. She saw he was scanning the room. "Don't worry, we're alone. My roomie is on leave until Monday."

Richard smiled broadly and walked over to the bed and sat down. "Your hallway smells like weed. Are there any rules in this temple?"

"Of course," she replied. "Don't ask, don't tell. Why don't you turn the overhead light off and get comfortable."

They made love for two hours. Stacie's sexual energy was unlike anything Richard had ever experienced. It wasn't like she was a seasoned professional. It was more like she had saved and stored a decade of passion over the years, and it was time to put it to use. She came across not with sexual prowess, but with heightened desire and sensitivity propelled by the touch and warmth of their bodies pressed together. For Richard it was an experience he had only dreamed of until now. They were falling off the cliff and there would not be an easy path back to anything resembling their previous mental states. Feelings of self-preservation and advancement were replaced with mutual empathy and desire.

Richard arose quietly and dressed. He gently kissed Stacie and whispered good night.

She placed a hand on his forehead and slowly slid her fingers down his face, tracing the outline of his nose and mouth.

"Don't make any other stops, cowboy. I'm not into sharing. Go straight home." She turned over, facing away from him and, in a muffled voice, said, "Good night, I love you."

Richard left the barracks undetected and returned to his quarters.

Chapter 8

Promotion Day

Two weeks after the briefing at brigade headquarters, Richard entered Captain Mason's outer office. The captain's administrative assistant was not at his desk. Richard heard what sounded like a coffee mug clanging against a metal desk, followed by the words, "Dammit to hell." The door to Mason's office was not fully closed. Richard slowly pushed it open. Captain Mason was sitting at his desk, wiping up spilled coffee and trying to pat dry the wet papers.

Richard said, "I'm sorry, sir, can I be of assistance?"

The captain remained focused on his task. "Come in, Lieutenant," he said, "and have a seat. We have some things to discuss. You remember Col. Sam Blaise."

To Richard's left, sitting on a cushioned chair next to a reading lamp, sat Sam Blaise. Sam, a highly decorated officer, had served in the Korean conflict and completed multiple tours in Vietnam.

The colonel stood and went to Richard and shook his hand. "Lieutenant, have a seat." Waving a hand, he said, "Captain Mason, carry on. This is your show." Colonel Blaise took a seat behind and to the side of Mason's desk.

Richard sat in a steel chair facing Captain Mason.

The captain dropped the wet paper towels into a wastebasket and looked up, pulling himself straight in his seat. "Richard, you've had a good first year here at Devens." Chuckling, he said, "As a matter of fact, you seem to be enjoying your time here more than most of us."

Richard was about to reply and agree with Mason, but paused when Mason leaned forward and stared at him eye to eye.

"Farnsworth, I've got some good news and some terrible news."

Richard knew what the terrible news was: Charlie Company was going to be deployed to Turkey. His mind went into a slump, and a dull, low-frequency hum in his head began to build in intensity.

Captain Mason interrupted his thoughts. "First the good news."

He stood at his desk, and Colonel Blaise and Richard rose as well.

Colonel Blaise moved to face Richard. "Lt. Richard Farnsworth, your service to the United States Army and your country has not gone unnoticed. From combat duty in Vietnam to the exemplary work you have completed here at Fort Devens, you have demonstrated unwavering leadership and loyalty to the country and to your men. In recognition of the excellent performance of your duties as an army officer, and with the authority delegated by the Secretary of the Army, you are hereby being promoted to the O3 rank of captain in the United States Army."

Richard was stunned, though his face did not show it. He wasn't due for an evaluation for promotion for another 22 months. The army had the authority to make advance promotions for various reasons, including the requirement to fill key positions for special-duty assignments. *Now for the terrible news,* Richard thought.

"Take your seat, Captain." Mason took a long sip of his cold coffee and sighed.

Before Captain Mason could speak, Richard said, "C Company is being deployed."

Mason raised his right hand, fingers splayed. "Not so fast, Captain. Colonel Blaise has an update to the Turkey briefing."

After they were seated, the colonel spoke. "Charlie Company will be sent to Turkey, but not right now. The threat in Turkey is much greater than we initially anticipated. We may end up adding an entire battalion-size force to the region. The Turkish government is more interested in removing US and Allied forces from their country. Before we commit any increase in our troop levels at Incirlik and Izmir Air Bases, we need to bolster our intelligence command and put in place a covert network of electronic and human surveillance capabilities."

After a glance at Captain Mason, Colonel Blaise said, "Captain Farnsworth, we need you to assemble a 10-man squad made up of your best commissioned and noncommissioned team members. You need to have signals intelligence, radio intercept, maintenance, and human intelligence capabilities. We have aerial intercept and locate resources, but the Turks know when and where our aircraft are, and they have their own voice and SIGINT intercept capabilities. The NSA and the CIA have listening devices and radio monitoring. However, their intelligence does not get shared with the US European Army Command until it is filtered through CIA Director Helms, DOD heads, and then Army Central Command. By the time our ground force commanders get the intel, it's old news. With Vietnam winding down, the ASA listening post on Sinop is primarily focused on Russian and German traffic."

Colonel Blaise stepped over to a side table and poured himself some water for a quick drink. He took his seat and said, "So, as far as Central Command and the other agencies know, your orders are to inspect and assess the army and air force signal intelligence tools, their range and effectiveness, and security level. What we want from your team is a unique, ground up, listening network manned only by need-to-know personnel with the proper clearances. Your SIGINT packets will be uploaded to ASA Command Center at Fort Belvoir by your contact in the 502nd ASA Group in Augsburg, Germany. He will establish the logistics of receiving your encrypted transmissions from your encampment at Izmir Station near Istanbul."

Colonel Blaise looked at Captain Mason and got a nod from him. Blaise said, "Battalion will work out your schedule and travel logistics. Send me a list of your team names and I'll work on their orders." Colonel Blaise rose and headed toward the door. "You and Captain Mason can handle their briefing. And, by the way, you and your team will receive level 4 Special Duty Assignment Pay. Hell, if anybody gets shot at, you will also get Combat Pay! Good luck, and congratulations on your well-deserved promotion. *Semper Vigilis*, Captains." After the required salutes, Blaise left.

A few moments later, Captain Mason and Richard went into the hallway outside of the office.

Mason said, "Let's regroup tomorrow at 0800. You and I can review the team requirements and come up with candidates for this mission." He paused, studying Richard's face. "You are in, right? Army regulations allow you to decline the promotion, but declining the deployment is not an option."

Richard replied, "Captain Mason, it is what I do. While Turkey is not my favorite vacation spot, my men and I are well equipped to carry out this mission. I am all in."

As they parted, Richard said, "Gene—sorry, Captain Mason."

Mason turned back toward Richard.

"I have a request. I need Sgt. Buster Browning to be part of my squad in Turkey. He has combat experience, and we need some bang-bang power if things go south in the land of Turks."

Mason replied, "Heard, understood, and acknowledged. Hooah."

Chapter 9

Walden Pond

"Hey, where are you, Captain? Are you okay? You've been staring into space since you first sat down." Stacie and Richard were having a light lunch at the PX.

Stacie grabbed his hand and said, "Let's go to Walden Pond this weekend. You can invite your compadre Buster what's his name."

"That sounds nice," Richard said. "We can pick up some wine while we're here."

"Oh," Stacie said, "I invited my friend Yvonne. I hope that's okay."

"It's more than okay, she is a looker! Buster will be all over her."

Stacie smirked. "Uh-huh, they will have a *lot* in common. They both like women! Richard, I told you she plays for the other team."

He smiled. "Well, maybe Buster can do some field trials and get her to change her mind."

"Not going to happen. I know her and I've seen how she is with women. She's a committed lesbian."

On Saturday the foursome loaded up their lounge chairs and headed to Walden Pond. The weather was perfect, the cloudless sky a beautiful soft blue. They set up their day camp near a picnic table along the edge of the pond. Except for the sound of Stacie and Yvonne's endless conversation, it was a peaceful and relaxing setting. The park was generally empty in late December. The temperature was chilly, but not unbearable.

Buster stood and announced, "Let's hike to the Thoreau cabin on the other side of the lake."

The cabin stood on the north side of the 64-acre pond. Henry David Thoreau built a modest cabin there in 1845. The land was owned by his good friend, Ralph Waldo Emerson.

Yvonne got up from her chair and said, "It sounds delightful. I'd love to join you."

"Come on," Buster said to Richard, "you and Stacie come with us."

Stacie pointed out that the cabin was really a recently built replica and didn't create the impressiveness the brochures described.

Richard said, "Buster, you two go ahead. Stacie and I will stay and guard the wine and our six-dollar lounge chairs."

Yvonne and Buster began the 30-minute walk to the historic site of Thoreau's 16- by 10-foot cabin.

Stacie spread a large blanket on the ground in front of the picnic table. The spot was shielded from the entry road and the walkways above the pond. At first she sat on the blanket, with her knees pulled to her chest. Then she lay down on the soft blanket which covered a bed of lush grass. She said softly, "Come join me, please. I want to be close to you."

Richard complied and stretched out next to her. The heat from the sun directly above them was comforting in the 58-degree air. In a move that was fairly predictable, he became aroused by the warmth generated by Stacie's body as she lay at his side. Her soft breasts were alluring, and he could not hold back his reaction to her seductive beauty.

With their clothes still on and coupled with some ingenious adjustments, Stacie and Richard made love in broad daylight in front of the rabbits, birds, and all of the Walden Pond wildlife.

Richard thought, *What could be better than this very moment?*

They lay there on the blanket and slipped into a state of half sleep with the soothing sound of the breeze blowing ripples across the pond. Life was good in Concord, Massachusetts, on December 19 of 1970.

They were awakened abruptly by the roar of four F-16 Falcons flying in formation 5,000 feet above their lakeside bed. Reality leaped into their picturesque setting.

Buster and Yvonne returned from their exploration. Richard and Stacie were waiting at the picnic table which they had draped with an army-olive-green bunk cover. They had some crackers, cheese, and two bottles of the PX's finest Chardonnay and Pinot Noir. Stacie had "borrowed" four mess hall water glasses repurposed for the occasion.

Richard and Buster walked to the nearest heavy brush to relieve themselves.

Richard asked, "How was your walk?"

Buster laughed and said, "You didn't tell me Yvonne was a lesbian."

With a serious expression, he replied, "So, is she still a lesbian?"

Buster turned and walked away mumbling something unintelligible.

That night, Richard told Stacie about his orders for Turkey. He was leaving four days after Christmas. She wasn't overly surprised. When Richard first heard about a possible deployment, Stacie had requested and received approval for a

10-day holiday leave and was actually leaving before Richard's departure. Stacie's mother sent her a prepaid flight home from Boston Logan Airport to Miami International. When Stacie returned to Fort Devens, Richard would be gone.

Chapter 10

The Republic of Turkey

apt. Richard T. Farnsworth flew on a commercial Delta flight from Boston to Atlanta's Hartsfield-Jackson Airport with three of his squad members. The other six members of Richard's team flew with four pallets of mission gear and supplies onboard a Hercules C-130 military transport plane headed to Fort McPherson Army Base in East Point, Georgia. Richard's group was transported by van to the base, where they joined the other team members.

In the lunch area of an unmanned warehouse on base, Richard assembled his team. The dimly illuminated space added a feeling of intrigue to the setting. After a sidebar with the ranking NCO Sgt. First Class Drew Hillyer, Richard addressed the squad.

"Take your seats, men. Let's get right to the point. This is not a standard combat deployment. Everything you see here, do here, or hear, is classified. You are not Bravo Squad or F Troop. We are an ASA Task Force with a mission to set up a covert network of ground-based intercept capabilities to collect intelligence from radio, telephonic, and video transmissions to and from select locations in Turkey."

Richard's team was charged with the task of installing a clandestine ground-based network of electronic signal intercept devices and listening stations. They were to collect and record the phone and radio transmissions into and from political and military offices in the Turkish government. The collected intelligence would be delivered to ASA Command in real time. The volatility of the political situation in Turkey was unfolding quickly, and the United States had to be ready to step in and safeguard US military personnel and bases.

Captain Farnsworth had been pacing in front of the group while briefing them. He stopped and faced them for emphasis. "The protection of our stockpiles of nuclear weaponry stored on US bases in Turkey is top priority," he said. "Our surveillance aircraft can track a soccer ball bouncing from 300 miles out, but their mission has been hampered by jamming signals produced by revolutionary Turkish forces seeking to overturn the government of Turkey."

After vaguely answering various questions from his men, Richard concluded the briefing. He was not specific regarding how long or how dangerous the mission would be. Not because it was on a need-to-know basis—he simply did not know the answers.

The next morning at 0500 hours, ASA Task Force "Grey Wolf" departed Fort McPherson and flew 5,800 miles nonstop from Atlanta to Istanbul. They were accompanied by a 10-man squad from the Tenth Special Forces. Even with the C-137's top speed of 600 miles per hour, the flight time was still just under 12 hours. Upon arrival they were processed by Turkish security agents and transported to Izmir Air Station 320 km southwest of Istanbul. The base was a temporary stop and not without some challenges. The previous year, on the first of July, 1970, the Turkish air force had taken control of the airfield and assumed the responsibility for support services to US and NATO operations on and off post.

Izmir wasn't really a base. The US and NATO administrative and other operational facilities were spread out in the townships of the historic city. The challenge for Richard's team and the Special Forces squad was to get their men and the ASA hardware off the plane and moved to a secure location off base.

After deplaning, Richard and Sergeant Hillyer met on the tarmac with Special Forces Capt. Michael Shad. They were joined by Army Maj. Thomas Dodson, an ASA contact charged with the logistics of moving the men and equipment to a secure off-base location. They discussed the plan for unloading the electronics gear and reloading it into the commercial vans. Military tactical vehicles did not have the space for three pallets of gear. They would also draw too much attention when entering and leaving the restricted areas of Izmir.

Major Dodson had arranged for three two-ton Ford vans to move the ASA squad and their gear. The Special Forces squad had other transportation and kept a much lower profile in the operation. They discussed and agreed on what a contingency plan looked like if their mission was compromised or impeded by Turkish forces.

Richard knew the Special Forces security squad had "fire when fired upon" orders. He hoped it would not come to that. It would likely kill the mission and possibly have fatal consequences for everyone involved.

As soon as darkness fell, Grey Wolf Task Force departed Izmir Air Station. The three vans staged their departures, placing at least one mile between the vans en route to their rendezvous point. The Special Forces squad split up into two different Turkish-built automobiles and one station wagon. They were interspersed in the caravan traveling from Izmir to a small hotel in the settlement of Buca, a main district of Izmir Province, its location five miles from the historic clock tower at

Konak Square. The Levantines settled there in the 19th century. The great mansions built in that century are still standing. Dokuz Eylül University, one of Izmir's largest universities, is in the Tinaztepe settlement in Buca.

Major Dodson had prearranged accommodations for the task force and Special Forces security squad at the ancient Nodrok hotel in the township of Konak. The hotel was purchased by the US State Department in 1952 and converted it into living quarters for the Allied Land Command. LANDCOM moved to newer accommodations in 1968, leaving the hotel maintained and mostly vacant for the past three years. It was perfectly situated, and the citizens and local government officials were used to seeing US and Allied military personnel in the hotel and surrounding settlements.

After settling in, two to a room, and securing the vans and their cargo, the task force assembled in the hotel's conference room. The Special Forces squad had their orders and knew their mission was to track and keep the Grey Wolf Task Force members and their equipment safe.

Major Dodson was the first to speak. He welcomed everyone and walked them through a list of local customs and cultural expectations they needed to be aware of and strictly adhere to. Dodson wished them well and instructed Captain Farnsworth to contact him with any concerns or problems while in Turkey. Dodson dismissed himself and Richard took over the briefing.

It was late in what had been a long day, and Richard ran through the steps which would take them into the heart of their mission. Four two-man teams were assigned to specific locations in the city that had been designated as high-traffic areas for electronic intercept hardware to be placed. For hardwired communications monitoring, the phone and data network hubs inside the buildings would be targeted.

Fortunately for the Army Security Agency mission, the Central Intelligence Agency and the State Department had done an extensive job of documenting the communications networks and the district's governmental organization and hierarchy. The DOD and NSA had access to the collected intelligence and had previously shared it with the ASA European Command. The new intelligence collected would be analyzed and identified with references to the sources and destinations of intercepted radio and phone traffic. While high-frequency microwave and satellite transmissions were possible, Turkey was a few years behind the US and its allies in the development of that technology. The US listening post in Sinop, Turkey, would easily pick up any high-frequency microwave voice, data, or facsimile transmissions.

Richard distributed briefing packets, along with maps, network diagrams, and building plans to each two-man team. The ninth man, a rover, would resupply the team and assist with any challenges or needs the teams might encounter. Communications between each team, the hotel command base, and the SF security squad would be accomplished with a newly developed VHF portable radio. The ammo-can-sized transceiver could operate in the 30–300 megahertz range. Compared to its predecessor—the 85-pound, 500 kilohertz, R-390A tube set radio—the portable PRC-25 VHF unit was easily carried and concealed.

Richard addressed the team further. "Men, get some rest. Report to the hotel mess hall at 0600 hours. Study your packets closely. For security reasons, they will be collected from you in the morning. You will have time after the morning meal to assemble your travel packs and comm gear."

In unison, the men responded, "Hooah," and headed to the doorway.

The captain had always liked the army slang "hooah," for "heard, understood, and acknowledged."

Richard hoped he had the right team for this mission. His gut said yes since he had studied the situation in Turkey. Chaos in the streets was rapidly unfolding; protests had turned to violence and mayhem.

The Turkish military memorandum issued on their arrival had described the chaos, which included closed universities, and students—dressed as urban guerrillas—robbing banks and even kidnapping US military personnel. Homes of university professors and others critical of the Turkish government were bombed by neofascist militants. The Islamist National Order Party rejected the modernist ideologies of republicanism and nationalism. Mustafa Kemal Atatürk, the founder of the Republic of Turkey, wanted to reform the political system and promote social policies based on science and reasoning. The Liberal and Islamist National Parties were pitted against the government and infuriated the Turkish armed forces.

Turkish Prime Minister Süleyman Demirel's government was paralyzed by the violence and unrest. The ultimate outcome would likely be a military coup and takeover of the country. Richard and his select squad of soldiers were marching right into an anarchist's battlefield. In some ways it was more stressful than his experiences in Vietnam. In the jungle there was clarity—find the enemy, kill the enemy. In the streets of Izmir, Kurecik, and Istanbul, the enemy was obscured by conflicting ideologies and outraged citizens and students.

Chapter 11

New Year's Day 1971

At 4:00 a.m. Richard was half asleep, thinking about Stacie. He pleasantly recalled every minute he had spent with her at Fort Devens. The feeling of the luscious soft curves of her body pressed against his had made an indelible imprint on his brain. He could hear her soft whisper of a voice saying, "I love you, Richard." He wondered if she would still be there when he returned to Fort Devens. He thought about Boston and how it was unlike any experience he had ever had with any woman.

Richard's alarm startled him at 0500 hours—*US 10:00 p.m. EST,* he thought. *Time to get up, shower, and dress for the day. Today … what will today bring? How many days?* The plan was to be in and out of Istanbul in five days, and then repeat the tasks in the other cities near US bases in Kurecik and Incirlik. After testing and signal verification with ASA contacts at the base in Augsburg, Germany, the mission would be complete. *I could be back in Boston by the end of the month.*

The soldiers from Task Force Grey Wolf mingled with Special Forces security team members at breakfast. Some sat quietly while others shared stories from their duty tours in Vietnam. Their mood was almost festive, and most of them saw this assignment as light duty. There would be no mortar fire or midnight attacks by a hundred crazed VC with rifles and long knives. The teams would be slipping into and out of office buildings and basements and placing electronic black boxes to capture phone and radio transmissions. Special Forces snipers on rooftops would be tracking their movements. Encounters with rioting students would be avoided as much as possible, and not engaged unless absolutely required for the safety of the men. If a situation became potentially lethal, every ASA soldier had a loaded 45-caliber M-1911 semiautomatic pistol with seven rounds and backup magazines. The SF guys had compact P-90 machine guns. They were lightweight (6 pounds, loaded) and small enough to conceal under a jacket. They also had M8 smoke grenades and M67 fragmentation grenades. The two snipers on the team used Remington's five-piece .308-caliber sniper rifle with a 20-inch barrel. It could be assembled after taking up a strategic position of fire.

Captain Farnsworth joined the team and took an empty seat next to his friend, Buster Browning. Buster was beyond thankful for Richard getting him out of the mess hall at Fort Devens.

Buster's face gleamed when he looked up at Richard. "Have a seat, sir, breakfast is on me."

Richard replied, "You get some sleep, pal?"

He grinned and said, "Yes, sir, I dreamed I was in Penang with my beautiful and talented Malaysian wife, Afrina."

Richard huffed, saying, "Do me a favor and please don't name any of your tribe after me, okay?"

At 0630, Richard excused himself and strode to the front of the room to address the men. SF Capt. Michael Shad joined him.

Richard said, "Good morning, men. When you finish your breakfast and have assembled your gear for today's work, meet in front of the hotel. Some of you will be traveling in the same vans that brought us here and others will be traveling in civilian automobiles driven by local drivers. Your drivers are paid US interpreters and will get you to each assignment. Should you encounter any resistance or other obstacles, the driver will attempt to negotiate safe passage. If that is not possible, then you will retreat and find an alternate route. You will not engage the protestors or any other factions you may encounter. Understood?"

"Hooah, Captain," was the instantaneous reply.

Next, Captain Shad addressed the group. "Gentlemen, you have the frequencies for contacting my men. You should only do so if you feel threatened by the situation, or you are assaulted by the student rioters or other belligerent forces. If the Turkish police or other government officials detain you, transmit the radio key codes we gave you to alert our team. We will get you out. That is all."

Richard and Captain Shad exited the room. SFC Drew Hillyer followed them out.

The first four days passed without incident. Most government and police officials were too focused on the street violence to notice anything unusual about the ASA's movements around the city. The mission in Izmir was nearly complete. Another day for final placement of equipment and the remote testing of voice-data radio reception, and transmission signals could begin.

Next stop, Incirlik Air Base. Incirlik, located in Adana, Turkey, was the home of the largest US military base in Turkey. It comprised a dozen air force squadrons assigned the security of NATO's southern flank, as well as other US allies. The base was originally opened in the fifties as an air force weather balloon launching site. The real purpose of the balloons was for airborne surveillance of the Soviet Union. The importance of this base could not be underestimated. The nuclear arsenal stored there was, of course, of the most important strategic and defensive value. Having the security of the base compromised by Turkish forces was not an option.

Just as they did in Azmir, Richard's team and the Special Forces would review the site maps and building plans that provided the location of communications hubs and strategic listening post locations. The network of interception hardware would be secretly positioned and tested. The radio signal, data, and voice recordings would be sent real time to the ASA ears in Germany, and on to ASA at Fort Devens and Command Central in DC.

On January 10, 1971, the men from the Grey Wolf Task Force headed across town toward the Government Complex. At least 2,000 protestors were also headed to the four square blocks of government buildings. This complication made entry into the buildings difficult. Blending in with hundreds of students and other rebel groups trying to gain entry was nearly impossible. Outside the perimeter of the buildings and the main courtyard, three of the team members were spotted when they gathered to discuss options. They were confronted by a student leading a small group of protestors that could have passed for a band of hippies from the streets of New York in the Hell's Kitchen neighborhood.

They yelled what were probably Turkish obscenities at the three men. As they closed in on them, one of the students began slapping his other hand with a bat-size metal rod. When he got too close, Sgt. Buster Browning reached into his belt under his jacket and pulled out a pistol. He held it up, but not directly pointed at the group of students. Buster gave them a round of obscene English phrases which caused them to back up slowly and turn to run. Buster being Buster, he ran after them.

Fifty feet into the chase, one of the students let his backpack slide to the ground. Buster ran 20 feet past the backpack and stopped, turned, and began walking toward the other two team members. The explosion shattered the windows in the buildings closest to the blast. Buster was blown five feet into the air, and slammed into a nearby oak tree trunk. Blood was streaming from his face and ears. His torso was contorted into a distorted mass, with his head and shoulders against the base of the tree and his body grotesquely twisted on the ground.

In the time it took to run 50 meters, two Special Forces men raced to Buster. The first man lifted Buster in one motion over his shoulder. The other Special Forces soldier attended to the other two Army Security Agency techs kneeling on the ground, each holding their head and ears. Their faces were covered in dirt from the blast. A third SF soldier was driving the van across the park and over to the soldiers. Buster was loaded into the back of the van and the others entered by the side door. They pulled onto the street and drove quickly but not frantically away from the scene. The crowd was less aware of the van and now focused on the other injured students at the blast scene.

Back at Incirlik, Buster was loaded onto a gurney and wheeled into the emergency unit of the base hospital. The other injured Grey Wolf soldiers entered the ER on foot. Richard and Captain Shad had been alerted by radio and were already in the ER waiting area.

Richard said to Captain Shad, "This is nuts. Students bombing buildings, and my men! What the hell? Fucking politicians and their ideologies are going to get a lot of people killed."

Shad replied, "Yes, sir, another year, another war. High office corrupts men with power and they start believing their own bullshit."

Richard put his palms to his temples and sighed. "Buster was my friend. I brought him here."

Mike Shad placed a hand on Richard's shoulder. "Captain, Buster is a warrior. He knew the risks. We all do. Besides, he was breathing and had a heartbeat when he got here. This base has the best doctors in the European theater. If he can be saved, they will save him."

The other two injured men were released. Their hearing and vision would be temporarily impaired; they would recover enough to remain on active duty after treatment and some rehab time.

The SF team and Grey Wolf Task Force were standing down for a few days while the mission at Incirlik and Adana was revamped by ASA Command in Germany. Meanwhile, the street violence in major cities across Turkey was escalating. Students were joined by the Workers' Party members and activists of the newly formed Nationalist Action Party. The danger for the people of Turkey was real. A faction of senior Turkish military officers was organizing for the likelihood of a government regime change. The importance of maintaining control and security of the three US military bases in the country was no longer a clandestine operation. Infantry, armored, and air force squadrons were on full alert. Back home, ASA and other regular army battalions were also on alert.

The remaining six men from the ASA Task Force joined Captain Farnsworth at the base mess hall for breakfast. Richard updated them on the condition of the injured men. As for Buster, he was stable, and not much else could be disclosed about his injuries. He was scheduled for surgery to repair broken ribs and a collarbone. His spinal injuries prevented him from any significant movement. The steel and leather brace limited his body movements to hands, mouth, and eyelids only. His eyes were open. He could not speak. The trauma and bruising to his internal organs filled his urine drainage bag and catheter with blood.

Before dismissing the men, Richard said, "Lay low today and tomorrow. Command is flying some brass in later today for a US and NATO joint forces meeting here on base. We should receive new orders after that conference."

After breakfast Richard went to the Air Force Command Center on base, where he had been assigned a small office. A phone extension on the desk could be patched to an outside line. He dialed the main number for the Army Security Agency Command offices at Fort Devens, Massachusetts, and asked to be connected to Capt. Gene Mason.

In his earpiece Richard heard Mason's scratchy yet enthusiastic voice: "Richard, how are you? It's good to hear from you."

Richard replied, "I'm in good health, Gene. What's the word on the streets of Washington?"

"Hey, I heard about Buster. Dammit, that's a shame. How are the other guys? Is Sergeant Hillyer okay?"

Richard took a breath and said, "Yes, sir, the two others at the blast will be fine. Sergeant Hillyer's team was on a separate installation, away from the incident. However, things are heating up here. ASA Europe Command has a joint meeting with NATO reps here on base. I guess I shouldn't have shared that. This is not an encrypted line."

Gene replied, "It's okay. We got a briefing from Colonel Blaise yesterday. We know about the meeting. Which means the Russians probably know as well."

Richard chuckled. "You tell Sam you are ready for the next promotion, and hey, if you need some R&R, I'll make room for you here in the palace of the Turkish Empire."

Mason ended the conversation with "Copy that, Captain, but don't hold your breath. I'd rather get busted at the Mousetrap in the Boston Combat Zone."

Richard reported to the Base Command Headquarters conference room. He arrived early and the room was empty. It was January 15, 1971. The next day was his birthday. He was thinking about his mother back home. *I should call,* he told himself. He squinted at the fluorescent ceiling lights. With his eyes closed he could picture Stacie standing in a doorway, studying him and curling her finger in a "Come here, big boy" gesture. He stared at her and thought, *When is Stacie's birthday?* It was not something they had discussed. It was right there on her dog tags, next to her blood type. *How could I have missed it?*

Capt. Mike Shad and two of his staff entered the room and took their seats.

Richard half rose and shook Shad's hand. "Hello, Mike, how are you?"

He replied, "It's all good. How's your man Browning?"

"Still in pretty bad shape. He'll be here for a month before being shipped home for a long rehabilitation period. He'll most likely be a civilian next time I see him."

Three more men entered the room. The highest-ranking officer was a full bird colonel named William Henry White. With his white hair and tall stature, he looked more like a senator or president. Everyone stood and saluted. Clearly, White was tired of the routine formality and returned the salute with a halfhearted slash of his arm as he dropped into a chair.

Colonel White cleared his throat and began the meeting. "Gentlemen, your mission has been abbreviated. As you know, the situation here in Turkey has escalated to the point that a full-fledged military response could be required at any time. The dissident officers running the Turkish People's Army have imposed martial law in a third of the provinces. The ASA post in Sinop will turn their ears toward in-country SIGINT traffic. Your friends in Augsburg will pick up the slack on Russian communications. The radar station at Kurecik is on full alert for any threats from Russian mobile missile units."

After noting the men's keen attention, Colonel White resumed the briefing. "Captain Farnsworth, you and what's left of your task force will report to INSCOM at USASA Field Station at Augsburg and await further orders. Captain Shad, your team is being reassigned to the 39th Weapons Security Forces at Kurecik Radar Station. You are acquainted with Maj. Thomas Dodson at Izmir. He will arrange your transportation to Germany. Be prepared to join the flight sometime in the next few days. Dodson will direct from here and provide the details."

Chapter 12

Augsburg, Germany

Richard and his ranking NCO, SFC Drew Hillyer were settled in their quarters at Field Station Augsburg. The city, founded in 15 BC, was one of the oldest in Germany. The base was one of the newest, having opened the previous year as a base for the United States Army Security Agency, or USASA. It was a techy place running 24-hour monitoring operations, intercepting Morse code, voice communications, and other radio frequency transmissions. Base operations included cryptanalysis of the recorded traffic and RDF (rapid deployment force) operations documenting the source and location of the gathered intelligence. Richard would fit right in this work environment. He and SFC Hillyer were temporarily assigned to the 701st Military Intelligence Brigade.

With the Vietnam War winding down, two platoons from MACV-SOG were also on base. The Military Assistance Command, Vietnam, Studies and Observations Group was the most effective and secret special operations organization in the Vietnam War. They operated inside and outside of South Vietnam. They carried out covert operations in Laos, Cambodia, Thailand, and North Vietnam. Why they were here in Augsburg was puzzling. SOG skill sets included reconnaissance, sabotage, and search and rescue operations. Richard could only assume it had something to do with Russia and the Cold War activities in Moscow and West Berlin.

Two days passed without contact from ASA Command or the office of the Military Intelligence Brigade. His orders were to stand by for orders. So he did. Though the newly opened base had a thrown-together appearance, a small reading room off the PX contained an ample supply of current magazines from the States. After devouring 20 or more issues of *Life* and *National Geographic* magazines, Richard felt as though he could easily prepare a doctoral thesis on a myriad of subjects, including the sex life of Congolese Bondo apes.

At 0600 hours on January 20, 1971, Richard was dressed and enjoying a cup of army coffee in the vestibule of his sleeping quarters.

A knock on the door startled him and he arose to find a sharply dressed private who promptly saluted and said, "Good morning, sir."

Richard returned the salute and stepped into the doorway.

"Captain Farnsworth, sir, I have a message for you from the MI battalion commander."

Accepting the paper, he said, "Thank you, Private."

They exchanged salutes again and, with parade execution, the messenger pivoted and marched away.

The official memo was from Col. Michael "Spike" Simmons. Richard had seen his name before and knew he was the commander of the now famous prisoner rescue operation at Sơn Tây prison camp about 23 miles west of Hanoi. The instructions were to report to headquarters at 0800 hours. No other notations or subtext, just be there.

At the appointed time, Richard approached the admin desk outside of Colonel Simmons's office.

The army specialist stood and said "Sir, the colonel and others are inside, and you may enter now. Thank you, sir."

Opening the door, Richard saw a dozen Special Forces soldiers standing behind a small sofa where three other officers were seated. Colonel Simmons's booming voice got his attention.

"Come in, Captain. No formalities, take a seat."

As he did, Richard recognized some of the faces and knew they were from Special Operations Command.

"Captain Farnsworth," Colonel Simmons said, "your orders for Augsburg were not an accident, and you are not here in transition to anywhere. We have an emergency situation requiring the army's very best effort and all the skills we can bring to bear. You have the electronic intelligence skills we need and you have combat experience."

Richard thought, *We're going back to war.*

Colonel Simmons looked at the other men and back at Richard. "Like you, the men you see in this room are handpicked for this mission. We have a delicate and dangerous situation that requires immediate action, with success as the only acceptable outcome. An army officer, 2nd Lieutenant Broughton, has been kidnapped and we believe she is being held somewhere in or near Munich. In any other country, we would plant a helicopter squadron of Special Forces troops on them and blast our way in and out with the prize.

"The diplomatic situation in Germany prevents us from visibly escalating our activity. The German government would like nothing better than to kick us out of the country and close our bases. Our operations here are too valuable to put at risk. From our air bases and listening posts, we can track the flights of every aircraft taking off in Russia and Germany, and any missile fired will be intercepted and destroyed."

Simmons glanced through the window to the street below. He turned to the group. "You need to understand the sensitivity and the enormity of this mission." He paused as if to think about what to say next.

Special Forces Capt. Walter Lee took advantage of the break and asked, "Colonel, may I ask a question?"

Simmons turned to Lee and nodded.

"With all due respect, sir, this seems to be an inordinate amount of effort for one nonessential gold bar."

Simmons walked to the opposite wall covered in framed portraits and tapped a photograph. "You may not have been made aware of it, Captain, but President Nixon has appointed Adm. Thomas Moorer as chairman of the Joint Chiefs, and that move put Army Maj. Gen. Thaddeus Broughton as head of the J2 Intelligence Directorate of the Joint Chiefs of Staff."

It instantly hit Richard—the missing Lieutenant Broughton was the general's daughter.

The room was silent.

Colonel Simmons said, "That's right, young Ms. Alyson Broughton is Gen. Thaddeus Broughton's daughter. We don't know all the details, and have to assume she was not taken at random. What started as students protesting capitalism and a lack of recognition as a student-led political party, evolved into more violent acts of bombing and burning buildings and kidnapping. Of greater concern is the involvement of a gang of more violent members bent on assassinating what they call the members of the imperialist power structure."

Richard was familiar with their history: Following the presidency of Heinrich Lübke (a suspected Nazi architect), in 1969, the students organized to fight what they perceived as a generation of criminals ruling postwar Germany. The Socialist German Student Union (Sozialistische Deutsche Studentenbund – SDS), led by Alfred Willi Rudolf "Rudi" Dutschke, was at the forefront of the protests.

Colonel Simmons said, "The movement has been supported by outside influencers, namely the KGB's Foreign Counterintelligence Group led by Maj. Gen. Oleg Kalugin. We must assume the KGB either knew or now knows who Lieutenant Broughton really is. That being the case, they will want to move her to East Germany and hold her as leverage. Perhaps for a prisoner exchange. Whatever the reason, we know from past abductions that the SDS and certainly the KGB are brutal in their treatment of captives. If we don't get to Broughton before they cross into East Germany, our chances of success are dismal."

Richard thought, *To call the SDS members student protesters falls way short of what they have become. They kidnapped German business leaders and even hijacked a Lufthansa passenger airplane en route to Mogadishu, Somalia.*

No one spoke, and Richard was about to ask a question when Colonel Simmons turned to him and said, "Captain Farnsworth, we have been flying ASA missions and intercepting every phone call and radio transmission made within a hundred-mile radius of Munich for the last five days. We think we have the coordinates of Broughton's general location from the intel we have gathered and analyzed. We are missing one leg of the triangle. I can tell you what complex of buildings we think she is being held in, but not which floor and not which room. We can't take out the whole building, so I need you and one of your men to get into the buildings with your equipment and determine which floor and which room Lieutenant Broughton is in. From there, Captain Lee and his Special Forces team will handle the extraction and rescue of Lieutenant Broughton."

Richard was thinking how bizarre this whole thing was. His choice for the second man was easy. Sgt. First Class Drew Hillyer had been with him through Tet, Turkey, and now Germany. He had more knowledge and experience with the portable electronics equipment they would need than anyone in the military. He had come to the army from the civilian world of electronics. Drew was the "Thomas Edison" of signal intercept technology. Richard knew that except for Drew's youth and questionable antics at MIT, he would have been in his class at West Point. If not for the war, he would have at least been sent to Officer Candidate School from Fort Devens.

The day after meeting with Col. Spike Simmons, Drew and Richard were taking inventory of the army's available SIGINT hardware. They found an impressive cache of electronic signal intelligence devices. Richard and Drew now realized why they were chosen, or, more generally, why the ASA was involved in the operation. The portable equipment they would use to locate Lieutenant Broughton was highly classified and anyone seeing and using the newly developed, sophisticated devices would require Top Secret Clearances and special access approval. Due to the secrecy involved and the cost of the equipment, the hardware was stored in a secure area.

The equipment used would pinpoint the precise location of any range of voice or radio transmission. The traffic could be locally analyzed or transmitted to a remote receiver for more detailed decryption. The portable RDF device, manufactured by Applied Signals Intelligence in the US, weighed less than 10 pounds and fit into a small backpack. It operated in a wide range of frequencies, covering 10 to 15 miles.

Richard smiled at Drew. "This will be a piece of cake."

Drew replied, "Copy that, sir. I heard that the new stuff was portable, but had no idea it had this kind of range and accuracy."

Later that same afternoon, Richard was summoned to Colonel Simmons's office, where he was joined by Studies and Observations Group Capt. Wally Lee. The three men sat together in the colonel's private dining area. A stainless steel coffee dispenser and three olive-green mugs were on the utility table.

Colonel Simmons poured himself a cup and added what seemed like an enormous amount of raw sugar. "Help yourself, gentlemen. This is straight from the Brazilian hills of Sao Paulo."

After taking a seat, he said, "Captain Lee, you are from Greenville, South Carolina. My mother was born there. Her family goes back four generations. Her mother was a teacher at the Baptist female college there on Reedy River Bluff. ... Okay, let's get to it. Are we ready to go for tomorrow?"

Wally and Richard answered in unison, "Yes, sir."

Richard said, "Colonel, why wait? We can go tonight."

Colonel Simmons took a long drink of his coffee and said to both men, "The State guys in Munich are sending a liaison officer to us in the morning for a briefing. General Broughton is distraught and impatient. He brought the CIA into the picture, and they want control of the operation. We will reconvene at 0700 hours tomorrow. With or without the State Department's blessing, we are going to get that young lady tomorrow. She may be in poor shape by now. Hopefully she is mobile enough to walk out of there on her own. Whatever her condition, you will bring her home. Understood?"

Again, in unison: "Yes, sir."

Chapter 13

The Rescue Mission

January 21, 0630 hours: Richard and Captain Lee stood outside the Army Security Agency Command Building, drinking coffee and discussing the procedures for locating Lieutenant Broughton.

Lee said, "I don't know what the spooks have planned. This is what my team has put together." Gesturing with his free hand, he walked Farnsworth through the extraction, step-by-step. As soon as Richard and SFC Hillyer had confirmed the floor and room and approximately how many targets were in the room, Lee's men would breach the door, take out any armed inhabitants, and remove Lieutenant Broughton.

Captain Lee gulped the rest of his coffee and said, "Broughton will almost certainly be drugged and, possibly, unconscious. One of my men will carry her out and two others will cover your exit. If any onlookers or other obstacles are encountered, they will pop a smoke grenade and hold position until the entire team and the prize are out of the building."

Richard and Captain Lee were directed to a conference room that could have served as a corporate boardroom, with 12 chairs around an oval table, and coffee service and pastries on a sideboard near the doorway. After a few minutes, Colonel Simmons entered the room, followed by a shorter man dressed in a dark navy suit.

In a voice that substantiated his reputation as Col. "Bull" Simmons, the colonel opened the briefing. "Gentlemen, this is Mr. Richard Beckwith from the Munich Consulate. He has some intel to share which will help you with our operation today. Mr. Beckwith has recapped what we need to know about Alyson Broughton. She is five feet, six inches tall, weighs 127 pounds, with dark brown, shoulder-length hair. Her slender size will be a relief to the man charged with carrying her out of the building." Simmons gave a nod to Beckwith.

CIA Agent Beckwith said, "We'll have a six-man extraction team in the field with you."

With raised eyebrows, Wally Lee looked disapprovingly at Farnsworth.

"At Colonel *Simmons's* insistence," Beckwith said, "the CIA team will be in a standby and guard mode through the operation. Should your team become compromised by injury or other restrictions indicative of mission failure, our team will take over the mission."

Colonel Simmons asked, "Any questions?"

Captain Lee spoke up. "Yes, sir. Colonel, what are our bang-bang orders?"

Beckwith answered, "Captain, the building is full of students. We cannot afford an incident that involves a student getting shot by stray gunfire or injured in a grenade blast. If possible, I suggest you make your hands, or as a last resort, the Ka-Bar your weapon of choice."

Colonel Simmons spoke next. "I know how you young folks enjoy your music these days. Fortunately for us, the Munich Center for the Arts is hosting a rock concert in Englischer Garten park two blocks from the Arabella Hochhaus. The

Arabella is a 23-story hotel and apartment building where Lieutenant Broughton is being held. The students will be in the park and the building should be mostly empty."

Everyone agreed this was the best of all scenarios.

Farnsworth smiled and asked, "What rock band will be performing?"

Bull Simmons snorted, saying, "They are called the Rolling Rockheads."

Richard Beckwith chuckled. "Sir, they are the Stones, the Rolling Stones."

Colonel Simmons folded his hands and said, "We go at 1800 hours. By the time we are in position, the students will be at the music festival. With all the activity, noise, and food trucks, the BMW SUVs provided by the CIA should go unnoticed on the street in front of the hotel. If everything goes as planned, by 1830 hours Lt. Alyson Broughton will be safely on her way to the base infirmary."

Simmons stood and the others followed. Operation Rolling Stones was set in motion.

***

The Arabella Hotel building had an adjacent tower of residences. The first floor contained a lobby and lounge area with a wide set of stairs to the service rooms and meeting rooms on the second floor. There was also a corridor connecting the apartment tower to the hotel tower. From an empty meeting room, Richard and SFC Hillyer could set up their equipment on the second floor and monitor the voice and radio communications, and heat traces, as well as acoustically monitor conversations and footfalls on the floor above. If the anticipated traffic was not detected, they would repeat the setup on the third floor in an unoccupied apartment provided by the hotel's manager. The kidnappers would very likely be holding

Lieutenant Broughton on a lower floor to provide for a quick exit if needed.

Richard had his devices set up and activated within 10 minutes after arriving at the Arabella. As suspected, the chatter from the third floor was immediate and clearly identified as person-to-person conversations regarding "the American." The "army bitch" they repeatedly referred to was, without a doubt, Lt. Alyson Broughton. Hearing no responses from Broughton, the team had to assume she was either unconscious, gagged, or both. She'd of course be restrained with handcuffs, plastic cuffs, or maybe plain old duct tape. Counting the clearly audible footfalls and heat patterns, Richard ascertained there were four people and which rooms they were in. One of the four in the apartment was a lighter person, possibly a woman, most likely not Broughton. The steps were too frequent and moved back and forth between the living room and bedroom.

Captain Lee and three other operators were in position in staggered locations on the stairwell. Despite the advice to use caution regarding gunfire and avoiding collateral casualties, they were armed with live ammunition and a clear understanding that lethal force was not only the first round of defense, it was an integral part of their plan. They knew exactly what the extraction procedure was and had not only practiced it many times, they'd had live experience with Col. Bull Simmons's son, Tay, and his raid in Vietnam. The whole operation would take less than one minute. When Lee gave the order, operator number one would open the door with a master key supplied by the hotel's manager. Operator number two would take the lead position and enter the room, shooting the first targets encountered. Number three would move to the number one spot as number two entered the adjacent bedroom, repeating the process. Captain Lee would follow and move toward the prisoner's location. After securing the prisoner, all four would exit the building's stairwell and leave in the waiting vans.

SF Specialist 5 Charlie White silently turned the key in the door and opened it slowly at first, then pushed it wide open as M.Sgt. Vincent Korman took two steps inside, shouting, "Don't move! Show me your hands!"

Korman was simultaneously sweeping the room for a target and preparing to shoot the first person in his path. Before he could adjust to the light, a gunman fired from behind a living room sofa. The first round hit Korman in the chest of his bulletproof vest. The second round struck him slightly higher, above the vest and through his neck. His pulverized carotid artery instantly pumped large amounts of blood down his chest as he slumped to his knees and onto the floor.

Sergeant Major Wallace was the third man at the door. He tossed an M84 stun "flashbang" grenade into the living room. The gunman positioned behind the counter in the adjoining kitchen was firing blindly into the living area. Regaining their senses after the blast, Captain Lee and Sergeant Major Wallace crouched in the entry hall and returned fire. The smoke from the grenade, coupled with the stunning effects of the light and sound of the explosion in the small living space, obscured the vision of the two Special Forces soldiers rushing into the space. Charlie White was on his hands and knees attempting to drag Sergeant Korman to safety. Richard and SFC Hillyer were already in the corridor when the first shots were fired. Sergeant Hillyer immediately began assisting White with Vincent Korman. The bullet had ripped open the side of Korman's neck and blood flowed steadily onto the floor around them. Hillyer and White each sensed he would not make it.

While Sergeant Major Wallace and Captain Lee were open targets in the apartment, their exchange of gunfire kept the two kidnappers trapped in the kitchen. Capt. Richard Farnsworth was no stranger to gunfire, and he ducked through the doorway with only one thought in mind—find Lieutenant Broughton. He entered a bathroom door just to the right of the entrance. The bathroom was a Jack and Jill and the next door connected to the bedroom. He blasted through the door and found the third captor huddled in a corner with her hands up.

"Please don't shoot me! Please!"

She was crying hysterically, and Richard yelled at her, "Where is she? Tell me now!"

The terrified young student could barely speak as she pointed at a closed closet door.

Richard opened the door and found Alyson Broughton sitting on the floor, her mouth gagged with tape and cloth, and her hands and feet bound with wide silver duct tape. Her eyes were bulging and staring up at him in terror.

He grabbed her hands and snatched her forward and out of the closet, saying, "You're okay. We've got you."

Alyson looked up at him and for a second or two, she found his eyes. Richard struggled to remove the gag in her mouth while moving her toward the door. They exited the apartment through the adjoining bathroom. In the stairwell he was joined by SFC Hillyer. Richard had his arm tightly around Lieutenant Broughton and they walked down the stairs and into the waiting SUV.

SFC Hillyer and Charlie White carried the limp body of Vincent Korman down the stairs and into the second vehicle. Captain Lee and Sergeant Major Wallace had neutralized the gunmen, cuffed the girl to a cast-iron stove, and were slowly backing down the stairs. Wallace had his pistol raised, ready to shoot anyone pursuing them. Thirty long seconds later they were on the street.

The CIA driver of the lead vehicle conferred briefly with Captain Lee and spoke into his handheld radio in a deadpan voice: "Cleanup on aisle 3, two hams, one live chicken."

Both SUVs were back on base within 25 minutes. The one carrying Master Sergeant Korman drove wildly through the base to the hospital's emergency entrance. Korman was placed on a rolling gurney and rushed through the open glass doors.

Drew Hillyer cursed out loud, "Shit-shit-shit!"

He put a hand on Charlie White's shoulder. They knew he was gone.

Farnsworth, Hillyer, and Broughton, in the second vehicle, had Lieutenant Broughton stabilized, and she was slowly beginning to catch her breath. She was a soldier. She was not crying or whimpering in pain. Lt. Alyson Broughton was a very pissed-off woman. Richard understood she had suffered the trauma of captivity and her reaction was more of a defense mechanism than real toughness. In addition, Broughton had survived an experience that would haunt her for the rest of her life. She would cry. Maybe not now, but one day soon the reality of the near-death experience would hit her like a land mine.

The next morning at 0700 hours, Richard and Captain Lee were being debriefed by Colonel Simmons and one of his senior staff members, Maj. Tracy Jenkins. Jenkins was actually a psychiatrist from Jacksonville, Florida. Her assignment in Germany and in Colonel Simmons's battalion was to lead a PSYOPs effort to interpret and combat the Russians' program of covertly influencing German citizens and the student population of protesters and anarchists. Things simply did not add up. The protests and obscure demands of the students were weak and unworthy justifications for the violence and mayhem in the major city centers throughout Germany, Poland, and Turkey. If there was a Russian brainwashing plan in place, it was working.

Colonel Simmons opened the discussion by saying, "I'm sure you know by now that the master sergeant was DOA. The goddamn captors were tipped off to the raid. We had the hotel manager arrested and interrogated. It wasn't him. Hell, it wouldn't surprise me if the CIA tipped them off to create an incident—to create traffic and movement from the Russian implants. The students must have had eyes on the street that saw the BMWs unloading. These kids." He sighed, shaking his head. "These murdering bastards knew the exact moment we entered the building. I underestimated their resolve and Vincent Korman paid for my poor judgment with his life. Master Sergeant Korman was a third-generation warrior and he knew the risks. What he did not count on was the stupidity of a group of 20-year-old brainless dimwits." Simmons paused and said, "The hysterical woman—God dammit—the stupid-ass girl you left strapped to the stove in the apartment has no clue about anything. She was the clueless girlfriend of one of the dead captors. The German liberal press is going to have a Pulitzer-winning field day with this fiasco."

***

After a week of doing nothing, Richard was getting impatient. Finally he received word that new orders would put them on a plane back to the US. Richard and SFC Drew Hillyer were going home. The Special Ops guys? They were off to another Top Secret mission.

Richard and Drew Hillyer joined a squad of regular army soldiers headed home after serving a 24-month duty assignment at USAG Stuttgart Army Air Base 30 miles outside of Munich. The happy soldiers filled the 12-hour flight with raucous laughter and beer drinking, while Richard and Drew sat without speaking, trying unsuccessfully to sleep. After two days of processing at Fort McPherson outside of

Atlanta, Richard and Drew Hillyer were on an MC-12 twin-engine turboprop mail carrier (King Air 350) headed to Ayer Massachusetts Municipal Airport and the familiar gates of Fort Devens Army Security Base.

Chapter 14

Fort Devens – February 1, 1971

In a Tennessee Southern drawl inherently part of Capt. Gene Mason's personality, he reached out his hand to Richard, saying, "Soldier, I am damn glad to see you in one piece! Welcome back to the zoo."

Richard was glad to be back, but nothing seemed the same. He was disoriented and walking around in a daze. He no longer had a command, and Stacie was teaching in California at the Army Language Institute. It was the first Monday in February, and she and Richard had not had any communication since he'd left for Turkey after Christmas. Following the tumultuous events of the past month, the prospect of resuming command of an Army Security Agency company of trainees at Fort Devens was not inspiring for Richard.

Captain Mason said, "Richard, why don't you get some rest. Take the week and get checked out at the infirmary. Colonel Blaise is in DC for a few days. He wants to see you when he returns. I'll have my clerk contact the colonel's admin and set something up for next Monday."

"Thanks, Gene," Richard replied, "I think I'll do that. My head needs some rearranging."

Now that Richard was on base, he could not stop thinking about what his future looked like in the army. Not only that, he could not get the image out of his mind of Lt. Alyson Broughton staring up at him when he'd pulled her from the closet in Munich. Her eyes held him only for a second, yet it was as if he had known her before. Maybe he could stick it out for another 14 years and retire as a field-grade officer O6, or higher. To Richard, at 27 years old, that seemed like a lifetime away.

February 8, at 0700 hours, Capt. Richard Farnsworth was in his neatly starched uniform and ready for a meeting with the battalion commander, Col. Sam Blaise. After an uninterrupted breakfast in the officers mess hall, Richard walked the short distance to brigade headquarters. Upon his arrival at Colonel Blaise's office, the front desk clerk told him to go right in; the colonel was expecting him.

Richard entered the office, which was unlike most ASA Garrison offices. Daylight streamed in from the large windows commanding a view of a five-acre field of trees and grass which separated the administrative buildings from the barracks and mess hall buildings.

Colonel Blaise bellowed, "Come in, Captain, have a seat."

Though Colonel Blaise had a gruff, commanding voice, his demeanor was unexpectedly pleasant. Blaise had served in the Korean conflict and multiple campaigns in the Vietnam War. The witnessing and causing of violent death broke a man's spirit, leaving him with a tough outward appearance, yet also a vulnerable persona that understands what is really important in life.

"Captain," Blaise said, "I just returned from the Pentagon and more 4-stars than I could count. I don't know what you did over there in Germany, but you are either in deep shit or up for the Medal of Honor. I had a meeting with the head of the Intelligence Directorate of the Joint Chiefs. One Maj. Gen. Thaddeus Broughton knows you by name. He directed me to issue your reassignment orders to embassy duty in Washington, DC. Captain, we hate to lose you and your book of knowledge on SIGINT operations, but I have no choice in the matter. Your orders will be ready this afternoon. You have three days to pack up and drive yourself to Fort McNair Army Base on the Potomac River, and report for embassy duty in DC."

Chapter 15

The District of Columbia

Before our country was called the United States of America, it was referred to as "Columbia" in the Revolutionary War (feminine name for Columbus). Three hundred years after Christopher Columbus discovered America, the federal government bestowed the name "District of Columbia" to the capital city of the United States of America. Richard's new duty station was to be Fort McNair in Washington, DC, at the intersection of the Anacostia and Potomac Rivers. The two-century-old base was the original home of the US Department of War.

Lt. Alyson Broughton was more than just a commissioned "army brat." When she was only 11 years old, she started and directed her own foundation. As an army child she learned about pain and unbearable suffering from her childhood friends who lost their fathers in the Korean War. Her best friend lost her dad to the war and was devastated. The child's father was weeks away from returning home from the war and had written to his daughter, promising a family trip to Disneyland in California. His death took away the family trip and irreparably broke Alyson's friend's heart.

Alyson took up the challenge to raise the money for her friend's family trip to Disneyland. Within a month's time she raised more than enough for the family to visit the world-famous amusement resort. Alyson continued to raise money for families suffering from wartime losses. While living at the home of the famous Third Infantry Battalion at Fort Stewart in Hinesville, Georgia, 16-year-old Alyson Broughton was named "1961 Army Military Child of the Year." At a Military Kids' Appreciation Parade ceremony, Janette Morse, with Operation Homefront, said these things about Alyson Broughton: "Alyson is an amazing young lady who has endured multiple deployments and moves, and understands the sacrifices so many children make. She puts others first and brings smiles and joy to children who have lost so much."

Lieutenant Broughton was not a graduate of West Point. In 1965, women were not allowed admission to the academy. Alyson enrolled in what was arguably the equivalent of West Point, as one of the first female ROTC cadets at George Washington University. The Hoya Battalion of female cadets quickly grew to 20 percent of the ROTC program at GW University. Alyson was also among the battalion's first female cadets to graduate from the US Army's Airborne School. In 1969 when she was interviewed by NBC News' *Today* show host Barbara Walters and was asked about going to war, Lieutenant Broughton had this to say: "Freedom of thought and expression, my family, and my lifestyle—they all mean a lot to me. I'd be willing to fight for them if I had to. I know I'd be scared to death. Anybody would be. If I have to go, I'll go." Lieutenant Broughton was not called to go to Vietnam.

In the late sixties and early seventies, military service tours in Germany were the first choice as rewarding assignments. The US had military bases in Kaiserslautern near the borders of Belgium and France. The bases in Heidelberg and Stuttgart were close to the home of the Mercedes and Porsche manufacturing plants. Career soldiers returning from the war in Vietnam often preferred Germany when they extended their enlistments and commissions. Alyson Broughton chose Germany and duty at the army base near Munich. While at George Washington University, she studied international relations. When her commitment to the army was completed, she had her sights on international service in the US State Department. She hoped that being assigned to duty in Germany would give her access to the people and workings of our US Embassy in Germany. She was technically on a 24-month duty tour at Stuttgart Army Base, and her work assignment was at the US Consulate in Munich.

The US Embassy was located in Berlin, 300 miles to the north. Just steps away from her small office at the consulate was the vast expanse of the 900-acre Englisher Garten. It was in this park that Alyson had been abducted while taking an early evening stroll along the artificial stream running the length of the park. She was going to the reconstructed Chinese Tower in the Garten when three young men approached and forced her into a nearby car. She was blindfolded, gagged, and her feet and hands bound. A painful sting to her right thigh was the injection of a drug that knocked her out. When she regained consciousness, she was in a cramped space with her knees pressed to her chest. She could not see in the darkness and only heard the blaring of a German television station and the muffled sounds of people arguing.

Alyson's kidnappers were students at the Ludwig Maximilian University of Munich. Established in 1472, it is among Germany's oldest universities. The large student population is generally made up of legacy students from wealthy German families and a significant number of international students. It is historically known for traditional academic programs in the sciences, philosophy, medicine, jurisprudence, and theology. The kidnappers came from a curriculum centered on futuristic societies and the Parmenides Center's Study of Thinking. The reason Alyson was targeted and kidnapped was simply because she was in the US military. She was also a female of slight stature and more easily handled than an athletic male target. The Russians had German-born agents who infiltrated the student protests in major cities in Germany. It was well known by the student protestors that they could easily exchange captured American tourists and military personnel for up to 20,000 Deutschmarks (5,500 USD, 1971). When she was rescued, Alyson was a day or two away from being handed off to the Russian agents.

Monday, February 15, 1971: Capt. Richard Thomas Farnsworth was dressed in his Class A uniform which displayed his military regalia. He had a driver assigned by his new CO at Fort McNair. They completed the five-mile trip in under 15 minutes. It would take another 30 for Richard to clear security and get to the section for the J2 Intelligence Directorate and the office of Gen. Thaddeus Broughton. Even though the Pentagon is over 6.5 million square feet, once you are inside the five-sided structure, the time walking the longest distance between two points is less than ten minutes.

General Broughton's staff of five assistants included civilian and military personnel. They were seated at gray metal desks in a front office area. Everyone seemed busy doing whatever a general's assistant does. Richard sat alone in a row of eight chairs arranged in a straight line along a half-height wall separating the work area from the corridor. The area was quiet except for the *clickety-click* of typewriters and the hum of a photostatic copy machine. He felt like he was back in high school, waiting to see the principal for a reprimand. Company-grade officers—Lt. O1 through Capt. O3—did not usually meet with or speak to generals of any rank. Even though Richard knew well who General Broughton was and this obviously had something to do with the rescue operation in Germany, it was still an unusual meeting.

Capt. Richard Farnsworth entered the vestibule of Broughton's office and was met by a 40-ish-looking Maj. John Eller, who greeted Richard with a handshake and escorted him to the inner office where Gen. Thaddeus Broughton sat behind a massive oak desk.

Not sure of the protocol, Richard approached the desk, came to attention, and saluted with a report of, "Sir, Capt. Richard Farnsworth reporting, sir."

The general rose from his chair and walked to the front of the desk. "Have a seat, Captain." Broughton turned to Major Eller. "John, please excuse us. I would like to speak to Captain Farnsworth in private."

Richard remained standing while Eller left.

The general put out a hand for an extended and hearty handshake. "Thank you for coming, Captain." Broughton returned to his seat and Richard sat in a straight chair in front of the desk.

General Broughton said, "Captain, I'm sure you know why you are here. I'll get right to the point. You saved my daughter's life and I wanted to thank you personally." The general paused, apparently hung up emotionally.

Richard replied, "Sir, I did not act alone, and—"

"Son, my daughter is the most important person in my life. If you and the others had not rescued her, she would likely be dead right now. Alyson would have fought the bastards to the end. You and I both know that if the East Germans or the Russians had gotten hold of her, she would have been raped and beaten into submission." He paused again to regain his composure, and Richard waited without speaking.

"Once they found out who she was, she would have been put in a hellhole prison cell in Moscow until a ransom or a prisoner exchange could be arranged."

Richard knew all this was true and felt great empathy for the general's emotional state.

Aside from the sheen of excess moisture in his eyes, General Broughton was back in command mode. "Captain, it is your face my daughter saw and your words she heard when you said, 'You're okay. We've got you.' At that point you might as well have been Jesus Christ Almighty! She knows your name and she will never forget it. I am here to thank you for saving the most important person in my life."

Once more, Richard was about to speak when the general raised a hand slightly. "Captain, I know your history and I know about your exemplary service in Vietnam and Tet. I also know you were wounded. Your missions in Turkey and the intelligence that was gained saved lives you don't even know about. In Germany, well, we know about Germany. Now that you're here in the US, you do not have a command. Your current orders assign you to the State Department's Office of International Security. You are going to get lost in that policy-making bureau. They want you to create briefings for the deputy secretary and write field guides for the spooks to use to learn about the latest intelligence intercept tools and methods. The tedium of working with a bunch of paper pushers is going to suck the life out of you. I would like to offer you the opportunity to join my staff. Before you say anything, I know you are not cut out for the confinement of an office building and administrative duties. You also do not have enough time-in-grade for a promotion to major. You can, however, accelerate the process by attending the School of Advanced Military Studies at the US Army Command and General Staff College in Fort Leavenworth, Kansas. By the time you complete the

10-month course and return to DC, you will qualify for a field-grade promotion. From there your options are numerous. You can continue your formal education at MIT, or Stanford, or assume a command in army intelligence. You could return to the ASA and Fort Devens, but I will tell you confidentially that the ASA will eventually be absorbed by a new agency called the US Army and Intelligence and Security Command. This information is not to be shared. Understood?"

Richard replied, "Yes, sir, understood."

General Broughton closed the meeting by telling Richard, "Think about what I am proposing for your future in the army. You are in a perfect position to advance through the ranks and create a rewarding military career."

Richard returned to his quarters at Fort McNair. General Broughton had asked him to strongly consider the offer and give him a response after meeting with the State Department and the Assistant Secretary of Military Affairs at the US Consulate. The captain already knew returning to Fort Devens was a dead end. He would likely die from boredom working as a staff officer in the Pentagon. Accepting the command and general staff college assignment would require an extension of his military service. Even early retirement was still 10 years away. Being stuck in limbo was unnerving and he needed to get things settled.

That afternoon at 1630 hours there was a knock on his door. Richard opened it to find an attractive young woman dressed in gray civilian clothes and a blue scarf covering her head. The dark brown hair and piercing hazel eyes caught Richard's attention. Except for her five-foot, six-inch height, she could have passed for Cher Bono. Richard recognized who she was.

The woman stuck her hand straight out and stated, "Lt. Alyson Broughton."

Richard shook her hand while she inquired, "May I come in?"

Slightly stunned, he managed to say, "Yes, of course. Please do. I'm sorry the place is not really set up for visitors."

They entered his temporary bachelor officers' quarters and sat opposite each other in a sitting area containing one chair and a love seat.

Alyson smiled briefly. "When I found out you were here, I had to come see you. I know you were in my dad's office this morning. I wanted to join you there, but the general wanted a private moment with you."

She reached out and took one of Richard's hands in both of hers, and as she was about to speak, she had to take a deep breath. "You saved me, you saved me from unspeakable things." Her eyes were watering. "I cannot find the words to adequately thank you."

Richard cut in. "Lieutenant Broughton, I was not alone."

Alyson squeezed his hands to stop him. "Please," she said, "please call me Alyson."

"Alyson, I was part of a team. *We* rescued you, not just me."

She knew this, and even though she had not been given the names of the special ops guys, she was aware that one of them must be dead or seriously injured. From the closet where she was being held, she'd heard the yelling and the gunfire. She saw Master Sergeant Korman being carried to the SUV parked outside of the Arabella Hotel. His uniform and face were soaked in blood and he showed no sign of life.

Holding her hands to her head, Alyson sobbed, "He's ... dead ... isn't he?" She looked up at Richard, who was reluctantly nodding his head.

Alyson said, "I don't know how to handle this. I want to cry. I want to get angry and scream. I'm numb, like my brain has switched off."

After a few moments of silence, Richard sat up straight and said, "War is pure hell. It never ends. Even when the fighting stops, the visions, the anguish, and hatred continue to boil in your head. What you have been through is no different. Evil people doing bad things and good men getting killed and maimed in indescribable ways. Our brains cannot process the horrible, unnatural acts we see and sometimes do. So, yes, you are numb and it's a good thing. You'll slowly compartmentalize the memories from Germany. They'll be in a box. A box only you can open, and from time to time it will flood your thoughts without warning."

Alyson sat up and wiped her eyes. "Richard, you are a good man. What I will always remember is your face and your words. When you pulled me from that closet and out of that hellhole, I was 1,000 percent dependent on you and your strength and determination to get me to safety and away from the most horrible experience I have ever known. Thank you. With all my heart and breath, thank you."

They stood up. Richard reached out a hand.

Alyson brushed it away and wrapped her arms around his waist. She pressed her damp face to his chest, whispering, "Thank you, thank you, Richard Farnsworth."

He told Alyson if she ever needed to talk, she should call him or send a message. He said he didn't know how long he'd be at Fort McNair or what or where his next assignment would be. She gave him a phone number written on her dad's personal stationery. The paper had the Maryland address for General Broughton's private residence.

Alyson's face brightened as she said to Richard, "Captain Farnsworth, don't make any plans for the weekend. Your orders are about to change."

Chapter 16

The Eastern Shore

Tuesday morning a delivery arrived at Richard's quarters: an itinerary for the week and a box of books and pamphlets from the US Consulate's Office in DC. Richard learned that his original generic "embassy duty" orders were actually an assignment to work for the State Department's Office of Missile, Biological, and Chemical Nonproliferation located in the Truman Building at 2201 C Street NW, four blocks from the White House. Today, he was to thoroughly acquaint himself with the physical and operational aspects of the US Embassy and the various offices in the State Department. He was to report to the Assistant Secretary of the Bureau of International Security and Nonproliferation Executive Director at 0800 hours Wednesday morning.

The Bureau of International Security and Nonproliferation existed to prevent the spread of advanced weapons. The mission included identifying areas where proliferation was already in place and creating responses to roll back the threats from those countries. The bureau would work closely with the Departments of Commerce, Energy, Treasury, and Justice. Richard now acknowledged to himself the general was right. He'd be stuck in a policy-making rut, while the CIA carried out the actual intelligence and special ops missions.

The next morning Richard reported to the BISN's Assistant Deputy Secretary, Miss Jane Miller. She gave him a tour of the building and introduced him to some of the people he'd be working with. The five-story building measured over one million square feet and was occupied by more than 5,000 civilian and military personnel. Richard would be reporting to Lt. Col. Joseph P. Lemire. The colonel was out on sick leave, so Richard would be joining one of the existing task forces assigned to the US State Department and embassy in Istanbul, Turkey. Richard knew well that the issue of security for the nuclear weapons stored in Turkey was a top concern for the United States and NATO. He was assigned a desk and locker and given more pamphlets from the military equivalent of the office of human resources. He joined the daily preparation meetings where they worked on the content for weekly White House briefings to be conducted by the Undersecretary of State for Arms Control and International Security Affairs. After a grueling day of doing essentially nothing, Richard's biggest takeaway was that these people used a lot of paper and printer ink.

Sitting at his desk on the fifth floor of the State Department wing, Richard felt like a business secretary working for a large public corporation. The feeling was one of being nonessential. He did not like it. Staring blankly at an org chart of the department and a list of the US embassies around the globe, he was interrupted by the ringing of his desk phone. No one outside the department knew his phone number. *Hell, I don't even know it.*

The voice on the line said, "Listen! Friday at 1400 hours you will get a call requesting your presence at McNair. Don't question it. Just be there. I will pick you up in front of the BOQ at 1600 hours. Got it, Captain Farnsworth?"

Richard was smiling. "Alyson, it's good to hear from you. How are you doing?"

She replied, "Never mind me, I'm fine. You be there on time, in civilian resort wear. Bring a jacket and whatever you need for two nights. It can be chilly at the seashore."

Alyson paused, and Richard said, "Seashore?"

She replied yes and clarified it was the general's home on Maryland's Eastern Shore. Alyson called her dad "the general" because she did not like saying Dad or Daddy while wearing the uniform.

Richard responded, "Ah, yes, the address on your dad's stationery."

"He has a family farm there and a guest cottage on the beach. I don't know if the general will be there or not, but he happily expressed his approval for your visit."

Thaddeus Broughton had been raised in Maryland, and he spent every weekend he could at the three-century-old family estate. During the week he lived in an apartment in McLean, Virginia, 10 miles from the Pentagon.

Friday afternoon at 1600 sharp, Richard was standing outside his quarters with an overnight bag. He was wearing a Yankees ballcap, long-sleeved navy linen shirt, and khaki pants. He couldn't remember the last time he'd worn tan loafers without socks. Alyson pulled up in a bright red 1970 Mercedes-Benz 280SL convertible. She popped the trunk, and Richard placed his overnight bag and a plastic garment bag holding a blue blazer and two dress shirts into the trunk, and gently closed the trunk. They drove toward the post's exit.

En route, Richard asked, "You were not in uniform when you stopped by on Monday. How is that possible?"

Alyson explained that when she returned from Germany and was released from the hospital, she was given a mandatory 30-day medical leave. She had three weeks remaining before she had to report to duty at the Pentagon. Her dad had secured a cushy communications position for her in the army chief of staff office under Gen. William C. Westmoreland. General Broughton and Westmoreland had been classmates in West Point's Class of 1936.

The drive to the farm in Trappe, Maryland, took a little over 90 minutes. Richard and Alyson talked continuously. More accurately, Alyson did most of the talking while Richard listened intently. Trappe, a very small town, counted only 400 residents. It sat on the Eastern Shore of the Chesapeake Bay, near Saint Michaels and Oxford.

Alyson asked Richard, "Have you ever been to the Eastern Shore?"

Confidently, he said, "Sure, I have. I know Trappe well. It is the home of Dwight Eisenhower and the famous Yankees third baseman, Frank 'Home Run' Baker." Richard had never been to Trappe or even Maryland.

Alyson laughed. "You are full of it. You have never been anywhere near the Eastern Shore."

He chuckled and said, "You're right. I looked it up in an old encyclopedia set at the base library."

Richard and Alyson pulled up to the entry with tall brick columns and a majestic iron gate. An arched trellis over the entry held a sign with 12-inch black letters spelling out the name CHOPTANK FARM. The electrically operated gate slowly opened to a long, white gravel road leading to the main house. The estate sat on the banks of the Choptank River, which extended southward from Chesapeake Bay. To call this place a farm was an understatement. Four hundred acres of waterfront wilderness with structures built in the 18th and 19th centuries included a main house, a guest cottage, a beach house, a pool, and tennis courts—not the kind of setting normally found on a farm. Even the barn was built in the early-19th century.

They drove past the barn and majestic old-growth trees to a circular drive and wide white-painted brick steps leading to a spacious front porch. The entry foyer provided a long view through the house, to French doors looking over the imposing lawn and the Choptank River. Flanking the foyer on each side were matching parlors with fireplaces and hand-carved 18th-century mantels. The three-story house had a total of eight fireplaces.

A housekeeper and one other well-dressed woman met Richard and Alyson as they exited the convertible. "Ms. Broughton, would you like the car to be moved to the garage?"

Alyson responded, "No, thank you, Donna, we will be going to the guest cottage after I show my friend the main house."

Donna was the farm's operations manager. Some dairy cows and beef cattle grazed the pastures east of the house. Alyson knew the farm maintained just enough agricultural activity to merit the lower property taxes assessed to farmlands.

"Donna Griggs, I'm pleased to introduce Capt. Richard Farnsworth. He'll be staying with us this weekend."

Richard extended a hand, which Donna ignored and, after a polite curtsy, she said, "I am very pleased to meet you, Captain. Please let me know if you need anything. Alyson, it is so nice to see you. Betsy will attend to your bags."

After touring the 17th- and 18th-century wings of the estate, Richard and Alyson drove to the beach house on the Trappe River. The river was officially known as La Trappe Creek in the La Trappe Creek Preserve. It wasn't a creek at all. The wide expanse of water was more of a bay on the east side of the Chesapeake. The beach house was nice, but too far from the main house where Alyson would be staying. Richard was assigned to the guest cottage, which was a second garage for two automobiles. It also housed a well-appointed one-bedroom suite.

While walking the grounds of the estate Richard noticed a historic bronze plaque. The inscription read as follows:

"THE CHOPTANK"

PART OF THE PRESENT HOUSE BUILT IN C. 1700. HOME OF DANIEL MARTIN AND SON NICHOLAS, WHO WAS CAPTAIN IN THE 38TH BATTALION OF MARYLAND MILITIA DURING THE REVOLUTIONARY WAR AND DIED HERE IN 1808. NICHOLAS MARTIN'S SON DANIEL, ELECTED GOVERNOR OF MARYLAND IN 1829, ADDED A LARGER PORTION OF THE HOUSE C. 1810.

MARYLAND BICENTENNIAL COMMISSION
AND MARYLAND HISTORICAL SOCIETY

Richard sat alone on the rear porch of the main house while Alyson unpacked and changed clothes. He was already experiencing feelings of insignificance before arriving at the general's impressive estate. After seeing the 271-year-old property and thinking about the history extending back to the Revolutionary War, his self-esteem had imploded to new levels of irrelevance. The troubling thoughts he had on whether to stay in the army or enter civilian life seemed trivial in the historic setting of the Choptank River.

Alyson descended the grand staircase and joined Richard on the porch facing the beautiful gardens. Flowers bloomed even in the winter months. Every month during the cold weather in December through March, the gardener had fresh plants shipped from Homestead, Florida, to the farm.

Standing next to Richard, Alyson announced, "We're having dinner at the beach house tonight. The farmhands are preparing an old-fashioned bonfire and a traditional Chesapeake crab bake just for the two of us. You will love it!"

After dinner Richard and Alyson sat by the fire and stared at the stars.

He turned to Alyson and said, "What am I doing here? What are we doing here?"

She wasn't sure about the answer. She put her hands over her face and sighed. "I don't want to be alone. I'm scared. I know it makes no sense. It's just a feeling of dread that keeps popping into my head."

He placed a hand on her knee and fixated on her eyes. "Alyson, you are going to be okay. It's only been a few weeks since you were blindfolded and locked in a closet, not knowing if you'd be killed. You need time to heal. After I was wounded in Vietnam and released from the hospital, everything tormented me. Being injured by an exploding rocket that I had no way of avoiding gave me a feeling of helplessness. It took away my will to live. The only thing that saved me was seeing the other severely wounded soldiers at Walter Reed Hospital. Young boys with amputated arms and legs and horribly burned faces had more spirit for living than I could muster at the time. I knew they'd trade places with me without thinking. I would get better, I would look better. They had a lifelong condition that would punish them every day and every night. You will get better. I promise."

After a few moments of silence, Alyson stood up and said to Richard, "Let's walk."

They strolled along the river's edge. Though they called it a beach house, its land wasn't like the white sandy beaches of the Atlantic coastline. The riverbanks were sand and mud with rocks and oysters and marsh grass. Alyson and Richard meandered on a neatly bordered gravel path which followed the serpentine banks of the Choptank. Subtle ground lighting illuminated their route. The bonfire in the background crackled, its flames lighting a large area surrounding the firepit.

Alyson stopped walking and turned to Richard. She put her hands on his waist and pulled him toward her. Her body shivered from the chilly night air. She leaned up and kissed him gently on the mouth. "Thank you, Richard. Thank you for everything."

He circled his arms tightly around her and pressed his face to her cheek. "You're welcome, Lieutenant Broughton. The pleasure is all mine."

Saturday morning, they had breakfast on the veranda, near the gardens and pool. Gas heaters mounted on the ceiling of the covered area kept the temperature at a steady 75 degrees. Miss Betsy served them a traditional breakfast of poached eggs with crabcakes and tomato slices on sourdough toast. Hot coffee and orange juice completed the resort-style meal service.

Richard stared across the wrought-iron-and-glass table at Alyson. "I could get used to this lifestyle, Ms. Broughton." Facetiously he added, "What's next? Tennis? Croquet?"

"Neither," she said. "We're going sailing!"

Richard's eyes crossed. "I don't know how to sail."

Alyson pushed away from the table and stood up. "Well, soldier, you're in luck. Because I was the captain of my sailing team at GW."

The *Bonito* was a classic 1912 design. The 26-foot Herreshoff sloop had a mainsail and foresail. The compact cabin housed a storage locker and a V-shaped bunk. The boat's name was not for the streamlined saltwater fish. It was Portuguese for "beautiful woman." Alyson and Richard walked along the long wooden dock toward the sailboat moored to a floating section of dock and accessed by stairs from the fixed dock above.

She asked Richard, "Can you swim?"

He replied, "Most assuredly, I can. Although it's not something I had in mind for this adventure."

They laughed and agreed that swimming was not on the itinerary for the day.

Alyson climbed aboard and removed the canvas that covered the seating and steering console. She flipped open the hatch to the cabin to check for fuel fumes and water under the floorboards. She reached into the open hatch and turned a key that started the boat's small inboard engine.

They untied the boat and slipped slowly away from the dock. Alyson steered upriver to the mouth and into the bay. She instructed Richard on how to raise and set the mainsail and the gaff-rigged foresail. With the sails up and the halyards secured, she pulled the mainsheet and jib lines tight and secured them to the capstans just forward of the helm. They were under sail and headed on a northwest course toward Chesapeake Bay.

With a steady 10–12 knot SW wind, they sailed briskly along the coastline, passing the Choptank Lighthouse at Cambridge and rounding Tilghman Island, toward Annapolis, 50 miles to the north. Once they were in the open water of the bay, the boat began a steady cycle of pitching through the low swells.

Alyson asked Richard, "Are you okay? How are your sea legs?"

He raised his hand in a thumbs-up gesture. "I'm fine. This is so beautiful. I can see why you love sailing and visiting the farm."

She shifted herself forward along the U-shaped seating and said to him, "Here, you take the helm." She stepped over Richard's legs, and he slipped into position and took the wheel.

Alyson said, "You look like a proper yachtsman, Captain Farnsworth."

He gazed across the water and thought, *This is a good way to live.* He briefly considered that maybe he should have gone to the Naval Academy instead of West Point—no snipers, tigers, or snakes in the ocean.

Alyson was peacefully observing the skyline and thinking how nice it was to be on the water again, and how nice it was to not be alone.

Richard watched her intently, her shoulder-length dark hair dancing in the wind. She was beautiful, and normally he would be on her scent with the dedication of a prize hunting dog. Still, he could not stop thinking about Stacie and how much she would enjoy sailing on the Chesapeake. He wondered how and what she was doing in California. He knew that having grown up in South Florida, she would manage just fine in the land of grapes and sunshine.

After an hour of sailing along the scenic eastern shoreline, Alyson gripped Richard's arm and said, "Okay, Skipper, it's time to come about. When I tell you, turn the wheel hard to starboard. When the boat turns, duck your head under the boom as it swings quickly over your head and turn the wheel to the middle position. If you forget to duck, you will know why it is called the boom!"

Richard did as instructed, and the boat came about. They took up a course back to the Choptank. The cruise was peaceful; both of them needed the therapeutic essence of being on the water.

That night they enjoyed an informal dinner at a round wooden table in the kitchen of the main house. The housekeeper, Mrs. Betsy Wilson, had prepared a shrimp and yellow rice casserole and left it in the oven warmer. Betsy was a true Southern lady from the historic Daufuskie Island on the coast of South Carolina. She had moved to the Eastern Shore of Maryland after her husband, Ralph, got a job with the Chesapeake Ferry Service. Betsy had set out a bottle of Jordan Chardonnay in a wine chiller placed on the picture-window sill next to the table. There was also a plate of crispy fried strips of quail breast and hot honey mustard for an appetizer. Richard and Alyson finished the first bottle of wine before the main course. They talked about their childhood years and family struggles. Richard kept most of his more traumatic childhood memories to himself.

He shared a sentiment with Alyson that his friend Buster Browning had told him in Nam: "Family! Sometimes it can be the American Dream, and other times it's just another f-word."

After dinner they sat on a wooden swing suspended from the substantial cypress ceiling beams on the back porch.

They were halfway through a Willamette Valley Pinot Noir when Alyson took Richard's hand in hers and said, "I don't want to go back."

"You don't have to," he said. "I'm sure I can find a ride to the base."

She squeezed his hand. "No, Richard, I don't want to stay in the army. I'm not a career soldier. When my four years are up, I'm getting out. I only joined ROTC at George Washington University to please my dad. My mother spends most of her time in the Hamptons, looking after her parents. They are both in their eighties and not doing well at all. My mother was a Morgan, as in great-granddaughter of the late John Pierpont Morgan."

Richard stared at her with a blank look.

She said, "J. P. Morgan, banker, super-rich Morgan. As in Morgan Stanley."

Richard apologized, saying, "Yes, sorry. Got it."

Alyson disclosed that they were not close, and her mother was up there protecting her interest in the family estate and the codicil to seven centuries of jewelry.

After finishing the second bottle of wine, Alyson rested her head in Richard's lap. She said abruptly, "I have to go to bed." She sat up and stepped off the swing.

Richard rose as well and stumbled into her. He said, "I'm so sorry!"

She held him and said, "I'm not. Why don't you stay here with me tonight. There is no one around, and the night watchman will not enter the house unless I summon him. Donna, the farm manager, will not show up until after church and maybe not at all." Alyson began pulling Richard by the hand, into the house.

The next morning Richard woke up early and gathered his clothes from the floor of Alyson's bedroom. She was out cold. He partially dressed and walked to the guest cottage, hoping no one would notice him. The sun was already up and over the horizon. It looked like a summer day, though it was still February and the temperature would probably not get out of the fifties.

After a long shower and getting dressed for the trip back to the base, Alyson showed up at the cottage door with a tray of coffee and fresh fruit. They sat at a table in the kitchenette.

She said, "I hope your preference is regular coffee, black, no sugar."

Richard smiled and said, "Yes, perfect. Thank you."

Alyson reached across the table and grasped Richard's hands. "I'm a bit fuzzy about last night."

His eyes met hers, and he said, "Nothing happened. Yes, we spent the night in your bed. You insisted over and over that I stay. Then you rolled over and instantly fell asleep. I stayed awake for a while, hoping you'd not be sick or wander through the house searching for me. So I stayed. Again, nothing happened."

Alyson appeared more concerned than relieved. She pushed her lips out and said, "That's too bad. I wanted something to happen." She placed a hand to her head and sighed. "I'm sorry, Richard. I should not have had that much wine. It doesn't change the fact that I'm glad you're here. I need you."

The drive to the base was quiet except when the radio blasted the latest number one hit from Crosby, Stills, Nash & Young, "Teach Your Children." Alyson dropped Richard off in front of his quarters at Fort McNair. Leaning over from the driver's seat, she kissed him lightly on the mouth. "I'll be at my apartment tonight, if you want to call … or come over."

Richard stepped out of the car, and Alyson revved the engine in park before accelerating and slightly spinning the tires, leaving Richard in a plume of dust.

***

Richard arrived at the Truman Building early on Monday. He sat through the first intelligence briefing, taking it all in. The war in Vietnam was the topic of the day. The discussions centered on how to end the war and achieve 100 percent withdrawal by the end of the year. The United States Conference of Mayors was calling for complete withdrawal. The hawkish US Senate continued to reject legislation that would mandate the withdrawal. Protests were ongoing in DC, and in the predawn hours of March 1, 1971, there was an explosion in the Capitol Building. A revolutionary group called the Weather Underground claimed responsibility for the bombing.

National Security Advisor Henry Kissinger was saying the war could not be won, and promised the North Vietnamese that the US would withdraw all troops by the end of the year in exchange for release of the American POWs. Congress was reducing authorization for the military draft to 150,000 per year. US soldiers in Vietnam were getting news of the pending withdrawals and the end of the war. The confusion prompted some combat troops to unlawfully refuse orders for patrols outside of the protective perimeter of field bases in Vietnam. The Paris peace talks were entering their third year, without much progress. The true measure of the progress of the war was in the number of dead soldiers. In the last 12 months, 2,414 Americans lost their lives in combat. Over 22,000 South Vietnamese were also killed.

The presentations and debate proceeded throughout the day. What Richard wanted the briefing package to say was SNAFU—meaning "Situation normal, all f'd up." For now, it looked like the rest of 1971 would bring more bombing, more draftees, and more death. Though Richard was a warrior and a patriot, he believed the civilian leaders in the Defense Department and the confused, misinformed politicians had destroyed any chance of winning the war. The objective was when to quit and at what price. General Westmoreland, the commander of the Military Assistance Command, Vietnam, was running the war and his current appeals to Congress were for funding drug treatment programs for 60,000 American soldiers abusing heroin, cocaine, and amphetamine drugs in Vietnam. To use another of Buster Browning's favorite acronyms, the war in Vietnam was FUBAR, f'd up beyond all recognition.

That evening Richard returned to his BOQ and, in lieu of dinner, he polished off half a bottle of Blanton's bourbon whiskey. He wasn't feeling sorry for himself so much, but more for the guys still in Vietnam. He wondered where his friend Buster ended up after Turkey. Maybe someone in General Broughton's office could track him down. Richard lay fully dressed on his bunk, thinking about Stacie. She had probably moved on. He should write to her and let her know what was going on in his life, and find out how to get in touch with her. Richard thought about Boston and their night of lovemaking at the Godfrey Hotel. He thought, *Lt. Stacie Shatner, I miss you. Where are you and what are you doing?*

The rest of the week was a repeat of Monday's preparation meeting. The task force was putting together a briefing to be delivered by the Undersecretary of State for International Security and Arms Control. The Undersecretary would then have his staff develop a briefing for him to deliver to the Secretary of

State, along with the other reports from other Undersecretaries. While administrative in its nature, the information was critical and often classified. In addition to the opaque messaging about the Vietnam War, the situation in Turkey was volatile, and the security of our nuclear arsenal stored there and in other parts of Europe was an ongoing concern. Failure to maintain control and security of nuclear weapons was never an option.

Monday morning at his desk, Richard was reading through the newswires to find international headlines. The most prominent news was an AP article dated that day, March 1, 1971. "Serving under an appointment by President Richard Nixon, George H. W. Bush became the United States Ambassador to the United Nations." Bush was a politician and previously a US congressman from the Seventh District of Texas. The news wasn't all that important to Richard; still, he did admire Ambassador Bush's record as a 19-year-old World War II naval aviator. While serving in the navy he'd received the Distinguished Flying Cross and three air medals. He was an extraordinary young man and graduated from Yale after only two and a half years. Richard thought it was good to know the ambassador viewed world events and challenges through a warrior's eyes. One of Richard's task force members was a semi-famous University of Florida running back by the name of William "Bill" Dennis. He had a girlfriend who worked in General Broughton's office. Richard had met her briefly at the base mess hall with Bill. Her name was Sharon, and she was, as they said, "Easy on the eyes." Richard arranged for Sharon to deliver a note to her friend in the G-1 Army Personnel Office. Richard was looking for the current location and APO mailing information for Sgt. Buster Browning and 1st Lt. Stacie Shatner.

Richard had the phone number for Alyson's apartment. He thought he should call and check on her and make plans for dinner one night that weekend. Except for the weekend at Choptank Farm, he had not been in the company of a woman for over two months. Richard did call and they agreed on plans for Friday night. Alyson made a reservation for them at the famous Old Ebbitt Grill in downtown DC. Old because it originally opened in 1856. Famous because Presidents Ulysses S. Grant and Theodore Roosevelt had been among their most famous clients.

Knowing they'd be drinking wine and maybe a cocktail or two, Richard took a cab to the restaurant. Army officers arrested for driving under the influence did not fare well in the ASA. Richard needed to maintain his clearance level and SI access. He arrived 30 minutes early and ordered a Heaven's Hill Manhattan at the bar. He surveyed the bar and the adjacent raw bar. Tonight was going to take a sizeable chunk out of his O-3 paycheck. Army captains received $600 per month plus housing and meals. For reasons unknown to Richard, he was also still getting $65 per month combat pay supplement.

The restaurant was beautifully decorated and the architectural wood paneling on the walls gave the place the feel of a living room. The glowing fireplace and the mix of table conversations and music from a piano bar set the stage for what would be a romantic evening. Richard felt a tapping on his shoulder and turned to find Alyson dressed in a stunning Bill Blass sleeveless, black cocktail dress with straps crisscrossing her perfect cleavage.

He quickly stepped from his bar seat and, putting his hands on her shoulders, exclaimed, "My God, Alyson, you are beautiful!"

He pulled her toward him for a kiss on the cheek. She put her hands on his face and planted a lover's kiss that released unbridled passion.

Richard leaned back, dazed, and managed to say, "And it's very nice to see you too!"

When he asked for the bar tab, the bartender said, "It has been taken care of, sir. It was my pleasure to serve you."

Before Richard could respond, the bartender bowed slightly, turned, and moved away.

In a whisper, Richard said, "That was a surprise. I'm not even in uniform."

As they approached the hostess stand, Alyson took Richard's arm. She looked over her shoulder to the bar and winked at the bartender. The maître d' smiled broadly and reached out his hand to Alyson, who took it.

He bowed and gently kissed the top of her hand, adding, "It is such a pleasure to see you, Ms. Broughton."

"And you as well, Mr. Aleman. I'd like to introduce my friend and fellow soldier, Capt. Richard Farnsworth."

Alyson and Richard shared a Rhode Island calamari appetizer and two cups of New England clam chowder. Richard devoured a Cedar River Farms ribeye steak, while Alyson enjoyed an Alaskan sockeye salmon salad. They started with a half bottle of Schramsberg Blanc de Blancs and emptied a full bottle of Domaine Droughin Pinot Noir. The dinner was a geographical smorgasbord. The conversation was pleasant and centered on Alyson's adventures at George Washington University and her officers' leadership training at Fort Hood, Texas, after being commissioned.

Following a short break in the conversation, Alyson took Richard's hand in hers. She smiled and said, "I'm two months past due for a promotion to first lieutenant. When I go back to work after sick leave, we have a small ceremony planned, and I hope you can be there. I will probably not stay in long enough to make captain. Still, this is important to me, and especially a big deal for my dad."

Outside, while waiting for Alyson's car to be brought to the valet stand, she snuggled up to Richard and said, "I know the perfect spot for a nightcap."

He groaned and said, "I may have had enough to drink for one night."

"Come on, Captain, you can have hot tea or coffee. It's only two miles away and I'm okay with driving. Afterward, you can catch a cab back to base."

One glimpse at Alyson's beautiful face and her perfect body wrapped in a winter-white mink-and-leather topcoat, he knew he had no choice but to comply.

She drove to her townhouse at the foot of Wisconsin Avenue in Georgetown. She pulled the car into a red brick building which aesthetically enclosed a parking garage. They went across an elevated connecting walkway to her apartment building. Alyson's townhouse afforded a view of the Three Sisters River and Theodore Roosevelt Island. You could see the lights from Pentagon City from her balcony. There was even a European-style riverboat moored on the river's edge below.

Richard said, "You continue to amaze me. You actually live here?"

She answered, "It was owned by my mother before she and Dad were married. It's mine now. How about that nightcap?"

Alyson switched on a stereo on a bookshelf in the living room. Frank Sinatra was softly singing the 1966 hit, "Summer Wind." Alyson poured them each a cordial glass of amaretto.

Accepting his glass, he said, "Why, Lieutenant Broughton, I do believe you are trying to seduce me."

Alyson laughed. "Captain Farnsworth, I had you at hello."

They set the liqueur aside and leaned into each other on the sofa. He kissed her lightly at first and then, with his arm around her shoulder, they took on a lovers' embrace. She moved her fingers through his hair as he reached low on her back with one hand and placed the other on her nearly exposed breast.

Richard murmured, "My God, you are beautiful, Alyson."

She placed a hand over his mouth and said, "Come with me."

As they walked toward her bedroom, she removed her earrings and bracelets and set them on a dresser in the beautifully appointed bedroom suite. It was a sea of blue and white colors and intricate patterns. The lush white carpet looked as though it had never been stepped on. Next to the bed, they embraced again with the passion of new lovers. She unbuttoned Richard's shirt and pulled off his necktie. Alyson stepped backward and carefully removed her silky dress and slipped out of her black lace bra and panties. She turned down the bed comforter while Richard removed his shirt and pants. He gently pushed Alyson backward onto the king-size bed. Their lovemaking had the controlled pace and passion of lovers well acquainted with the other's body and desires.

Richard observed that Alyson's figure was slightly fuller than her appearance disclosed when fully clothed. Her perfectly formed breasts were also fuller than one would expect on a slender frame. Everything about her was perfect and luscious. He had never seen or experienced any woman so stunning. They made love a second time and rested on the soft sheets.

Alyson asked, "Do you want to stay? Saturday is open for me. I can show you parts of Washington you have never seen, and maybe drive to Annapolis for lunch on the waterfront."

Richard rolled to his side, facing her. "I'm not sure what we're doing here. I *am* sure I like it. You are an amazing woman. To answer your question, I don't have any clothes for sightseeing. I'll get a cab to base and return about ten thirty. We'll have the day together. The weather is supposed to be clear and sunny."

Alyson smiled and said, "Okay. And you may want to bring more than one change of clothes. In case we get snowed in."

He slid closer to her and pressed the full length of his body against hers. He could think of no place he would rather be than right there with Alyson. She wasn't just voluptuously attractive; she had a magnetic alluring beauty that was inescapable.

She kissed him and said, "It looks like the captain has come to attention. We'd better fall in for some more PT. How about a few more pushups, soldier!"

Chapter 17

Annapolis, Maryland

With Richard at the wheel of Alyson's Mercedes convertible, they made the 30-mile drive from DC to Annapolis on US Highway 50 in about 50 minutes. Along the way Alyson gave Richard a streaming history of the city. The original town, in 1649, was on the north shore of the Severn River. It was named the "Town at the Severn." Later, in 1683, it moved to the southern shore of the river and became "Town at Procter's," and in 1684 it was renamed "Anne Arundell's Towne." In 1694, the capital of the Royal Colony was moved to Anne Arundell's Towne and renamed "Annapolis," after Queen Anne of Great Britain.

Annapolis, the capital city of Maryland, had a population of more than 30,000 people, per 1971 figures. The small city was well known as the home of the United States Naval Academy, established there in 1845. What was not as well known: in 1783, after the signing of the Treaty of Paris ending the Revolutionary War, Annapolis became the first temporary capital of the United States. The capital followed the meetings of the Confederation of Congress and moved to New York City, then Philadelphia, and ultimately in 1791 Pres. George Washington decreed the capital would be constructed between the bordering states' boundaries, in a new federal territory named the District of Columbia, after the great explorer Christopher Columbus. After 10 years of construction, the 100-square-mile capital city became known as Washington, DC.

When Alyson finished Richard's history lesson, she noticed he was serenely focused on the surrounding countryside.

She turned to him and asked, "Did you hear anything I said?"

He replied, "What? Of course. It was fascinating. Especially the part about the loose Lady Anne hooking up with elderly Lord Cecilius of Baltimore. There was more going on in that little village than just oyster-packing and sailmaking."

Alyson exclaimed, "Okay, I get it! Enough history for today. Let's talk about something more important, like where we're going to have lunch."

The most historic 140-year-old restaurant in Annapolis was the Federal House—one block off Main Street, one block from the waterfront, and one block from the Naval Academy. Richard sighed and told Alyson he had spent an entire semester at the academy in his third year at West Point. The two academies provided the opportunity to seven students each year to participate in a scheduled exchange program between the academies.

The couple pulled into a parking place near the end of the Carrol's Creek waterway in the heart of downtown Annapolis, close to the restaurant on Main Street.

Taking Alyson's hand, Richard said, "Let's enjoy a nice lunch, and then I'll personally walk you through the Naval Academy. The full guided tour will take too long. After we're cleared for entrance, we can visit the Naval Museum and Memorial Hall."

The museum was founded in 1845 and was housed in Prebble Hall. It contained 6,000 prints that recorded European and American naval history, along with an amazing model ship collection donated by Henry Huttleston Rogers.

During lunch Alyson and Richard talked about their college years and childhoods and anything that helped to avoid any conversation about their immediate futures.

Toward the end of their meal, Alyson looked at Richard with a serious facial expression and said, "My mother is coming home next week."

Richard responded, "Why do you make that sound so ominous?"

"Don't get me wrong," she said, "my mother is a good and generous person. She's just different. She comes off as aloof and haughty. She can't help it. Growing up with all that wealth in a rigid—formal—lifestyle permanently shaped her personality. I tell you this because you will initially, and most assuredly, not like her."

He thought about this and simply said, "She will adore me. I will put forth my top-shelf personality with all the charm and charisma befitting that of an esteemed member of the elite Army Officer Corps."

Alyson shook her head, saying, "It won't be enough."

Chapter 18

The Hay-Adams Commemoration

After another week of going through the motions with meetings and general assemblies, Richard was sitting in his BOQ struggling to read the last chapters of J. D. Salinger's *The Catcher in the Rye*. He could readily identify with the mental struggles—feelings of not belonging, loss, sex, and depression. He was interrupted by a sharp knock at the door.

Opening the door, he found a sharp-looking enlisted WAC dressed in a two-piece army-green wool suit with a white shirt, black tie tab, and garrison hat.

She snapped to attention and saluted. "Good afternoon, Captain Farnsworth, sir. I have a delivery from General and Mrs. Broughton."

Richard returned the salute and thanked the female soldier as he closed the door.

The invitation was in a fine ivory-colored stationery envelope with the handwritten calligraphic lettering addressed to:

Captain Richard Thomas Farnsworth
Officers' Quarters, Unit #7
Fort McNair, Virginia

The formal invitation read:

The General and Mrs. Thaddeus Morgan Broughton
request the pleasure of your company at the
Commemoration Dinner for the
Distinguished Lieutenant Alyson Christine Broughton
Saturday, the 20th of March, 1971.
Cocktails at 6:45 p.m., Dinner at 8:00 p.m.
Formal Attire
The Hay-Adams Lafayette Dining Room
800 16th Street NW
Washington, DC 20006

Richard knew the dinner was planned to celebrate Alyson's survival from the ordeal in Germany, as well as her promotion to first lieutenant in the United States Army. He was not aware that the Broughtons had reserved the entire restaurant at the Hay-Adams. Formal attire meant army blue mess jacket, high-waisted trousers, white dress shirt, black bow tie, and cummerbund. Fortunately, he had all the pieces carefully stowed in a hanging bag in his BOQ closet. It had been more than a year since he had worn the uniform, and he was hopeful the pants and jacket still fit.

On Friday, Alyson and Richard had lunch at the base mess hall. She informed him they were expected to join the general and her mother for a pre-dinner reception at the general's apartment in McLean, Virginia.

Richard said, "I'll take a cab. What time should I arrive?"

She corrected him. "Take a cab to my place around four o'clock. The general's driver will pick us up there at five. We won't be at the McLean apartment any longer than necessary. You'll meet my mother and have time to get acquainted before the more formal setting at the Lafayette. She'll ask you about yourself. Don't share too much detail. While she may seem genuinely interested, trust me when I say she is not. Her vision of my future is to marry a legacy of one of her friends in the elevated echelons of Boston's circle of wealthy families."

Why bother going at all? he asked himself.

Alyson noted the expression on his face. "Richard, I'm so sorry. I've offended you. Oh God, forgive me. I'm not like her. I don't share her dream. Please just go through the motions with me and we'll get through the evening together."

He pressed his lips together and stared at her. "Alyson, I'm the one who should apologize. This evening is a special moment in your life. Your family and friends will be there to celebrate the blessing of your survival from a horrible experience. I'll be there with them to toast and salute your achievements. Your father is right to be proud of your promotion. The Women's Army Corps consists of about 12,000 female soldiers, and only 1,000 are staff officers. It was just last year that the very first female officer became a general in the Women's Army Corps. You're one of fewer than 200 female first lieutenants. I'm one of 35,000 captains in the US Army. So, yeah, tonight is pretty damn special. I am more than lucky to be here."

The general's apartment in McLean was a townhouse in a 100-year-old building converted to residences by Theodore Lerner, a wealthy Jewish philanthropist and real estate developer in Virginia. The neighborhood was populated with wealthy politicians, movie stars, and other influential people with business in the DC area. Upon Richard and Alyson's arrival at the general's home on Chainbridge Road, a security officer dressed in a black suit met the car and escorted them to the courtyard and front door of the residence. The home was within eyesight of the famous Hickory Hill residence of John F. Kennedy and Jacqueline Bouvier Kennedy. JFK's brother, Robert Kennedy, had bought the home in 1956.

A tuxedoed servant met the couple and directed them to the sitting room, where they joined the general and Mrs. Broughton. General Broughton made the introductions and Alyson's mother extended a hand to Richard, which he gently grasped and air-kissed while bowing slightly. Champagne was served.

General Broughton welcomed Richard to his home and offered a toast to his daughter. "To the second most amazing and important woman in my life! You have my love and respect this day and in all days to come."

Mrs. Christen Morgan Broughton was dressed in a full-length black velvet Hubert de Givenchy ball gown accented by a triple strand of graduated natural pearls. A 10-carat diamond-clustered heart pendant sparkled. Her earrings were simple four-carat diamond studs with gold lace backing. With her five-foot-nine-inch height boosted by three-inch Arpels black heels, she cut a stunning figure that would turn heads in any setting. Richard was appropriately impressed with the 50-year-old Christen Broughton.

Alyson's mother was the first to speak. "Captain Farnsworth, I would like to add my deepest gratitude for you and your role in saving our daughter. When I think of the unspeakable things she avoided, I shrink helplessly at the thought."

The general stepped in. "Now, Mother, please, we are here to celebrate. Let's move to the den and enjoy a few moments at the fireplace before we leave."

"Okay, yes, of course," Mrs. Morgan said, "and Captain, you must tell us about your family. Except for your military service and that you are a West Point graduate, Alyson has shared very little with us about you."

They moved to a spacious cypress-wood paneled room featuring a granite stone fireplace and settled onto the soft leather furniture. Above the hand-carved walnut mantel hung a portrait of General Broughton's grandfather, Confederate Gen. Hugh Mercer Broughton.

Richard gave the Broughtons a brief history of his family and listed many of the important inventions and contributions his father had made while working at RCA.

Impressed, Mrs. Broughton said, "Your father is quite a nice gift to society. Television, cameras, and nuclear fusion. That really is amazing. Your mother sounds like the one who held the family together. I hope you have her visit sometime."

Richard responded, "Thank you for those kind words, Mrs. Broughton." He had almost used her first name, Christen, but caught himself in time. He added, "Yes, my mother is truly a blessing. I owe her more than I can ever repay."

General Broughton stood and said, "It's time to get moving. We will take two cars. It is likely you younger folks will remain vertical longer than these old knees will hold out."

The setting at the Hay-Adams was elaborate. As they entered the John Hay Reception Room, they were entertained by a duet of flute and violin musicians from the Georgetown University School of Music. A hostess representative took their topcoats and a second host announced each of their names and titles as they entered the room. They were led to a lavishly decorated high-top table adjacent to a towering flowing fountain containing a statue of none other than Mr. John Hay and Mr. Henry Adams. Drink orders were placed for the cocktail reception. Roving servers offered hors d'oeuvres, champagne, and other wines.

The program was printed on off-white linen stationery. At the end of the reception line, guests were instructed to be seated in an area adjacent to the John Hay Room. The scene was much like a wedding ceremony. The general and Mrs. Broughton were standing at the head table, along with two other flag officers and their wives. Richard escorted Lt.

Alyson Broughton to the front of the room and presented her to the general. Alyson and Richard turned toward General Broughton and saluted.

Alyson said, "Sir, Lt. Alyson Broughton reporting as ordered, sir."

Richard backed away three steps from the podium.

General Broughton turned to the audience. "Ladies and gentlemen," he said, "welcome to the commemorative dinner for my daughter Lt. Alyson Broughton. You are here tonight as representatives for all the brave men and women who serve in the armed forces of the United States of America. You are also here as our friends. As senior members of the military, we have a responsibility for the well-being and advancement of the officers and enlisted men and women that we command. Before I begin the official ceremony, I want to personally thank one of the brave men here tonight who rescued my beautiful daughter from the violent, depraved revolutionaries protesting in Munich, Germany."

Richard approached the podium. Mrs. Broughton stepped up to the podium too, next to her husband.

"Capt. Richard Thomas Farnsworth," General Broughton announced, "you have my respect and admiration. Your actions and bravery are duly noted in the record books of the United States Army." Thaddeus put an arm around his wife's shoulders and said, "In my house, you and your acts of valor are indelibly recorded in our hearts and minds, and we will forever be thankful to you for saving the life of our daughter."

The emotionally moved audience stood and applauded for a full minute.

Mrs. Broughton, Alyson, and Richard took their seats at the head table.

When they were settled, General Broughton said, "Ladies and gentlemen, please take your seats."

The two other flag officers, Brig. Gen. Peter Hummel and Maj. Gen. William "Sandy" MacArthur, took positions at each side of the podium.

General Broughton read, "Attention to orders: The president of the United States, acting upon the recommendation of the Secretary of the US Army, has placed special trust and confidence in the patriotism, integrity, and abilities of 2nd Lieutenant Alyson Christine Broughton. In view of these special qualities and her demonstrated potential to serve in the next higher grade, 2nd Lieutenant Broughton is promoted to the grade of 1st lieutenant in the Women's Army Corps of the United States Army, effective the 20th day of March, nineteen hundred and seventy-one, by order of the Secretary of the Army."

The general congratulated Alyson. They exchanged salutes, and Thaddeus Broughton, the father, leaned in and hugged his daughter. The audience erupted with applause. After the head table stood up and began moving toward the Lafayette Dining Room, the other guests did the same.

The dining room was arranged in a formal U-shaped fashion. White tablecloths were a classy backdrop for the numerous pastel-colored floral centerpieces. The silverware and fine crystal glassware represented the classic Hay-Adams style.

After everyone was seated, General Broughton and Mrs. Broughton stood, and the general announced: "Honored guests, please join my wife and me in a prayer of thanks, led by Col. Barnum McCarthy from the United States Army Chaplain Corps."

Colonel McCarthy stood and offered this prayer: "Our Father in heaven, hear our prayer. Bring strength to soldiers in the fight for freedom around the world. Give wisdom to the leaders of brave men and women in the fight against evil. Bring peace and healing to the hearts and bodies of the broken and injured. Father, we thank thee for our many blessings and beseech thee to forgive our many sins. We offer prayerful thanks for all the things thy goodness sends. In the name of our Savior Jesus Christ, we pray. Amen."

The attendees replied "Amen."

General Broughton said, "Please enjoy your meal and fellowship, and thank you again for joining this evening of commendations and appreciation for the service of my daughter and all the members of the United States Armed Forces."

Chapter 19

Springtime in Washington

The cherry blossoms were in full bloom, and the churnings of the governmental machines of Washington were humming along with more than 250,000 federal employees working in 50 buildings spread around the nation's capital. Alyson and Richard moved through the motions in their jobs and saw each other regularly. Student protests and violence continued to dominate the news from Germany and Turkey. Richard's days consisted of situation assessments and signal traffic analysis for the US Army Security Command and European combatant commands. Richard's group played what-if war games on paper and analyzed Army Security Agency SIGINT reports from the ASA Field Station in Augsburg.

Tensions proceeded to mount in Turkey through 1971, and President Richard Nixon and Secretary of Defense Melvin Laird ordered the newly commissioned USS *Trenton* to deploy to Izmir, Turkey. The 16,000-ton naval transport ship carried 2,000 marine combat and supply troops, along with six Sea Knight helicopters. The *Trenton* joined the historic Midway-class aircraft carrier USS *Franklin D. Roosevelt* and other warships in the aircraft carriers' strike group. The move was not an attack posture. American forces were there to deter any move by Turkey to take over US bases and the nuclear arsenal staged there. The show of force had the desired effect, and Turkish President Cevdet Sunay stood down and assured US President Nixon their relationship was intact and no further advancements would be made regarding the control of US bases in Turkey.

Richard was relieved that he would most likely not be ordered back to Augsburg. He did, however, wonder about Stacie. He hoped she was still in California and not in the mess brewing in the European theater. He had not heard from Bill Dennis or his girlfriend, Sharon, regarding the whereabouts of Stacie and Buster. Richard made a mental note to follow up on his inquiry the following week. The April weather in DC and throughout Virgina and Maryland was perfect. The month of May promised similar temperatures, in the mid-sixties. While Washington, DC, was not his favorite city to live in, the proximity to other attractions and outdoor activities made his life seem like an extended vacation. Even with the idyllic conditions, his thoughts frequently wandered to the Vietnam War. He harbored a sense of guilt that he was here and safe, while young boys and men were still dying in the jungles of Vietnam.

"Hello …. Richard, where did you go?"

Richard and Alyson were driving east on US 301, toward the coast en route to Choptank Farm. The idea of sailing and spending another weekend with Alyson was appealing to him. Still, he remained distracted and unsure of the direction his career in the army was headed. His old vision of embassy duty in Washington, DC, had lost its appeal. He felt as though he was in a holding pattern, but for what?

"I'm sorry, Alyson. I've been distracted by work. Thank you for arranging this weekend. I know you love it at the farm. Maybe you can teach me some of the basics of sailing."

The weekend at Choptank was idyllic. They went sailing on Saturday and stayed on the water most of the day. They had lunch at a quaint marina restaurant located on the docks in St. Michaels harbor. Alyson, as usual, looked perfectly beautiful, in calf-length khaki pants and a stunning navy-trimmed blood-red knit top which zipped up the front. She was quite an attraction on the St. Michaels dock. After lunch they took a walk through the historic dockside museum. The museum had been previously housed in the Hooper Strait Lighthouse before being relocated to the Navy Point property in 1966. The restaurant was built the same year, on the property that was previously the home of the Coulbourne and Jewett Crab and Oyster Packing House.

On the slow trip back to Choptank, Alyson and Richard huddled closely in the chilly spring air. The sounds of the water slapping at the hull and the rigging whipping about was peacefully soothing to Richard. The smell of Alyson's hair and the warmth of her body pressed against his put Richard in a delightful trance. He was no longer thinking about Stacie or Turkey, and Vietnam was a distant shaded memory 8,000 miles away.

That evening they enjoyed a tranquil dinner on the rear porch of the main house. The bacon-wrapped grilled quail was a welcome break from Maryland's usual crab entrées. A Willamette Valley Pinot Noir and a crackling fire in the porch fireplace set the perfect medium for another romantic evening with Alyson.

Sailing had not been a physically strenuous activity that day. Being on the open water and exposed to the sun and wind for nearly eight hours did cause some fatigue. As lovely as the dinner setting was, by 9:45 p.m. Alyson and Richard were in her bed on the second floor. The balcony doors were partially open and a soft breeze gently cooled the room. The sound of the wind in the trees and the water lapping at the rocks along the shoreline offered the perfect ambiance for sleeping. Sleep did come, but not before an hour or so of lovemaking in the truest sense of the word. They were intertwined in a spell which neither of them could unwind.

April 4, 1971. After a light breakfast, Alyson told Richard about a concert at the National Mall. The iconic folk rock duo Simon & Garfunkel were staging a reunion concert to celebrate Palm Sunday. "The Sound of Silence," "Bridge Over Troubled Water," and "Mrs. Robinson" would reverberate from the Lincoln Memorial Reflecting Pool to the Washington Monument.

Richard replied, "Sounds great, Alyson. It's a perfect way to wrap up an amazing weekend."

The "spell" was securely cast and there was no exit path for Richard or Alyson.

Chapter 20

Alyson's Episode

April turned into May and the business in Turkey was old news. Most of Richard's days concerned meetings and briefings. Saturday morning, May 1, 0700 hours, Richard's phone rang sharply.

"Richard! It's Broughton."

Startled and half-awake, Richard replied, "Yes, sir, what—"

"Just listen. I am at Fort Bragg, and Christen is in Boston. Alyson is in the ER at Walter Reed Hospital."

Richard's heart sank and before he could respond, Broughton said, "She is not injured, thank God." Broughton paused and again before Richard could speak, he added, "Alyson was walking her neighbor's dog this morning. She was fully dressed in her Class A uniform for a presentation at St. Patrick's Parish. She encountered a group of those damn Yippie protesters outside her Georgetown apartment. They saw her in uniform and began harassing—"

"General," Richard said, "I can leave right now. I will call you when I arrive."

In what would later be called the May Day Protests, 40,000 people had assembled in West Potomac Park for a demonstration. Metro Police showed up in riot gear and ordered the protesters to leave. The group dispersed and a few individuals who remained were arrested. Half of the group reassembled in nearby churches and college campuses. The following Monday, President Nixon ordered 10,000 federal troops to patrol the DC Metropolitan area. Just 15 miles from the White House, at Andrews Air Force Base, 4,000 paratroopers from the 82nd Airborne Division joined 2,000 DC National Guardsmen and more than 5,000 DC Metropolitan Police.

Nixon's overwhelming response was based on the previous activities of the Youth International Party (YIP). As innocuous as the Yippies name sounded, they had a disruptive and violent history, beginning with war protests in 1967. They shut down the New York Stock Exchange and Grand Central Station in 1968. The Yippies staged antiwar protests at the 1968 Democratic National Convention in Chicago. Millions of viewers watched the mayhem unfold as police battled the protesters on live television. The Yippies' loosely bound organization was intertwined with members of the White Panther Party and the Freedom Party. They foolishly idolized the Communist leaders Chairman Mao and Ho Chi Minh. When 50,000 antiwar protesters, led by the revolutionary Abbie Hoffman, staged the "March on the Pentagon," the group's notoriety gained a new level of attention from the Nixon White House.

On Saturday morning, May 1, 1971, Alyson was walking her neighbor's six-year-old German shepherd named Rocky. When the protesters approached her, one of them got up close and in her face, shouting, "You fu__ing baby killer, you should die, not babies!" The protester reached out his hand to grab Alyson's hair. She reacted with a throat punch to the protester's neck. Rocky reacted simultaneously, biting the struggling and now kneeling man on the arm and thigh. Others in the group joined in to pull the dog away. Two of them grabbed Alyson and began dragging her along the sidewalk.

Alyson was screaming and trying to fend off the assailants. Her mind was instantly in Germany, where she was dragged in a similar fashion and taken prisoner by the SDS. Her body continued to fight, but her mind went blank.

A passing patrol car spotted the group and responded. The car's PA system blared out, "Stop! Put your hands in the air!"

Two officers rushed out of the car while a second police vehicle approached the scene. With guns drawn, they ordered the two men holding Alyson to get on the ground face down. While the men were being handcuffed, two other Metro police officers helped Alyson up and tried to calm her. She was shaking uncontrollably and shouting words in nonsensical phrases.

When Richard arrived at Walter Reed Army Medical Center, two uniformed members of the DC National Guard met him. The compound, as impressive as the Pentagon, was equally complex in its layout. They escorted Captain Farnsworth to the seventh floor, Eagle Zone, in Building 9. Alyson was no longer in triage; she had been moved to a secure room for further evaluation. Richard was introduced to the attending physician, a female doctor named Arpitha Yettick. Captain Yettick was head of the center's internal medicine department. She explained to Richard that her duties were for the comprehensive management of Alyson's inpatient care while she was at the center. Dr. Yettick had spoken to General Broughton, and he had authorized her to share Alyson's condition with Captain Farnsworth. She went on to say that Alyson was in exceptionally good physical health and had not sustained any injuries during the incident in Georgetown. She was sedated and would be asleep for at least two more hours.

Dr. Yettick told Richard that while it was early in the process, the evidence pointed to a psychotic episode. She said, "The general told me Alyson has a history of mental trauma. He said you could fill in some of the details."

Richard gave Yettick a summary of the events in Germany.

She asked, "Does Alyson use any drugs not on her list of prescriptions?"

Richard responded that he was not aware of any recreational drug use or anything other than an occasional Tylenol for headaches and monthly female issues.

He called the number which General Broughton had given him. No answer. Richard figured the general would have terminated his activities at Fort Bragg and was probably on a superfast Sikorsky helicopter headed back to Washington. Alyson's mother would also be on her way to the hospital.

After an hour of watching Alyson breathe in and out, he saw her stir in the bed and roll over, facing him. She stared at Richard intensely, but no words came out of her mouth. It was like she wanted to say something. He looked at her and saw no signs of fear or anxiety, just a blank face. Occasionally she jerked her head from side to side and then quickly settled into a deadpan expression, staring blankly at the ceiling.

Richard knew Alyson carried the trauma from Munich in her head. She would never talk about it, and he assured her that one day it would come spilling out. It had to. He had seen it many times. Soldiers returning from combat in Vietnam had no outlet to relieve the horror stored in their tormented minds. The memories of unspeakable scenes of death and injury simply had no place in daily conversations. Alyson would need months and perhaps years of therapy to deal with the darkness hiding in her thoughts.

General Broughton and Christen Broughton arrived at Walter Reed at nearly the same time. Richard could hear them speaking with the medical team and he figured they would want time alone with their daughter. He gathered his cover (uniform hat) and topcoat and straightened his uniform. The general held the door for his wife and they entered the patient suite. Richard was standing and arranging the chairs for the Broughtons to join their daughter.

In a low tone, Richard acknowledged the general and his wife. "General, I will leave you with Alyson. If you need anything at all, please let me know."

The general did not speak, merely nodding his head. Mrs. Broughton was holding Alyson's hand and the general stood next to his wife with his hand on her shoulder.

Alyson remained in the psychiatric evaluation and treatment center for 30 days. The specialists provided daily cognitive behavioral therapy designed to create routines that gave her mental stability. She also received antipsychotic medications to regulate the dopamine and serotonin in her brain. Richard attended a couple of the family therapy sessions, and he generally felt out of place. By the end of week three, Alyson was beginning to resemble the woman he had come to love. She was playful and getting her wit and sarcastic demeanor in order. After returning home and back to duty, she was, in her words, "at 100 percent." Richard knew it was more like 90 percent; there would always be a wound which would never quite heal.

June slipped by, and July in Washington was marred by more than 12,000 war protesters being arrested. Protesters had exploded a bomb in the Capitol Building. Over 60 percent of the country opposed the war in Vietnam. While trending downward, the US had 200,000 troops still fighting a war in Vietnam. Bombs were still falling from the sky and young men were still dying. Richard's thoughts often slipped into a dark place as he wondered what his future held. The country was a perplexing place. He thought, *We have men walking on the moon while the Russians are burying their dead cosmonauts from a failed attempt a month ago.* The Ku Klux Klan, protesting desegregation, was blowing up school buses. Richard questioned if everything had to be a life-and-death conflict.

Richard and Alyson were locked in a solid loving relationship. Each of them needed the other to maintain some sort of stability in their life. On a crisp afternoon in September, Richard and Alyson were sitting on a stone wall above a row of Civil War cannons in Rock Creek Park. They had strolled to the park, which was only five miles from Alyson's apartment in Georgetown.

She took Richard's hand and said, "Did you know Abraham Lincoln stood on this very wall during the Civil War? He was addressing the Union troops at the same time the Confederates were preparing to attack Fort Stevens."

"I did not know that. You are my historian. Thank you."

"Did you also know that my birthday is in 22 days?"

Richard began standing up. "You got me again, Alyson. I did not know that either. So, you'll be 24 years old."

She shook her head. "Wrong again, Captain, I'll be 25."

From their location, if you could find a high enough perch, you could see the White House three miles to the east. Alyson and Richard resumed their walk through the park.

A couple of minutes later she stopped and turned to Richard. "I'll be in Boston for Christmas."

He replied, "That's nice. I assume your mother will be there too."

"Yes, she's there now, and will stay through the holidays. My grandparents aren't doing well. They'll require full-time nursing care soon."

Richard asked, "When do you leave?"

After a moment, she answered, "I pull out on Sunday, December 5."

Richard sensed there was more. "You pull out? That sounds ominous. What are you not telling me?"

Alyson reached for Richard's arm to turn him toward her. "I have new orders. I report to the Department of Defense at the army's Natick Soldier Systems Center. I'll be assigned as the executive officer for supply logistics. The center is only 15 miles from the Morgan family home on Beacon Street in Boston."

They carried on walking and did not speak for a while.

Alyson squeezed Richard's hand and said, "When my 24-month assignment is up, I'm getting out."

That evening they had dinner at a French restaurant recently opened by a Frenchman named Patrick Moulet. The food was exquisite and the prices, while beyond the regular "diet" for army captains' salaries, were acceptable. Richard and Alyson discussed what the next few months might entail. They'd continue to see each other, and in December, everything would change. Boston was nearly 500 miles from Fort McNair. A train ride would take all day. Two days of travel for a one-day visit was possible; given their duty schedules, it was not sustainable.

Alyson was torn between her family obligations and her love for Richard. She knew the general had to remain in Washington, as much as her mother needed to be in Boston. She realized life was sometimes just not fair.

Knowing it had been nearly a year since he last saw his mother shrouded Richard with a burden of guilt. Alyson and Richard would not share this Christmas together.

Chapter 21

The New Year – January 1, 1972

Even though troop levels in Vietnam were continuing to decline, the battlefield was heating up. North Vietnamese forces had crossed the demilitarized zone and advanced into South Vietnam. President Nixon was stepping up the bombing campaign. The strategies of gradual advances and sustained engagement of the enemy imposed by the Johnson administration and Secretary of Defense Robert McNamara were a total failure.

Richard was temporarily assigned to lead a task force to review and analyze SIGINT tools and strategy for a joint Army Security Agency and air force analysis of the Top Secret bombing campaigns in Hanoi and Haiphong. Poor weather and a lack of actionable intelligence on enemy troop locations were hampering the air offensive. Many of the long-range B-52 bombers did not have the latest electronic countermeasures installed, and that made them highly vulnerable to the dozens of surface-to-air missile sites in Hanoi and Haiphong.

Richard's days were occupied by analyzing the reports from ASA field commanders regarding enemy locations and troop movements. The bombing campaign was effective, but came with a cost measured in civilian lives lost, and the loss rate for B-52 bombers was at an alarming rate approaching 10 percent. Richard's team was developing a new form of intelligence intercept tools which would help the air force and marines create a more efficient use of the planes and the hundreds of tons of bombs dropped on every mission. A more accurate attack plan that would reduce the total time-over-target and increase the accuracy of the strike locations was the foremost objective for Richard and his team of analysts.

On Tuesday morning, February 1, 1972, Richard received a call from General Broughton's schedule coordinator. Richard was directed to join a meeting of the Joint Intelligence and Security Command (INSCOM) and present in person the SIGINT/MASINT Interim Report that Richard's team had submitted to INSCOM five days earlier. The report gained significant traction after one of McNamara's staff officers read it and briefed the Secretary of Defense. Vice Joint Chiefs of Staff Chairman Broughton had also read the report.

On Wednesday, February 2, at 0900 hours, Capt. Richard Farnsworth entered a secure conference room in the JCS section of the Pentagon. He saw five members already seated, which included INSCOM Chairman Gen. Thaddeus Broughton, brigadier generals from the marines and the air force, along with their field-grade support officers.

General Broughton opened the meeting and directed the meeting coordinator to table the presentation of past minutes. They would proceed directly into the presentation from the ASA Task Force. General Broughton gave a brief update from the US Military Assistance Command Vietnam. "We have reliable reports that North Vietnamese leaders in Hanoi are planning a major offensive in the Bình Phước Province. The capital city, An Lộc, is most likely the primary target. They have pushed across the DMZ, into the Quảng Trị and Thừa Thiên Huế Provinces. With our troop levels below 200,000 and the outnumbered ARVN forces struggling to contest the advancing VC in the northwestern provinces, our only option is to increase US air power and escalate the intensity and frequency of our bombing missions. General Abrams is bogged down in South Vietnam, and sending more aircraft to the south is not going to win this war. Major General Duval will continue with a summary of directives from President Nixon."

General Duval, the commanding general of the Intelligence and Security Command, got to his feet. "Gentlemen," he said, "the president has issued orders directly to JCS Chairman Admiral Moorer to plan and implement a two-day attack against SAM sites from the DMZ to targets at the 18th-, 19th-, and 20th-degree latitudes to the north—25 miles north of the DMZ. This effort will hopefully motivate the North Vietnamese to rejoin the peace talks in Paris. He has instructed Admiral Moorer to prepare for additional bombing campaigns in Hanoi and Haiphong if the North Vietnamese do not respond." Duval then delivered additional details and official notices regarding the authority and protocol for the implementation of President Nixon's directives. With a nod to General Broughton, he took his seat.

General Broughton gave some background on the troubling results of the current air campaign. "In the past three years we have lost over 7 percent of our B-52 bombers to SAM sites north of the DMZ. The People's Army of Vietnam are being supplied with Soviet and Chinese jets, artillery, and surface-to-air missiles. On the ground, the Army of the Republic of Vietnam is facing a barrage from PT-76 amphibious tanks and T-54 medium tanks. The cover of the jungle and lousy weather make our mission even more difficult. We can bomb cities and other known targets using established coordinates. The locations and movement of the enemy tank battalions are difficult for us to track. Radio transmissions are present, but if the RC-135 spy planes can't fly, they can't locate the tanks. We are carpet-bombing at record rates, but the kill ratios are not sufficient to warrant the expenditure associated with the effort. B-52 Stratofortress bombers with over 100 Mk82 500-pound bombs are being shot down before they can complete their mission."

General Broughton introduced Capt. Richard Farnsworth and summarized his military and combat history, specifically his skills in electronics intercept and signal intelligence gathering. Broughton relinquished the floor and Richard began his presentation.

"Good morning. You are all familiar with Combat Skyspot, so I will skip the explanation and discussion regarding enemy positioning using triangulation of intercepted SIGNET. Communications Intelligence tells us what is being transmitted and sometimes who is transmitting. We can also analyze the intervals of the transmission occurrences. With airborne support and instrumentation, we can locate and intercept ground and air radar systems. We can jam the signals and send deceptive return signals, creating false data for the radar and missile targeting systems.

"A subset of SIGNET is our computer-controlled electronic signal intelligence intercept software, ELINT, that can provide rapid time-stamped signal acquisition with operator-defined emitter sorting and identification. We can 'soft kill' radar and missile sites from a great distance."

General Broughton interrupted. "Captain, if we can locate and take out the radar, we can do the same to their troops and tanks?"

Richard responded with confidence, "Yes, sir, I am coming to that precise explanation."

After receiving a nod from the general, Richard said, "Today's problem is the significant impedance to our efforts that comes from foul weather. Most of the SAM sites north of the DMZ have been identified and can be targeted by artillery assets regardless of weather conditions. General Broughton has told us that a large offensive is expected from the North Vietnamese now that they have crossed the DMZ and moved forces into South Vietnam. Tracking the movement of troops, tanks, and other hardware is difficult, if not impossible when our planes cannot fly. Higher altitudes diminish the accuracy of our intelligence. Flying at lower altitudes exposes the B-52s and other aircraft to ground fire. Even at optimum altitudes, we are losing one out of 10 planes on most missions.

"We know from field reports that Russia and China have supplied amphibious tanks and other medium-class tanks to the People's Army of Vietnam and the Viet Cong. The ARVN forces in the south will not be capable of addressing this new threat. US air support is the only solution that will sustain the South Vietnamese positions. In simple terms, the bad weather prevents us from using our air-based SIGINT and COMINT to locate and track the movement of troops and tanks in the dense jungle. The current strategy of blindly carpet-bombing the suspected locations with 500-pound dumb bombs has not been effective. The air force and naval planes are also at great risk when we do not have the locations of the mobile missile launchers. The ground forces and encampments will be decimated by the enemy tank battalions."

General Broughton slapped the arm of his chair. "We know the problem. Get to the solution."

Richard answered, "Yes, sir. The project we have been working on is ready for deployment. MASINT is a computer-driven measurement and signature intelligence system. Our existing ASA Traffic Analysis technicians intercept and measure the frequency, repetition rate, and other emitted characteristics of a broad range of transmission frequencies. This is augmented by overlaying infrared and magnetic signatures that can identify the targeted assets. The computer-based algorithms are designed to distinguish individual signatures for tanks, troops, missile launchers, and other rolling hardware. The software employed by remote systems can access our master database at Fort Devens, as well as Mission and Installation Contracting Command at Fort Belvoir, Virginia, and our field station analysts at Two Rock Ranch, California."

With an upraised hand, General Broughton stopped Richard. "Gentlemen," he said to the group, "we have employed order of battle plans since the Revolutionary War. Like many planning systems today, we now have computer-based war games software that integrates our SIGNET and COMNET data and human intelligence to create an electronic order of battle that provides the most effective battle plans, and the expected outcomes right down to equipment losses and body counts. The innovative ASA software components developed by Captain Farnsworth and his team of specialists will significantly enhance the EOB plans beyond our expectations."

Richard and General Broughton fielded a few questions. One in specific terms was how the measurement and signature intelligence system differed from the capability of the existing electronic intercept and surveillance systems.

Richard added more details. "MASINT scans the unintended signals generated in the magnetic and infrared spectrums and matches them to reference profiles in the database. The background noise and the static and recurring wavelengths from the asset and its onboard equipment are compared to the known profiles of enemy tanks, ships, aircraft, missile launchers, and even assembled troops. In addition, the instantaneous analysis allows the information to continuously upload from moving troops and equipment."

He scanned the room for questioning looks and went on. "In short, we can locate, confuse, and destroy the tanks moving in the jungles through North and South Vietnam, regardless of the weather conditions. It is like seeing someone in the dark and knowing if it is a friend or foe."

General Broughton rose from his seat. "Gentlemen, that's enough for now. I think you will agree this is an amazing advancement in our intelligence capabilities. Captain Farnsworth, please express our appreciation and thanks to your team. It goes without saying, gentlemen, that everything you have learned today is Top Secret with SCI level access only. Thank you, we are adjourned."

Chapter 22

The Battle of An Lộc

On April 13, 1972, the People's Army of Vietnam and Viet Cong divisions launched a major advance to take over the capital city of Bình Phước Province. The Easter Offensive, known as the Battle of An Lộc, was underway. Three enemy divisions were advancing toward Saigon. South Vietnam's 10,000-man strong Fifth ARVN Division was outnumbered three to one. On the same day, the People's Army of Vietnam forces invaded Loc Ninh 20 miles to the north. An enemy victory there would cut off supplies to the ARVN troops in An Lộc. Five days earlier, PAVN forces overran a base camp in Quản Lợi. This became a staging ground for PAVN units coming from Cambodia to join the siege of An Lộc.

The intelligence task force created by General Broughton had previously produced a report which predicted the strategy and the target cities the NVA and Viet Cong armies would attack. The beginning of the Easter Offensive now revealed the timing of the advance on Saigon. As Richard's team had indicated, the South Vietnamese forces lacked the strength and resources to stop the attack. US air support was essential to the battle to stop the enemy advance on Saigon.

Following the SIGINT/MASINT intelligence script from the Pentagon, the United States Air Force joined with the ARVN First Airborne Brigade. As predicted, on May 11, the Fifth and Ninth PAVN divisions launched a full-force assault on An Lộc with infantry and T-54 tanks. The MASINT system that designed the order of battle created a grid of boxes measuring 1 km by 3 km each. USAF B-52 Stratofortress bombers were guided to the designated grids by ground-based radar. Every hour for 30 hours, 170 B-52s carried out the bombing missions.

On May 12, the People's Army of Vietnam forces regrouped for a new attack—on Ho Chi Minh's birthday. They were stopped by US air support and a counterattack by Army of the Republic of Vietnam paratroopers. PAVN forces continued to attack, surrounding bases through May, and the South Vietnamese cavalry and infantry divisions defeated the advances. The end of June brought the final destruction of the PAVN strongholds, and the battle for An Lộc was declared to be over.

Back in Washington, General Broughton summoned Captain Farnsworth to his office in the Pentagon. Richard presumed it was related to the war and the fighting in the Ben Phước Province.

The general was alone in his office when Richard arrived. Broughton waved him in and toward a seat in front of Broughton's massive oak desk. Richard was right. General Broughton summarized the An Lộc battle and added that the fighting was ongoing. The South Vietnamese had gained control of strategic hill positions, allowing them to target advancing troops with air and artillery fire. General Broughton added that with the arrival of the heralded ARVN's 18th Infantry Division, the fighting in that region would be over by the Fourth of July.

The general briefly held up a file folder and said, "Captain, the intelligence plans you developed played a decisive role in the Battle of An Lộc. A loss in that capital city would have brought about the fall of Saigon. You may not have been there physically in the battle, but your intelligence plans saved hundreds and maybe thousands of US and South Vietnamese lives."

After a reflective pause, Broughton said, "You won't be on the cover of *Life* magazine. The victory is being downplayed at home. In the last days of the fighting and before the press could react, we lost a deputy field commander. Brigadier General Tullis was landing at An Lộc and was met with PAVN artillery fire. Three men were killed, and General Tullis died later at a field hospital in Saigon."

Richard expressed his condolences and thanked General Broughton for his words of acknowledgment.

General Broughton clasped his hands together and leaned toward Richard. "I need you on my team. I need you here in the Pentagon. We have a war to fight and we need to win it! We can accomplish this, and you can help me do it, and reduce our casualties while we close out this damn war. Three things are going to happen. First, you are being advanced to the rank of major. This is a wartime promotion. Your time in grade and command staff training will be deferred for now."

Richard stood, saluted, and reached out his hand to the general. As he was about to express his thanks, General Broughton said, "Sit down, Major, there is more news."

He sat.

"Your old CO at Fort Devens is being replaced. I need you to return to duty there and assume his command. It is only temporary. You will resume your assignment here in DC after we replace him."

Richard asked, "May I speak, sir?"

"Yes, of course."

"Sir, I don't understand. Captain Mason was an exemplary soldier. I served with him in the 303rd in Vietnam during Tet. He is a third-generation army officer."

General Broughton put up his right hand. "Settle down, soldier. Mason was one of my commissions. I've known him since he was a cadet. There is no finer soldier in this army. For reasons you will understand, I cannot share many details." The general sighed and added, "Richard, Gene Mason is sick. Bad sick. He has cancer and it is inoperable. He needs to spend his final days with his family."

Chapter 23

Fall in Massachusetts

Richard sat at Capt. Gene Mason's desk in the Command Headquarters Building at Fort Devens. The base was in Ayer, Massachusetts, just 40 miles from Boston. The fall season was winding down and winter was creeping in; cool air was turning cold. Schools with winter commencement ceremonies were graduating students around the country, and a small percentage of them would be simultaneously completing their swearing-in ceremonies and pledging their allegiance to the flag and country. Some of them were opening a letter from the US Department of Defense which informed them they had a winning military draft lottery number.

The new year would bring a fresh class of recruits to Fort Devens's ranks in the Army Security Agency. Richard assumed command of the Battalion Support Group for Electronic Warfare Training. He had oversight and direct command of the training center and curriculums for ASA enlisted and officer ranks. The school also provided electronic intelligence and electronic warfare training to platoons from the Tenth Special Forces Group stationed at Fort Devens. The ASA had more than 50 military occupation specialties and the initial training for 20 of them was provided at Fort Devens. Cryptanalysis and electronic intercept traffic analysis training topped the list. First priority was also given to the DOD's Defense Foreign Language Institute based in Monterey, California.

Richard was where he'd started. The move revived the doubts he'd had before moving to Washington. He'd thought a promotion to major wouldn't happen for another two or three years. It was now a blessing and a curse. His plans to leave the army had taken a back seat to what could be a 20-year stint. The prospect of an extended army career brought even more unknowns to his daily thoughts. Being at Devens raised fresh thoughts and memories of his time there with Stacie. Concentrating on the training of the next generation of electronic warriors was becoming more difficult. He often thought, *What if I locate her or she returns to Devens while I'm here? What about Alyson?*

He found some relief from knowing his recent assignment was temporary. Fortunately, the mechanics of kicking off the classroom instruction for trainees was nearly automatic. The organization had not changed, but the content was changing monthly. The world of communications was shifting from a 70-year-old vacuum tube technology to transistor-based amplification and modulation of radio signals. Richard was up-to-date, but by no means an expert. His training staff was made up of seasoned career NCOs who picked up the slack. The army was very good at providing continuous learning experiences. Equipment manufacturers were also quick to understand they couldn't sell it if the end users could not operate and maintain it.

After only two months at Fort Devens, Richard received a teletype order commanding his appearance at a Top Secret briefing in the J-2 Intelligence Directorate's office in the Pentagon. The order was unsigned. Richard knew the directive came from the executive officer in General Broughton's office. At first Richard thought something may have happened to

Alyson. He also knew that a personal message would not have come in the form of an official DOD or army communication. If something bad had happened, Alyson would have called. Richard told himself not to overthink the situation. If he was being transferred again, the messaging would have included a moving order.

The next morning when Richard arrived at his desk at 0730 hours, a manila-sized white envelope sat in his inbox, embossed with DOD's official gold-and-blue emblem. It contained an itinerary, hotel information, and a commercial airline ticket to Washington National Airport. He was scheduled to leave in three days. There was no return ticket. The envelope contained a smaller envelope, plain and unmarked. Inside was a handwritten note from his pal Bill Dennis. The note read:

> *Sgt. Buster Browning, Medical Discharge, Feb. 10, 1972. No fwd. address.*
>
> *Stacie Shatner, last post, DLI (Defense Language Institute), Monterey.*
>
> *Current location – CLASSIFIED.*

The envelope also included a photograph of Bill Dennis and his girlfriend Sharon. An arrow marked on the photo pointed at Sharon and a caption read: "Fiancée!"

Chapter 24

New Orders – Field Station Shemya, Alaska

General Broughton's staff had made the arrangements for travel and accommodations for Major Farnsworth's DC visit. Richard arrived in Washington on Thursday, December 7, and was met at the arrival gate by a youthful-looking uniformed CWO1 warrant officer named Charlie Thompkins. He escorted Richard to a black sedan waiting in the pickup lane outside the terminal, which took them directly to the century-old Willard Hotel at 1401 Pennsylvania Avenue NW. Richard did not need to check in. He was given the key to a junior suite that was way above his pay grade. Warrant Officer Charlie Thompkins checked if he required anything else and said good night.

Richard skipped dinner and went directly to the hotel's famous Round Robin Bar for a Hayman's Gin martini straight up. The second round prompted his exit from the iconic bar, and he returned to his room. The next morning, he dressed in his Class A uniform, complete with the army regalia of a seasoned warrior. While staring into the mirror and finishing his morning routine, he heard a tapping at the door to his room. He opened it and a bellman was there holding a silver tray.

"Room service, sir."

Richard replied, "It must be a mistake. I didn't order from room service."

The bellman picked up an envelope from the tray and said, "You are Maj. Richard Farnsworth?"

Richard said, "Yes, I am."

The bellman handed him the envelope and left after thanking Major Farnsworth for the tip.

Inside, the folded sheet of paper read: "Enjoy your breakfast. See you tonight!" The initials *A.C.B.* were written at the bottom of the note.

Richard ate a hurried breakfast, and was again met by Warrant Officer Thompkins. Following the 10-minute ride to the Pentagon, Richard passed through the security gate and was directed to the Military Command Center. After a short wait outside General Broughton's office, the phone on his assistant's desk beeped once and she answered it and nodded.

She turned toward Richard. "The general will see you now."

"Come in, Major, and have a seat. This may take a while." The general looked up and added, "It's good to see you."

Richard wanted to ask about Alyson, but held back his questions. Something was up and he sensed it was important. He also knew from overhearing the end of the general's last phone call that this was not the time for catching up on family matters.

General Broughton pushed the intercom button on his desk phone and said, "Linda, please ask Col. Thomas Wesley to join us." Broughton turned to Richard. "I know you are familiar with the ASA listening post in Shemya, Alaska."

Richard replied, "Yes, it was rumored I might be stationed there when I was XO at Devens."

Broughton chuckled and said, "Only about a dozen men are stationed there. Except for an occasional visit by the CO, they are all specialists and noncoms."

Colonel Wesley joined Richard and General Broughton.

The general stood and said, "Let's move to the conference table."

After they were seated, Colonel Wesley unrolled a site map of the Army Security Agency Field Station Shemya. Next, he produced a stack of official military personnel files for SP4 Robert Cinotti, Electronic Warfare/SIGINT Interceptor; SP5 George Martin, Intelligence Analyst; E3 Ray Norton, Electronics Equipment Repairman; and CW4 Steve Rodgers, Analysis Technician.

Wesley and General Broughton exchanged a look, and the general said, "Proceed, Colonel. Major Farnsworth has clearance for this briefing."

Colonel Wesley began with a review of the location of FS Shemya. "The island is the next to the last island in the chain of the Aleutians. It is 1,400 miles from Anchorage, Alaska. It is also the same distance from Tokyo. There are approximately 1,000 soldiers stationed there. As remote as it is, the 5073rd Air Base Squadron is based there. They provide the amenities found on most military bases. The US Coast Guard and Air Force have troops stationed on the island of Attu, 35 miles to the west of Shemya. In World War II the Japanese landed on Attu with the hopes of invading North America. The US Infantry's Fourth Regiment had other plans and forced the Japanese out and built airstrips and barracks. Shemya became the home base for our B-17 and B-24 bombers that carried out missions over northern Japan until the end of the war."

Colonel Wesley unfolded a map of the northwest Alaskan coastline, which included the eastern regions of Russia. He was about to speak when there was a knock at the door.

General Broughton said, "Yes, come in."

His assistant walked directly to the general's seat and handed him a folded note. She left as quickly as she had entered.

Broughton glanced at the note, pocketed it, and said, "Continue, Colonel Wesley."

"The base was deactivated after World War II and reactivated during the Korean conflict. In 1957, Shemya became the home to Army–Air Force Joint Operations and the westernmost field station for the Army Security Agency. Today our mission is to listen to the Russians. At a distance of 500 miles, the Kamchatka Peninsula of Russia is closer to the island than mainland Alaska. Eareckson Air Station on Shemya is home to the largest radar ever built. Code-named the Cobra Dane, it is our best defense against missile attacks. With new digital technology, our submarines can transmit high-frequency multiplexed encrypted data that identifies the location of Russia's ships and submarines. ASA analysts combine the intelligence from our electronic signal intercept data with the bursts of intelligence packets from our Pacific and Bering Sea assets. Add that information to real-time MASINT radar intercepts of unintended transmissions, and we can tell you the location and movements of every Russian ship, sub, aircraft, and satellite in the Northern Pacific region. We can also monitor troop and equipment movements in western Russia. Cobra Dane has a range reaching well into Russia and 28,000 miles into outer space."

General Broughton spoke up. "Okay, enough of that. Let's get to the problem. Some of our spooks have switched sides. We don't know how, but everything we learn from our collected intelligence is being shared with the Russians. The pattern is simple. Not long after we learn the location of a Russian sub or ship, that enemy asset begins evasive maneuvers. They know what we know. Major Farnsworth, I need your team of experts to find out how they are getting our highly encrypted and guarded information. And we need to identify and punish the perpetrators of this traitorous act."

Richard's brain was spinning. He was already mentally assembling the electronic equipment and designs he'd employ to find the outgoing transmissions.

Colonel Wesley picked up the personnel files and spread them out on the table. "These men have been identified as the most likely suspects. Analysis of military records, personal family situations, and bank records make these four the most likely targets to be compromised by foreign agents."

Richard held up an index finger and asked, "Why not bring them in and shut down the operation?"

General Broughton answered, "Yes, we will do that. First we need to know if they are the right suspects, and more important, are they the only ones? We also need to know who the Russian agents are and what they have on the poor schmucks who have ruined their lives and betrayed our country."

"Surely," Richard said, "they will know something is up when I arrive with a cache of hardware and a squad of technicians."

Colonel Wesley said, "Major, you and your team will be sent in under the cover of being there to audit the capabilities of the intercept systems in place at FS Shemya. You will appear to be designing the physical footprint needed for new digital upgrades to the radar control modules and all other communications hardware."

General Broughton added, "Major, you already have the required personnel and equipment here at L. J. McNair. Special Operations Command North has recurring traffic into and out of Shemya. The 160th Special Operations Aviation Regiment will transport your team and supplies directly to Eareckson Air Station. If you need to do airborne intercept, they will provide RC-135 surveillance aircraft or helicopters as needed."

***

Back at his desk in the Pentagon, Richard was reading everything he could find about FS Shemya and the capabilities of the systems in place at the radar station. Cobra Dane was an L-Band radar operating in a range of 1175–1375 megahertz. It was pointed to the west with a 136-degree span that reached 2,000 miles into Russia and the Soviet Union. It could store and track 120 targets and provide precise tracking data to the US Sentinel Missile Defense System. Richard was aware that Army Green Berets from the Fifth Special Forces Group were deployed to Shemya—the same group that saved his ass in Vietnam during Tet.

Chapter 25

Georgetown

After returning to his Fort McNair BOQ, Richard reread the note from A.C.B. He changed out of his Class As and into civilian clothes. He reached for the phone on his desk. Before he could lift the receiver, he heard a tapping at his door. When Richard opened it, 1st Lt. Alyson Broughton was standing there, more stunning than before. She wore a form-fitting, low-necked black cocktail dress and stood tall in the doorway in her two-inch black heels.

She observed his astonished face and said, "Well, soldier, are you going to invite me in?"

As much as both of them ached to get undressed, Alyson convinced Richard to dress for dinner in town.

After he did, they held each other for an extended time and Alyson said, "We can talk later. I made reservations for us at the coolest restaurant in DC. It's on Blagden Alley and less than four miles away. You will love it."

Richard was dazed and delighted to have Alyson back in his life. He asked, "What are you doing here? I thought you were in Boston at the Army Natick Center."

She replied, "And I thought you had transferred to Fort Devens."

"You're right," he said. "Let's talk later. You look fabulous."

Alyson had arranged for a private driver. In the car she informed him she was visiting the general to personally deliver news regarding the situation in Boston with her mother and her dying grandmother.

"Ah, yes, the note you sent to the general this morning," Richard said, and asked her about the unlikely coincidence that both of them had been reassigned to bases in the Boston area. The US Army Natick Soldier Systems Center (NSSC) was a DOD logistics center charged with the sustainment of the military's food, clothing, shelters, and other soldier support services. Richard added that he was not sure how long he'd remain at Devens. He was on temporary orders pending the assignment of a replacement CO for ASA Charlie Company at Fort Devens.

"I had nothing to do with my orders or yours," Alyson said. "I'm sure the general arranged for me to be transferred to be there for my mother, and you already know the sad circumstances at Devens and poor Captain Mason. I feel so badly for his family."

Richard said, "How long are you in DC?"

"I'm on a three-day pass. It's up to the general. How about you?"

After a long pause, Richard answered. "Alyson, I have new temporary orders for an op that usurps my previously issued orders for Devens. I don't have an end date for my current assignment."

She stared at Richard and said, "Hmm. You're being vague and secretive."

In a soft voice, Richard replied, "Well, that answer will have to do for now."

The driver lowered the security screen separating the front seats from the passenger area and turned to Richard and Alyson, asking, "Shall we proceed directly to the Dabney?"

Richard took Alyson's hand. "You have to stop doing this."

"What?"

"You know what I mean. This! This lifestyle. You know I cannot afford to dine at the Dabney or any of the high-priced places you know so well."

She sighed and said, "Richard, I'm sorry, and I don't want you to be uncomfortable. We can go to my apartment and walk somewhere close by in Georgetown. I was just so excited when I found out you and I were going to be in DC at the same time, I wanted to plan a special evening for our reunion."

Now Richard felt guilty. Alyson had been through hell the last six months. "No, Alyson, you're right. I'm sorry for complaining. This is a special night, and I love you for the surprise. You scared everyone back in May, and tonight you are more radiant and beautiful than I have ever seen you. Most of all, you are here with me." He leaned over and kissed her gently on the mouth. He was careful not to smudge her lipstick or makeup. She really did look like a supermodel.

The evening at the Dabney was classic Washington elegance. The eight-course meal started with charred Millbrook venison and Metompkin Bay oysters. The main course of braised lamb was stuffed with Olive Farm pheasant and pork sausage and served with collard greens, sour corn, and Sea Island peas. A Sicilian Gambino family's Tifeo Rosso Etna provided a medium of excellence that rounded out the exquisite meal. Richard was again the student at the table where he learned more and more about fine cuisine and wines. His intimidation would be palpable if not for Alyson's down-to-earth approach to the extravagant aspects of her lifestyle.

At dinner Alyson recapped some of her recovery for Richard. She told him that if not for her father's influence, she would have been involuntarily medically discharged in June.

She disclosed that even with her current status as "fit for duty," she knew it was only a matter of time before she either resigned her commission or the army discharged her for medical reasons. Any sign of a relapse would be cause for dismissal.

Richard asked, "And then what?"

She was silent for a moment, and said, "I will remain in Boston ..."

Richard interrupted, asking, "To help your mother and grandmother?"

"No, not really. Mother has full-time nurses and caregivers who take care of everything that's needed. Grandmother is comfortably situated in a private suite in the extended care facility on the hospital campus. I just do not want to continue living in the DC area. Georgetown has been marred by the incident last May and may be a trigger for another breakdown, and I do not want to feel helpless or weak. It's like there is a demon that is not me and it's hiding in my head."

Richard leaned over and whispered, "Let's get out of here. No dessert, okay?"

"We can go to my apartment. Georgetown can't hurt me as long as I'm with you."

That night set new heights for passion. Except for visiting Alyson in the hospital last May, they had been apart for over six months. They made love in the truest sense of the word. She released her pent-up emotions with an energy that at times seemed more like an exorcism of the emotional pain she had stored away. Wave upon wave of extraordinary pleasure mixed with mental anguish swept through her body until she was spent. They created a stronger bond. It rose above what could have easily been a feeling of dependence on Richard. She needed him; they understood that. It was different this time and she could not envision life without Richard at the core of her existence.

The next morning they sat, enjoying coffee on the rear balcony of Alyson's Georgetown apartment. The balcony overlooked a peaceful garden area.

"Perhaps you can stay on at Fort Devens," Alyson suggested. "Maybe you can be a permanent replacement for Captain Mason's command. Or a position at the battalion or brigade level."

Richard wiped a hand down his face and said, "Yeah, I don't think that's what the general has in mind. He is focused on ending the Vietnam War as quickly and victoriously as possible. Our country is in turmoil and the antiwar movement keeps growing larger and more violent with every newscast. We are negotiating for peace at the Paris Accords and simultaneously pushing for more and more bombing missions over North Vietnam."

Richard took Alyson's hands in his and asked her, "Where will you live and what will you do in Boston?"

She responded, "Mother has an apartment in Beacon Hill. I can stay there. I can get a teaching position at Boston College. Mother knows the trustees and the family has been a longtime supporter of the university."

Richard said, "Sounds nice, but won't the apartment get a little crowded?"

Alyson laughed. "It's Beacon Hill. The apartment is a 10,000-square-foot single-family townhouse with a view of Boston Common. It has 12-foot ceilings and eight fireplaces. I can live in the au pair suite on the lower level and never see anyone else in the residence. I'll have my own parking garage and outdoor living space. You will love it there. The cobblestone streets are lined with gas lanterns and boutiques and restaurants. It's a setting from a bygone era."

As lovely as all of it sounded, Richard thought it did not conform to his vision for the future. He was uncertain about his future, but he knew that planting himself in the elevated echelons of Beacon Hill was not in his playbook.

Before leaving Alyson at the Georgetown apartment, he promised to return later for a late lunch at J. Pauls in Georgetown. In the cab ride to base, Richard contemplated on what to tell Alyson about Boston. It was out of his hands. The army made the decisions about when and where he would be going. He could not think about much of anything except Shemya. Richard and his team would be departing in four days. Alyson would be back in Boston and life would go on, one day at a time.

Richard returned to Alyson's apartment and stayed overnight. They had Asian takeout food for dinner. Alyson overserved herself with plum wine and saki. Richard paired his pork fried rice with a few good shots of Jefferson's Reserve bourbon. They watched back-to-back *MASH* and Kung Fu TV shows. Alyson talked and giggled her way through both shows. Richard was feeling guilty about being there with her … and about helping her fall in love with him and not being there to catch her when she fell. She was the best thing that had ever happened in his world. This night would be their last until he completed the operation in Alaska and returned to Fort Devens. His next stop after Devens would most likely be the Command and General Staff School at Fort Leavenworth, Kansas. Richard reminded himself that Leavenworth was only about 40 miles from Kansas City and 1,500 miles from Boston—about half the width of the United States.

The next morning Alyson was picked up by the same driver who had driven them to dinner the previous Friday evening. Richard took a cab back to Fort McNair. On the way he thought about the next few months. He was eagerly anticipating the Shemya operation. It made him feel like he still had a purpose; and while it wasn't a battlefield, he could at least apply his skills and lead a squad of specialists on a meaningful operation. Christmas was only 14 days away. He told himself he should call his mother that night. He wondered about his father and where he was. He recalled the bad history with his dad and wondered who had become more impersonal, more calloused—his dad or himself.

Chapter 26

Operation Polar Ice

Wednesday, December 12, 1972, Operation Polar Ice was on. Maj. Richard Farnsworth and his team were assembled in the conference room of the Joint Operations Center in Building #46 at Fort McNair. The squad received a final briefing from Col. Thomas Wesley before heading to Andrews Air Force Base in Morningside, Maryland. The flight from Washington to Anchorage was 3,400 miles. The team would be transported by the air force in a relatively new Lockheed L-1011 Tristar. The 700-mph three-engine jet would get them to Anchorage in less than seven hours. From there they would travel another 1,400 miles to Field Station Shemya in an MC-130 combat transport. They now knew the ETA was approximately midnight, and the weather would be 28 degrees Fahrenheit, with snow showers and 20-knot winds. It was not the best time of year to visit Alaska.

Richard's Special Operations team included specialists in cryptanalysis, electronic warfare operations, traffic and translator analysis, systems repair, and two armed agents from the Criminal Investigative Command.

At the briefing, he said, "The mission is to intercept any unauthorized outgoing transmissions from FS Shemya and the nearby island of Attu. FS Shemya and the ASA operators are there to intercept and receive communications from Russia's air and sea fleet and land operations. The only authorized outgoing SIGINT is the encrypted intercept reports and analysis sent to ASA Command Center and Language Institute at Two Rock Ranch in California and on to other DOD and ASA destinations. After locating the source of the unauthorized traffic, the CID agents will arrest and detain the suspects. They will be transported to Arlington, Virginia, and handed over to the provost marshal general for interrogation and prosecution. The traitors will most likely spend the rest of their days at Fort Leavenworth's military prison."

The approach to Eareckson Air Station was bumpy, with a ceiling of 150 feet. It wasn't really a ceiling. The cloud cover simply changed from dense to opaque blasting snow. In the darkness the wind sounded more like hurricane-force turbulence. A crosswind was blowing horizontally at 20 knots. The landing was a series of bouncing crashes, and the real concern was stopping the plane on the iced-over runway.

A couple minutes after landing, the copilot stood in the doorway to the cockpit and said, "Welcome to Shemya, boys! We arrived ahead of schedule. I'm afraid the restaurant and movie theater are closed. You ground pounders watch yourselves on the boarding ladder. Hands can freeze to the railings."

The Polar Ice team was met on the tarmac by CWO Brandon Bidwell. "Welcome, gentlemen. I'll show you to your barracks. Corporal Harrell and his crew will stow your gear in a secure locker in Building 6. The mess hall opens for coffee at 0530. Breakfast comes later, at 0700. The barracks, Building 46, is your home during your tour of Shemya."

Richard was thinking, *Building 46? There are only about a dozen structures on this six-square-mile flat rock 1,000 miles from nowhere.*

Shemya had been home base to the Fourth Regiment of the Seventh US Infantry Division during World War II. It did double duty by serving as an airfield for air force B-17 and B-24 air raids on northern Japan during the war. The base was closed after the war and reopened for the Korean conflict. The Army Security Agency chose Shemya as a field station in 1956. It was now the westernmost field station in the ASA. The US Air Force also continued its strategic defense mission on the island.

The next morning Richard and E5 Sgt. David Stevens went directly to Building 6 to inspect their gear. Once they were comfortable with the security and accuracy of the manifest, they headed to the mess hall. The buildings next to the mess hall had a few surprises. There really was a 500-seat theater. They also walked by an NCO Club, a bowling alley, a gym, and a chapel. Inside the dining room they found standard mess hall seating. There was not a separate officers dining room. A corner of the main dining hall was designated as the officers dining area. Officers were scarce on Shemya; most of the jobs and duty tours were filled by NCOs and other enlisted men. Richard and Sergeant Stevens chose a table near the front entrance. From there he and Stevens could intercept his squad members as they came in.

Richard had thoroughly briefed each team member before they departed for Shemya. He'd instructed them to avoid indoor conversations pertaining to the Polar Ice mission. They needed to develop and maintain a casual image of a group of technical specialists sent there to audit the performance levels and maintenance needs of the giant Cobra Dane radar installation. Measuring 120 feet in height and 95 feet wide, the radar was accurately described as being giant. The L-band phased array operated at 1375 MHz, with 35,000 radiating elements, making it the most powerful radar in the world.

For the next three days Richard and his team reviewed activity logs and met with key operators of the radar station. They set up monitoring instruments which recorded the signals across a broad range of frequencies: from 300 megahertz to 300 gigahertz. Outgoing transmissions were analyzed to determine the frequencies in the bandwidth of the radar. They checked wavelengths, time and frequency divisions, and any modulation of the signals that might indicate an embedded data transmission. They found nothing unusual.

As part of the simulated audit of the base operations, they interviewed the soldiers assigned to SIGINT interception, intelligence traffic analysis, and equipment maintenance and repair. Spec. 4 Robert Cinotti was the most interesting suspect. His electronic warfare military occupational specialty provided him the skills to pull off a covert operation that might include capturing the radar data and intercepted signals intelligence and resending it to the Russians. The question was how did he or his band of traitors transmit the reports. The team did not find it in the higher frequencies, and the limited transmission distance in the VHF bandwidth was not sufficient to reach Russia or its warships patrolling the Bering Sea between the Aleutian Islands and Shemya, Alaska. The Russian Kamchatka Peninsula where the Soviet Kura Missile Test Range was located, was about 500 km (311 miles) from Shemya.

Richard and the two Criminal Investigation Department officers also interviewed Intelligence Analyst SP5 George Martin and Senior Analysis Tech CW4 Steven Rodgers. CID's profile of Rodgers paid off and they caught him in more than one outright lie about his previous assignments. When asked about his nickname, "Ditto," he explained that his original military occupational specialty was O5H when he supervised electronic warfare signals intelligence using international Morse code. Electronics Repairman Ray Norton was interviewed and dismissed as a suspect. At least for now, they were pretty sure he had no idea what they were asking about.

Day 4 – Richard assembled his team and instructed them to "go low": meaning, start scanning a bandwidth that included signals in the range of single-sideband transmissions as low as 1800 kilohertz.

Sgt. David Stevens spoke up first. "Major, they have an old vacuum-tube RC-390 transceiver in the back office, next to the Cobra Dane Operations Room. The old heterodyne tube set radio can spin the dial to any frequency you want in that low-frequency bandwidth. If they are using international Morse code, it can operate in a continuous wave mode that is perfect for IMC transmissions."

Richard was sure they had them. It was only a matter of discovering who was involved and exactly how and what they were sending to the Russians.

Two days later at 1500 hours, Sergeant Stevens met with Major Farnsworth. He found Richard sitting at his desk in a makeshift command office.

"Good afternoon, Stevens. Would you like a cup of the army's finest coffee?"

Stevens replied, "No, thank you, sir. I was hoping you felt like taking a walk with me. The weather is in between blizzards, and it has warmed up to 27 degrees Fahrenheit."

Richard understood this to mean that Sergeant Stevens had some new intelligence to report, so Richard stood and grabbed his field jacket and gloves. They walked along the street toward the 10,000-foot runway that was originally built in 1943 to support the Eleventh Air Force. At the time, B-25 bombers flew 1,000-mile missions to drop 500-pound bombs on Japanese air bases.

"Major, we have identified the operating frequency and the IMC signals. We played a hunch and kept monitoring through the night. At midnight we began picking up the Morse code transmissions. They only lasted three minutes. At first I thought this would be a piece of cake. After two hours of listening to and copying the three minutes of code, we could not make any sense of it. SFC Ken Smith is the very best cryptanalysis specialist in the army. We know it contains conversation-length words and alphanumeric series that could be asset identifiers. It's gibberish. We don't need an IBM supercomputer to break the cyphers on something this small. It's just gibberish."

"I have a call scheduled for 1700 hours with General Broughton," Richard replied. "Let's see which ASA cryptanalysis group he wants to share this with. If we get some more eyes on it, maybe they can make some sense of it. Our primary mission here is to find out who is working with the Russians, and then CID will take over and detain them for transport to the folks in the Special Investigations Office at Fort Belvoir. The guys in Virginia will find out what we need to break the encryption code they used. Maybe our CID guys can get them to turn on each other here in Shemya."

Richard briefed the general and received his orders to send the recorded IMC and transcripts to Test Readiness Review's ASA Command in Petaluma, California. The traffic analysts at Two Rock Ranch deciphered the messaging. Meanwhile, the two CID agents assigned to Operation Polar Ice arrested Robert Cinotti and Ditto Rodgers. Cinotti clammed up; Rodgers started singing like a church choir soloist. He confirmed what Sergeant Stevens had said about the transmissions being gibberish. They were in fact encrypted by an unbreakable cypher. Richard had first encountered the cryptosystem cipher in Vietnam. The US Army Special Forces used the system known as "Diana" at communications stations in Vietnam, Laos, and Cambodia.

SP5 SIGINT Analyst George Martin did not report for his follow-up interview, and he was officially listed as AWOL.

Witnesses reported he was last seen leaving the barracks on a snowmobile. He did not return for the evening mess call. Shemya is only four and a half miles long and half as wide. In the subfreezing weather, Richard and CID knew he either would be found or voluntarily return to base. The other option was to remain in hiding and freeze to death.

The encrypted messages were sent over radio channels using Morse code. The cypher was in fact unbreakable. It used one-time pads (OTP) that provide letters and numbers which are applied to a simple handheld cardboard dual wheel that scrambles the messages into alphanumeric gibberish. Unless you had the OTP, the message was impossible to decipher. In the Polar Ice operation, there was only one OTP and it was reused for each transmission. This would make the decryption much easier for the ASA traffic analysts.

As General Broughton had advised Richard, the decipherment was not really that important. Broughton said, "We already knew they were telling the Russians what our intercepted signal intelligence was telling us. We knew what Russian naval assets were deployed and where they were located. We knew the frequency and routes for the Russian airborne traffic. After receiving the encrypted information from Shemya, the Russians were changing the locations and routes for their aircraft, ships, and troop movements. The assets would be re-detected, and the cat-and-mouse cycle went on like a game of Whac-A-Mole."

Day 7 – SP5 George Martin was no longer missing. A base patrol found his body about two miles from the base. He was lying in a snowdrift next to the overturned snowmobile. It looked like an accident, except for the large frozen pool of blood his head was resting in. He had an entry wound on his right temple and a gaping fist-sized exit wound on the left side of his skull. Suicide could have been a likely conclusion, but no gun was found at the scene. Any footprints or tracks that may have been made by a shooter or a second vehicle had been concealed by the ice- and wind-driven snow. CID would have an early and unfortunate Christmas present as they sorted it out. Richard and Sergeant Stevens surmised it was most likely a self-inflicted wound, but realized that an embedded Russian operative or even one of his own accomplices could have been the shooter.

The penalty for a finding of treason in a military tribunal could be a long prison term and even death by firing squad. SP4 Robert Cinotti and CW4 Steve Rodgers would be court-martialed and serve hard time at Leavenworth Military Correctional Facility. Unless they could be tied to the murder of George Martin, they would most likely receive 30-year sentences with no parole.

Chapter 27

December 20, 1972 – Back to Washington

Richard returned to Camp McNair late on Wednesday evening. At 2350 hours, it was closer to Thursday morning.

The next day Richard reviewed the Polar Ice operation with Col. Thomas Wesley. It was a successful op and executed in a short period of time. The colonel gave high praise to Richard and his team.

Colonel Wesley also said, "Richard, with the latest developments in our SIGINT and general communications tools, it is phenomenal that we were duped by simple Morse code and a cardboard Diana wheel. VHF, microwave, multiplexed time, and frequency encryption tools be dammed. The Special Forces used the same system all over Vietnam. Oh, well."

Richard replied, "I'm glad we were able to find and stop the transmissions. We are fortunate to have some of the best technical warriors in the agency."

Colonel Wesley shook his head. "And it is a damn shame about Martin. That Shemya tour is extremely hard on the men's frame of mind. Thirteen months of isolation on a frozen island would drive anybody crazy. We will be doing a top-to-bottom follow-up there. We need to know how long this mess has gone on and what their incentives were. The Russians are good at compromising young soldiers on leave in Anchorage and then blackmailing them into submission."

There was a knock on the door and Wesley's administrative staff officer stepped in. "Colonel, I'm sorry to interrupt. The Deputy Assistant Secretary of Defense is here."

"Yes, I'm expecting her. Please escort her in."

Colonel Wesley and Richard stood, and Ms. Anna Mayberry Valent entered the room. After the proper introductions were made, they moved to a small conference table.

Ms. Valent took the lead. "Major Farnsworth, I am here to brief you on a development that has the potential to become a matter of national security." Valent distributed a three-page document. Under the DOD insignia, the title read: "Night Train."

Deputy Assistant Secretary Valent said, "What began as a joint training exercise for Defense Department agencies has expanded to include the military services, selected DOD agencies, and seven unified and specified military commands. Over the past 12 months the operation developed planning options and reporting systems to address and expedite decision-making in emergency situations that involved the US presence in friendly countries, and specific requests for assistance from allied governments. The Army Operations Center, DOD staff, and seven major commands participated in the exercise."

Ms. Valent's eye contact was steady as she spoke. "As we know, our relationship with people around the world depends on our ability to effectively communicate. The subject matter can at times be extraordinarily complex, and the comingling of written and spoken messaging in multiple languages inhibits that intercourse." Valent went on to explain that the ideographic nature of written Asian languages presents significant problems for the Chinese, Japanese, and Koreans. The Chinese language, for example, was used by more people than any other language in the world. Transcription of ideographic languages to a written form suitable for printing and distribution involved a rare and laborious calligraphic process which inhibited timely communication in an emergency situation."

Valent opened a bottle of water in front of her. She took a few gulps, screwed the cap back on, and said, "Okay, let's get to the crux of the matter. We solved the communication challenges. We have developed a photocomposing machine with software that allows the linguistic operator to compose ideographic languages using a keyboard. The keys are struck in the sequence of the ideographic message to produce an ideograph containing the full text. The ideographic strips can be reproduced with standard printing processes. The machine can also punch tapes that can be transmitted over teletype to other remote teletype receivers. A machine on the receiving end can produce the transmitted texts at a rate of 500 ideographs per minute. The composing machine's influence on cultural and educational activities is obvious. Putting general information from the Chinese and Koreans in the hands of people and organizations on a timely basis has far-reaching ramifications. So much so that Secretary Laird has classified the dissemination of any information or product that comes from the development and future use of this new intelligence tool. For now, we need to further develop them and understand the strategic value this breakthrough brings to military and intelligence operations. To have real-time news and communications from China, Japan, and North and South Korea will enhance our national defense and the security of other allied nations." With a nod, she focused on Wesley.

He said, "This is all fascinating. Let's move on to the immediate problem. We assembled a team of experts to travel to our ASA bases in Europe for the purpose of training traffic analysts and ASA human intelligence operatives in the use of the ideographic machines. Two officers in the top ranks of this training operation were dispatched to the ASA field station in Chitose, Japan. There they were charged with training the Bravo Trainers Company, who would extend the training to the ASA field stations in Torii, Misawa, and Zama. The next stop was Diogenes Station in Turkey, also known as Sinop. The location of the geodesic domes and parabolic satellite dishes in that fishing village is highly strategic. The 300-acre base is situated on a 700-foot hill two miles from Sinop, and directly across from the Russian Black Sea fleet in Sevastopol on the Crimean Peninsula. After Sinop, they were scheduled to report to the 508 USASA Group at Yongdongpo, South Korea. They never made it to FS Sinop."

Richard took advantage of a pause as Colonel Wesley cleaned his eyeglasses. "Colonel, isn't this a matter for the Criminal Investigative Division? They have hundreds of agents based in Turkey."

Wesley responded, "Major, we have the CID's Executive Protective Group working on it as we speak. They know our folks left Japan on a commercial flight to the Republic of Cyprus. That's a 10-hour flight, so they would have spent the night. Their scheduled flight from Cyprus to Sinop had mechanical problems."

Deputy Assistant Secretary Valent gave a slight cough and said, "Actually, the Egyptair Ilyushin turboprop crashed in the Kyrenia Mountains en route to Nicosia. All 37 onboard perished in the crash."

Colonel Wesley spoke next. "Cyprus Airways took over the route to Sinop. This is where we lose the trail. We think they boarded the flight, but the manifest did not transfer properly from Egyptair to the flight to Cyprus. They posted the new passengers, and in the scramble to rebook the stranded travelers, Cyprus haphazardly added the Egyptair passengers from a standby list. They could have boarded the plane or sought out alternatives for travel to Sinop. The last information we received was that they were attempting to rebook on the Cyprus Airways flight."

Richard said to Colonel Wesley, "With all due respect, Colonel, my initial question still stands."

Deputy Assistant Secretary Valent raised a hand from the table and pointed at Richard. "Major, we know you had your friend Maj. William Dennis make an inquiry to the Pentagon desk about the location of your friends Buster Browning and Lt. Stacie Shatner. Rightfully so, Shatner's status was classified and not released. While stationed at the Defense Language Institute at Presidio of Monterey, Lieutenant Shatner was working with a civilian coder named William Meadows. They basically invented the Ideographic Composing Machine. Meadows's knowledge of software, coupled with Shatner's extensive knowledge and use of foreign languages, literally came about from their friendship at Presidio. The importance of their discovery was immediately recognized and, as I said before, classified."

Colonel Wesley spoke again. "Major, we also know you were stationed at Fort Devens with Lieutenant Shatner and that you two were very close. We hope to take advantage of your insight into the habits and thoughts Lieutenant Shatner may have employed in the current situation. Your intelligence skills and combat and special ops experience may bring us closer to resolving this potential breach of security. Of course, the safe return of Lieutenant Shatner and Mr. Meadows is paramount to the success of this recovery operation. You will be assigned to CID's Special Protection Group as a lead investigator."

Deputy Assistant Secretary Valent said, "Merry Christmas, Major. Turkey is quite beautiful this time of year."

That evening Richard packed for his trip to the Republic of Turkey. At 10 degrees Celsius it would be much warmer than Shemya. He had no chance of falling asleep. Not knowing Stacie's whereabouts was troubling enough. Now that he was aware she was in Turkey, he imagined a dozen different outcomes and all of them were bad. He should call Alyson, but could not come up with the words to express his thoughts. He figured, as usual she was one step ahead of him and knew about this development. He'd call the next day, after his flight plans were established. The flight from DC to Larnaca International Airport would take 16 hours, with a one-hour layover in London. Turkey was seven hours ahead of East Coast time, so it was already morning in Cyprus. He could sleep on the plane.

Alyson picked up after one ring.

"Good morning, Alyson."

She replied, "Is it really? Why send you? Isn't it a CID matter?"

"You know I cannot discuss this," Richard replied. "I'm as sorry as you are that I'll be away for Christmas. I assume you'll be with your family in Boston. Anyway, you know I'd be a fifth wheel in that setting."

Alyson shot back, "Only because you choose to be. You have a distorted perception of what our family is like. Yeah, the general can be a little gruff, but he mellows out when he gets away from the Pentagon and his official routines. My mother will be in her dream world with more Christmas decorations than a holiday shop in Manhattan. You might even enjoy yourself if you let down the walls—if you let me into that messed-up head of yours. When do you leave, Richard? Can you at least tell me that?"

"I don't have my flight information yet. I'm sure it's soon. Tomorrow at the latest. I'll call you when I know. The return is of course open-ended."

Richard felt bad about the tension he was causing Alyson. The situation was out of his control, and he could not think straight. His head kept pounding with *Stacie, Stacie, Stacie. Where are you?* He slept intermittently for the next six hours and finally gave up and got showered and dressed. Sitting in the mess hall he thought, *She is most likely dead, or worse.* He had to get a handle on this and clear his head. *I'm going to find her and bring her home, and then what?*

An attractive member of the Women's Army Corps approached his table and snapped to attention. "Major Farnsworth, PFC Matyi Maresma, sir. I have a packet for you from the Pentagon." She placed a large envelope on the table. "Thank you, sir." She tilted her head, smiled and winked, then turned and left the table.

Richard felt a tinge of guilt as he watched her stride away. He thought, *There must be a Victoria's Secret platoon at McNair.* The envelope contained his itinerary and tickets to Heathrow in London and on to Cyprus.

O3 Farnsworth, Richard

Friday 22 Dec. 1972: 12:10 p.m.–4:25 p.m.[+1]
British Airways – 1 stop LHR 16h 15m IAD LCA

Seats 3A, 3C

Additional contents included instructions for ground transportation and information about his contact in Turkey. He would be met by Army Maj. Keith Newman. His photo and brief bio were included. Newman was a CID intelligence officer. The photo was provided because, like Farnsworth, Newman would be in civilian clothes. The mission was not covert, and it was designed to not attract unnecessary attention while in Turkey. CID officers stationed in Turkey had already begun a standard public investigation into the disappearance of Lieutenant Shatner and Mr. Meadows.

Chapter 28

Return to Turkey

Larnaca International Airport was controlled by the Republic of Cyprus. While Turkey would have liked to claim the country as their territory, it was a separate island country of one million people, located on the shore of the eastern Mediterranean Sea. Like Turkey, multiple languages were spoken in Cyprus, including Armenian, Cypriot Arabic, and Greek. Its unitary presidential republic was governed by a president, a vice president, and a house of representatives.

Newman met Richard at the exit from airport security. They loaded his duffle and an oversized briefcase onto a luggage cart and handed it off to a CID agent who would transfer it to a car waiting outside the airport.

Richard and Major Newman met with the CID field agents in a sitting area outside and near the passenger loading area.

CID Agent John Rutherford opened the briefing. "We've got them. Not physically, but we know they left Cyprus. We have men checking the transfer in Istanbul. I suggest the two of you go on to Sinop. I will join you there in a day or possibly two, depending on what we find in Istanbul. There are no flights out of Larnaca. My office has booked your flights out of Paphos this afternoon, and rooms in Sinop at the Sinopark

Hotel. You could stay on base, but it limits your mobility, and you will find the accommodations to be a far sight better than Quonset hut living with TUSLOG troops. The hotel is right on the Black Sea. You can see our antenna farm from your balcony. From the air you can see the Crimean Peninsula. It is home port for the Russian fleet in Sevastopol."

Richard and Major Newman got into a boxy, gray 1968 Renault 10 sedan.

Newman said to Richard, "We have a 90-minute drive to Paphos Airport."

He answered, "Whoa, wait a minute. What about Larnaca? They were supposed to fly out of there to Sinop."

"Major, you heard the man. There have been no flights to Sinop since the Egyptair crash."

Newman pulled the Renault onto the highway and said, "Look for an exit or a turn-out in the median. Our folks have been all over that airport and every hotel surrounding it. We checked on dates five days on either side of their arrival day and planned departure day. Except for their arrival in Cyprus on Monday, December 18, they do not show up on any cameras and their names are not listed at any passport security checkpoints. Our agents interviewed ticket agents and security officers and showed them photographs. They did not board the Cyprus Airways flight or any other flight leaving Larnaca."

Major Newman glanced at Richard. "So," he said, "sit back and enjoy the drive. I was told the A6 coastal highway to Pathos is spectacular. We're going to the international airport. That would have been their only other choice for travel into Turkey. We already have agents in Paphos doing the airport interviews. They'll check with rental car agencies and talk to cab drivers. We should know something solid by this afternoon."

Richard relaxed and took in the views along the coast and the surrounding mountain range. He could see why the Cypriots wanted to maintain their independence as a sovereign country. Rural Cyprus was picturesque. The Troodos mountain range was surrounded by ocean vistas and populated with family-owned wineries in dozens of countryside villages. As beautiful as the scenery was, he could not stop thinking about Stacie. Every scenario he imagined had her being severely injured, tortured, or dead.

His thoughts were interrupted thirty minutes into the drive to Paphos. Major Newman's satellite phone rang with three short bursts.

"Hello, this is Major Newman." He listened for two full minutes and responded, "Yes, sir, I understand, 1800 hours, Universal Weather Aviation." Newman put the phone down. "There has been an incident in Sinop. The Turkish police are on the lookout for suspects involved in the shooting death of an Arabic cab driver. The alleged shooter was a 27-year-old civilian named William Meadows. His accomplice is an army officer, one Lt. Stacie Shatner. Blond hair, blue eyes, five feet, nine inches in height, and 138 pounds."

Richard exclaimed, "Holy mother of God—Stacie!"

Newman slowed the car and carefully pulled off the highway into a rocky truck pullout. He turned to Richard and said, "Change of plans. Operations Control has arranged a private flight for us to Sinop, out of the Universal Aviation FBO at Larnaca. We leave at 1800 hours."

***

Three Days Earlier

Stacie Shatner and William Meadows arrived in Sinop on December 19, 1972. Their flight plans changed after the Egyptair plane crashed. After losing a day in Cyprus and failing to report on Monday, the 18th, they were technically AWOL. After clearing the Turkish security checkpoints, they hailed a cab.

Stacie spoke to the driver in perfect Arabic: *"Sinopark al-funduq fadli."* ("Hotel Sinopark, please.")

He replied, *"Enta Too 'Mór."* ("As you wish.")

They proceeded to drive along the Black Sea coastline on the Inebolo Highway toward the hotel. They would arrive just after dark and in time for a nice Turkish meal. Stacie was thinking about Turkish flatbreads and stuffed vine leaves.

They could see flashing red lights ahead, and their driver slowed to a stop. A soldier in a Turkish army uniform, carrying what looked like a Heckler & Koch G3 submachine gun, walked directly to the driver's partially open door. They exchanged words. Stacie could only make out part of the conversation. She did hear the soldier say in Turkish, *"Kisiyi gozaltina alacagiz."* ("I am taking them into custody.") Stacie could see another soldier had exited the Turkish land forces vehicle and was standing in the roadway lighting a cigarette. The first soldier and the cab driver began arguing, each shouting in Turkish, *"Sik tir git!"* ("Screw you!")

Stacie grabbed William's hand and said, "We have to get out of here! Now!"

As they were moving to exit the cab, the first soldier pulled a Beretta 9mm pistol from his holster and shot the driver in the head. Before anyone could move or react, a fast-moving Imza red minivan struck the second soldier standing in the highway. When the shooter turned away from the cab, Stacie and William jumped out of the cab and ran down the embankment toward the sea. They could hear the gunfire ricocheting off the enormous boulders as they ran for cover. William stumbled and fell. He yelled to Stacie, who was 20 meters ahead of him. She stopped, turned back. William was on his feet and as he began to run, another burst of gunfire ripped through the woods. William yelled again, this time a scream of shock and pain. He fell to his knees as blood spread across his shirt and right shoulder.

Stacie crouched and searched for a path toward William that would not be in the shooter's field of vision. William was moving into the brush, toward her. The rough terrain prevented the shooter from seeing their location or the direction they were moving.

Stacie reached William and asked, "How bad is it?"

He replied, "I can move my arm. The bleeding is bad."

Stacie tried to rip the sleeve from her blouse. She could not get it to tear. Helping William up, she said, "We have to keep moving."

They came to the edge of a planted pine forest and could see through the trees to a lower road heading toward the bright lights at the Sinop Sports Stadium. Stacie had learned from a travel brochure that the sports complex was only a few miles from the Army Security Agency field station. They needed to get to a telephone. Stacie took notice of William's shoulder and opened his shirt. The blood still oozed from the entry wound. She unbuttoned her shirt and with a few contorted body maneuvers she pulled off her bra. She wrapped the elastic undergarment twice around his shoulder and underarm and clipped it tightly in place.

Except for one car approaching from the west, no one else was on the roadway. It would take a half hour to walk to the closest city center. William suggested they flag down the car and get a ride. The soldier with the gun would likely be in his vehicle and searching for them by now. Stacie waved her hands in a manner that communicated their desperation.

A small, light-green Turkish automobile came to a stop and the driver rolled down the passenger window. "Are you okay? Do you need help?" she asked.

Stacie replied, "Oh my God, you speak English! Yes, we need to get to a telephone right away."

The driver smiled and said, "Jump in. My apartment is just a few minutes away."

When they were getting into the back seat, the driver noticed William's condition. "Oh my God," she said, "you're injured!"

Stacie said, "You are American?"

She replied, "Yes."

"Please, we need your help. I am an American soldier, and my friend has been shot."

The driver worked as a bartender in a popular nightclub near the army base. She was familiar with the military presence in Sinop and comfortable around the soldiers who frequented the club. Stacie helped William settle into the vehicle, and the driver took off toward the city center.

The driver said, "I can take you to the hospital. It's not far from here."

William spoke up. "The bleeding has stopped. We should get off this road and to a telephone."

Stacie's mind was spinning. None of this made sense. She thought William was right. He needed medical attention. They should alert their field station contact. They were already a day late for their scheduled report time. The whole scene was not making sense. Something was off about the way the Turkish police officer had spoken. When he left his vehicle, he turned toward the car and said something to the other officer in the car. It was not clear; she thought she'd heard: *Hadhih hi waljasus alakhar.* ("That's her and the other spy.")

They were headed toward town and the sports arena. The driver glanced at Stacie and William in the rearview mirror. "My name is Jeanne. What the hell happened to you?"

"We were in a cab from the airport," Stacie said, "and we were stopped by the Turkish police. The police officer and the cab driver were arguing, and the officer pulled a gun and shot the driver in the head. Another van was speeding by and struck the police officer's partner standing in the road. In the confusion of the accident, we were able to escape and ran down the embankment into the forest. That's when William got shot by the Turkish police officer. We saw the lights and were trying to get to the village near the stadium."

Jeanne replied, "I'm off work for the evening, so I can take you wherever you need to go."

"That is so kind of you," Stacie said. "The phone at your apartment is perfect."

Stacie got William's attention and pointed to his forehead. He had spots of spattered blood from the impact of the gunshot the Turkish police officer had fired through the cab's open driver's door. Stacie asked Jeanne what she was doing in Turkey.

She said she was married to a Turkish professor and that he had died the previous year. She went on to say that while she didn't have Turkish citizenship, as his widow she was not required to leave the country. "This is my apartment building. I'm on the second level."

At Jeanne's apartment, William asked to use the restroom while Stacie called the base operator at Field Station Shemya. "Good evening. My name is 1st Lt. Stacie Shatner, ASA European Command. Could you please patch this priority call through to the OIC Nighttime Desk?"

The mention of Lieutenant Shatner's name to the desk of the Officer-in-Charge would trigger a series of calls. The operator responded, "Roger that, ma'am, right away. Stand by while I make the connection."

After several minutes, the operator came on the line and reported, "Lieutenant Shatner, your call is being patched through to a CID field officer who can help you. Maj. Keith Newman is on the line. Go ahead, ma'am."

Newman said, "Before you say anything, just listen. This is not a secure line. Answer my questions with brief responses. Are you or Meadows injured?"

Stacie said, "I am fine. Mr. Meadows has been shot and needs medical attention."

"Are you safe?"

Stacie responded affirmatively.

Newman said, "I am aware of the incident involving the cab driver and your encounter with the Turkish police. They have reported to their command that William shot and killed the cab driver. We know that is highly unlikely. What is important is that the Turkish army wants to take you and William into custody. They would like nothing better than to create an international incident and use it as leverage against the United States. The bottom line is they do not want us in Sinop, or anywhere in Turkey, for that matter."

Stacie cut in. "Major, neither William nor I had access to any weapon and we most certainly did not shoot the cab driver."

"Lieutenant, I understand. Can you stay at your present location until we can get to you?"

Stacie replied, "We're at the apartment of a good Samaritan who picked us up on the roadway and allowed us to use her telephone."

Major Newman said, "Lieutenant, listen to me. Do not go anywhere in public. The Turkish police know who you are, and you will be arrested. They are looking for you and Mr. Meadows, and they will undoubtedly check the hospitals and clinics on your route from the airport. They have your luggage from the cab and the baggage tags link directly to your identity. The airport security agents have images of your passports and military travel clearance documents. Your photos will be on the television news and you will be described as armed and dangerous. Fortunately, this call is physically patched through the telephone switchboard at Sinop and can only be traced back to FS Sinop."

Shatner replied, saying, "Yes, sir, got it. I'm sure we can stay put for a while."

"We will come to you," Major Newman said. "Do not say anything specific about your location. Are you in a house or a hotel or an apartment?"

"Apartment."

"Can you see the parking lot from your position?"

"Yes, I can."

Newman said, "We are in the area. Look for an unmarked white cargo van. When you see it, flash the lights in the apartment twice. Write down this number and call me if your status or location changes. We are boarding a jet for Sinop. I will call back in 20 minutes. We will find you."

Back in Cyprus at the private hangar for Universal Weather & Aviation, Richard and Major Newman boarded a sleek Gulfstream G-11 twin-engine jet bound for Sinop, Turkey. Universal was a US government services contractor working with the DOD and the CIA. They provided private transportation for CIA agents and other defense personnel in multiple European and Asian countries.

After takeoff and reaching cruising altitude, Major Newman retrieved a heavy black case and opened it. He powered up the defense satellite communications unit and dialed in a base station that patched him through to the number of the apartment where Shatner and Meadows were hiding. There was some static and noise from the jet engines ... a woman answered the phone on the second ring.

"Hello."

No answer.

Jeanne said, "Hello, who is this?"

Aware of the delay in the transmission of the voice signals, Newman replied quickly. "Good evening, ma'am. I am calling for your house guest. Please put her on the phone."

"Yes, of course. She's right here."

Newman said to Lieutenant Shatner, "We are on our way to you. Are you still safe?"

Stacie replied, "Yes, but Mr. Meadows may be in shock. He lost a lot of blood."

"Lieutenant," Newman said, "you must keep watch on the parking lot in front of your apartment. We will come to the most likely locations in the area you are in. A white van will enter each of the selected apartment parking lots and park. The driver will slowly tap out the IMC for SOS on the brake lights. They will remain in position and watch for your response. We have several agents in the area, so it could take some time, but we will find you. They could be at your location anywhere from now to 30 minutes, so keep watch. It is imperative we get to you before the Turks. When you see the signals, both of you proceed at a normal pace to the vehicle and get in."

Major Newman paused and added, "Lieutenant Shatner, I have someone here who wants to say hello." He handed the phone to Richard.

"Hey, Stacie, what's this about you being AWOL?"

"Oh my God, Richard, is that really you?" Her eyes filled with tears of happiness and surprise. She said, "I cannot believe it. You are coming to Sinop?"

He responded, "We'll be on the ground in 60 minutes."

When Richard and Major Newman landed at Sinop Airport, they were met on the tarmac by a CID agent driving an unmarked white passenger van. En route to the rendezvous point to meet the field agents, the driver's radio squawked. "We found the missing package. Repeat. The package is secure."

The driver responded, "Roger that, I copy, you have the package. Will pick up at the train station in 20 minutes." The train station was code for the pre-established rendezvous point.

Everything went as planned and Major Farnsworth and Lieutenant Shatner were transported directly to the Joint Command hangar at Sinop Airport. William Meadows was taken to the hospital at the base in Sinop. Richard and Stacie boarded an MC-12 King Air 350 and flew to Izmir Air Base, where they were met by two CID Executive Protection Agents. Together they were transferred to a Boeing 737-200 operated by the Central Intelligence Agency, and flew directly to Davison Army Airfield in Belvoir, Virginia.

Stacie slept for the first five hours of the flight. She was exhausted mentally and physically. Richard wanted to sleep too, but his mind was reeling with unsettling thoughts. *What about Alyson? What will I tell her? What do I tell Stacie about Alyson?* He knew no matter what his next moves ended up being, it was the start of a shitstorm in DC.

Stacie awoke and put an arm under Richard's, on the armrest. She pulled him to her and whispered, "I missed you so much. I didn't know if I would ever see you again."

They made small talk for an hour and Stacie told him about California. She loved it, but it was not home. She missed her family in Florida and she missed Richard. Stacie told him she was not seeing anyone.

Richard said, "What about Mr. Meadows?"

She responded by leaning into him and kissing his ear. "William is a friend. Thank God he was not killed. Richard, I have never been so terrified. I have never been shot at before or been in a situation where someone wanted to hurt or even kill me. How did you cope with it in Vietnam?"

He looked into her eyes and said, "You just live with it and let the memory fade away. It never really goes away. You put it in a box and try not to open it. Thank God you were not hurt." He was thinking, *How would I react if she were in a body bag instead of sitting here next to me?*

Stacie said, "William is a brilliant, boring computer nerd. We worked together. That's all there was to it."

"Yes," Richard said. "I know about the graphic composing machine. Maybe you can patent it and become a billionaire."

"That's funny," Stacie said, "or maybe not funny at all. William's brother is an attorney and he asked him to investigate the patent process. We could file for a patent, like any other private citizen, but the system is classified 'secret with limited access.' If the army or DOD declassifies the composing machine and the software, it could be deemed by the Patent and Trademark Office to be public information. So we could not get a patent. William's brother thinks we can fight it and eventually win."

Richard said, "Don't forget your friends."

She punched him lightly on the arm and asked, "What about you?" She quickly added, "You don't have to answer. It's a stupid question. Of course you're seeing someone, or several lucky ladies."

Richard took Stacie's hand and squeezed it. He held it to his lips and kissed the back of her hand. "No, not several, and yes, it's complicated."

She knew this was true, while hoping it wasn't. Turning away, she said, "I will not be a problem for you."

Richard sighed and pulled her by the shoulder to face him. "Stacie, you know how I feel about you. We had something special. Give me some time to sort things out. I'm just glad you are alive and safe."

"Yes, of course, Richard. I'm so glad to see you. Ignore me tonight. We can talk it all out later." Though she sounded confident, she was crying inside.

They landed at Davison Airfield early the morning of December 23. Stacie was provided temporary quarters at Fort Belvoir and Richard was driven to his BOQ at McNair. They were both informed that after a break to clean and dress, they were to report to the Pentagon for a debriefing with Col. Thomas Wesley.

Stacie had no civilian clothes. She picked up a Class A uniform set from the supply depot at Belvoir. A stop by the base PX provided her with enough of the personal essentials to get through a couple of days. Some women in Turkey would be wearing her clothes that had been confiscated by the Turkish military police.

Separate interviews were conducted by DOD Undersecretaries, followed by a joint session with Colonel Wesley and Deputy Assistant Secretary of Defense Valent. Secretary Valent offered her praise for the success of the rescue mission. She elaborated on the consequences a negative outcome would have had on the relations between the US and Turkey. In addition, she spoke of the strategic value of the military bases and airfields in Turkey.

Colonel Wesley informed Lieutenant Shatner that the European training mission would continue in their absence. He told her the excellent work they did with the Bravo Trainers at FS Chitose would allow them to suitcase the training to Sinop and other bases in the European theater. Colonel Wesley added, "Lieutenant Shatner, you will return to the Defense Language Institute at Presidio, and hopefully, Mr. Meadows will recover from his wounds and join you at the DLI. The two of you will be instrumental in the development of training modules for the ASA and the Tenth Special Forces Group at Fort Devens."

Richard sat without speaking. His future orders were not pertinent to the agenda for this session. Stacie wanted to ask about Richard's future assignment, but the tone of the discussion was not open to such a question. In the army, most conversations with command staff officers were one-sided.

After receiving a medical evaluation, Stacie would be given a 14-day leave before returning to California.

Following the debriefing, Richard and Stacie got a ride to Fort McNair. Stacie needed to make travel arrangements for a visit to her parents' home in Coral Gables.

After arriving on base, Richard asked the driver to drop them at the G-1 office buildings.

Stacie said to Richard, "I'm flying on a commercial flight, not military transport. I need a telephone to make my reservation. We can go to your office or BOQ."

Richard knew what was coming if they went to his quarters, and he was hesitant to go down that road with Stacie. Not yet, anyway.

He spoke to the driver. "Corporal, take us to the Officers' Club."

"Yes, sir," the driver replied. "However, on weekdays it does not open until 1600 hours."

That was two hours away. Richard decided on neutral ground, and they went to his office in the Joint Operations Building. Stacie made her calls and would be flying to Miami on a Delta flight departing at 0700 the next morning.

At near breaking point, Stacie was the first to speak. "Look, Richard, I get it. You have someone. Go to her. I will be fine." She was saying it while not believing her own words. She wanted Richard, right now, tomorrow, and every day after that. "I can get a ride to Belvoir, and you can go back to whatever and whoever was in your life before Turkey."

Richard put his hands over his face and rubbed his eyes briefly. "You know I care about you, Stacie. More than that, you know I want to be with you. Take your leave and enjoy visiting with your folks. We can sort this out later."

"Yeah, right! Are you coming to California? No, you are not. I cannot deal with this right now. Hell, my tour is up in a few months. I may just resign my commission, move to Key West, and shack up with a local Conch."

Stacie returned to Fort Belvoir and flew out of Washington Dulles Airport the next morning. She would arrive in time to celebrate Christmas Eve with her family. Richard had no current orders. He would report to his desk at Joint Command headquarters and wait on new orders or communications from Colonel Wesley or General Broughton.

Lying in his bunk, he considered this the best and the worst Christmas he had ever experienced. He got to see Stacie, and now she was gone from his life again. He thought he should have kept her with him or gone to Miami with her. The memories and visions of their time together in Boston were life changing. No one was more passionate or more beautiful. What in the hell was wrong with him? In his heart he had not rejected her because he loved Alyson. He was protecting Stacie. Protecting her from being hurt by his own confused actions. *I am not that good of a person*, he thought. *I should be with Stacie, making love, making a life. Dammit to hell.* He pounded the mattress with his fists and told himself, "Get up. Get dressed, get your shit together."

Chapter 29

Back to Devens

Richard got his orders three days later; he was going back to Fort Devens. He would report to the Army Security Agency Training Command. He realized this was not a career advancement. He suspected Alyson may have had a hand in convincing her father to influence the decision that would put him in Boston and close to her. Richard was, in a word, disheartened. Not by Alyson or Stacie. It was like he was on a downhill slide. Ever since he left Vietnam, and especially after recovering from his wounds at Walter Reed, he had lost his focus on what the future looked like. He mused, *I could stay in and make lieutenant colonel in four years.* He knew the system. He could put in a full 20 years and retire at age 42 as a full bird colonel. That prospect used to motivate him; now it seemed more likely to depress him.

He didn't call Alyson, knowing she was in Boston with her family. Her duty station at the army's Natick Soldier Systems Center was less than 20 miles from Fort Devens. He would see her soon enough. His last mission was classified, and unless the general told her Richard was in the US, she'd assume he was still in Turkey. Richard packed his gear and personal belongings. He had a flight on a C-130 leaving Bolling Air Force Base in 48 hours.

After getting settled in at Devens, Richard called Alyson. She picked up after the phone rang six times. He was about to hang up when she said, "Hello, this is Alyson."

"Alyson, it's me, Richard."

There was a pause that seemed longer than normal, and Alyson replied, "Oh my dear, it is good to hear your voice. I have a thousand questions. Can I call you back in an hour? … Richard, are you there?"

He replied, "I'll call you later today. I'm fine. I'm at Devens Training Center."

"Okay, call me. Bye."

Alyson was at her apartment connected to the family's estate home. Sitting in the interior courtyard, she said to her lunch guest, "I am so sorry for that interruption. Please excuse my bad manners. That was an old friend of mine from DC."

Her guest was an investment banker with the 100-year-old Welch & Forbes firm based in Boston, and a friend of the family. Alyson's mother knew he was visiting and hoped his interests extended beyond young Alyson's portfolio of investment assets.

***

December 28, 1972: Richard reported for duty at the ASA Training Center Command Headquarters Building Thursday morning at 0800.

I should be happy, he thought. *I'm safe, healthy, and no one's shooting at me.*

Two inches of fresh snow covered the ground. It was Thursday and the weekend was approaching. The weather was too cold for comfort. That night he went to the pub at the PX and had a few beers with a couple of the guys from the Special Forces platoon stationed at Fort Devens. The comradery and a six-pack of Schmidt's beer got him through the night. He should have called Alyson back, but did not.

Friday was no less dreary than the day before. Richard sat at his desk and attempted to edit the training manuals he was updating for the ASA human intelligence, a.k.a. HUMINT, classes. They were written by noncombatant staff members at the Brigade Command Center and read more like college philosophy textbooks. The technical instructions were accurate, but the field operations and procedures did not depict the real world in a combat zone. Richard knew firsthand that some procedures employed on the battlefield were better off being left out of any published training manual.

Richard was thinking, *Here I am, back in the States, writing manuals for warriors in the battle zone. I've become part of the bureaucratic war machine I criticized when I was on the front lines. I need a break.*

Richard picked up the telephone and dialed. "Good morning, Alyson. How are you?"

"Oh, Richard, it's good to hear your voice. I will see you tonight, yes?"

He answered, "Yes, that's the plan. I can meet you somewhe—"

"No, no, please come to my apartment first. I need to catch you up on some news."

That evening Richard drove his personal car to Alyson's apartment. Technically it wasn't an apartment; it was separated from the main house by a courtyard and had a private entrance from the street.

As soon as Richard stepped through the doorway, she literally leapt into his arms. Her long flowing brown hair had the color of dark chocolate and she smelled like fresh flowers. Richard admitted to himself she was the most beautiful woman he had ever encountered. They hugged and shared a passionate kiss.

Alyson stood and regained her composure, saying, "Come to the living room. I poured us some wine."

They sat, and Alyson gave Richard a rundown on the shitshow that was Christmas. Alyson's mother and the general had serious disagreements over what the next steps were regarding the care of Christen's ill and aging parents. Christen wanted to bring them home to live out their lives in the family estate. General Broughton understood the level of care they needed would mean a near constant calendar of frequent trips for scheduled and unscheduled trips to the hospital. It was not the way he wanted to spend what little time he shared with his wife in the Boston family home.

Richard took a large sip of his wine and said to Alyson, "I am so sorry your Christmas was less than enjoyable." He was thinking, *I guess Sinop, Turkey, wasn't so bad after all.* Richard took Alyson's hand in his. "That's behind you now," he said. "Where would you like to have dinner?"

"I don't care where we go," Alyson replied, "as long as I have you for dessert." She suggested the Boston Harbor rooftop restaurant at Rowes Wharf. She enjoyed the lights from the city along the harbor, which were beautiful in the winter. "You are not driving. The general's driver is available. He was standing by for my parents. They've decided to stay in for the evening."

Richard did enjoy being on or near the water for any reason. He later confirmed that Alyson was right: the lights along the harbor were spectacular. The food was also over-the-top. The seafood offerings in most Boston restaurants were far superior to anything in the towns of Ayer or Shirley, near the base.

After dinner, the couple sat in front of the fireplace in Alyson's apartment and finished the Pinot Noir Alyson had opened earlier. They made love that night and each of the following nights. Physically, they were made for each other. Their bodies meshed like they were genetically disposed to the act of sexual intercourse. From the shoulders up, they could not be more different. Not just the juxtaposition of male and female. They thought about things differently. Alyson's environment as a child and her educational background were very different than Richard's upbringing. Because of the way in which Alyson and Richard had met, their closeness, or mutual attraction, was more therapeutic than loving.

The war had taught him the ability to compartmentalize his thoughts. Somehow he excused the duplicity of his affection for two women at the same time. But like the memories of war and death, he expected there would be a reckoning one day. Burying the past horrors of war was not the same as deceiving two innocent women in real time. He told himself, *Alyson is here, Stacie is not.* However, he knew that was not enough to cure the guilt building with every day he saw Alyson.

Richard and Alyson spent New Year's Eve watching the sporadic display of amateur fireworks on Boston Harbor. The couple bundled up in heavy winter jackets and gloves and strolled along the waterfront. The amazing display of ice sculptures along the riverwalk was an annual theme for Bostonians. The main fireworks show would not begin until midnight, and they opted to catch that on television at Alyson's apartment.

She asked him, "Do you have to report for duty tomorrow? It's New Year's Day."

"Actually, I do have to be there," he said. "The classes are closed, and the admin staff is there for light duty and emergencies. I at least have to show my face at 0600 hours for reveille."

The next morning, Richard slipped out without waking Alyson. She had shown him how to deactivate the "stay" mode on the apartment's alarm system. On the 45-minute drive to Fort Devens, traffic on Massachusetts Route 2 was light. The snowdrifts along the highway were piled high and showed no signs of melting.

Richard and Alyson spent time together most weekends through January and February. In mid-January, Richard received a belated birthday card from Stacie. She was in California at the army's Language Institute in Monterey.

Richard's relationship with Alyson was not failing, yet it had changed. Things became more perfunctory. Neither of them had a solid plan for the future. The Paris Peace Accords were officially signed on January 27, 1973, ending the war in Vietnam. Richard was bored with his current assignment at Fort Devens, and Alyson was becoming more consumed with life in Boston and her new cadre of friends there.

Chapter 30

The Funeral

Monday morning on the 12th day of March, things changed for Richard.

His assistant, Corp. Olivia Rouse, stuck her head in the doorway to Richard's office. "Your mother is on line two."

Richard said, "What? Who?"

Corporal Rouse repeated what she had said.

Richard could not remember when he'd last spoken to his mother. He instantly felt an enormous wave of guilt sweep over him. He picked up the receiver and said, "Mother, is that really you? Are you okay?"

After a short pause, his mother spoke softly into the phone. "Richard, your father has passed away."

Now it was Richard's turn to pause. A thousand thoughts rushed into his head. He responded, "How did he die? Where?"

"We were back in Santaquin, at the old lake house. After almost two months there, it seemed like life would be good again. Gardner wasn't traveling like he used to. He had lost his penchant for trying to solve every technical problem in the universe. He was still drinking, but nothing like the old days."

She paused, and Richard could hear her softly sobbing and catching her breath.

She went on to say, "Three days ago, at two in the morning, he bolted upright in bed and began yelling my name. He was squeezing my hand so tightly I thought the bones in my hand would snap. He yelled, 'Eloise! Eloise! Bring my ….' He never finished the sentence. He fell back onto his pillow and never breathed another breath." She was crying again.

Richard said, "Oh, Mother, I am so sorry. I am so, so sorry." He got himself together and said, "I'm coming to you. Are you still in Santaquin?"

"No, I'm at home in Provo. Your father wanted to stay close to the university. We traveled back and forth to the lake house from there."

Fortunately for Richard's mother, Gardner's friends were supportive. He was the reason for their success, and for much of the recognition the university received. Not to mention the government-funded research grants bestowed on the school for their work on military defense projects. The funeral would be in Provo, Utah, and he would receive military funeral honors.

Gardner had scored high on the entrance exams and attended the United States Naval Academy after high school. He was eventually discharged early in his service commitment under a provision for being the eldest child in a fatherless family. The truth was that he wanted out so he could pursue his television projects. Even though he remained in the navy for only a short time, his connections in Annapolis made sure he received the honor.

Gardner Farnsworth had an impressive obituary. He invented an all-electronic scanning system which produced highly refined images. His work was used to create the first electronic television. He received patents for his work with televisions and, along with dozens of other related patents, also had patents for the development of electronic movie cameras. Companies like RCA and ITT funded much of Farnsworth's research. They purchased several patents and secured a right of survivorship over other patents, including his latest work with nuclear fusion.

While in Provo for the funeral, Richard was two weeks into a 30-day leave when he received a phone call from an attorney by the name of Charles Towers. Mr. Towers told Richard his father had a last will and testament, along with two trusts which had been set up for Richard and his mother. It had taken a couple of weeks to get things organized; the patents and stock issues had to be reviewed and valuated for income and estate tax purposes. Mr. Towers explained to Richard that his mother's trust provided her with a lifetime income generated from the assets in the trust. These included company stock dividends and capital gains from the sale of the patents previously controlled by his father.

Towers said, "In a nutshell, your mother will be very comfortable with her arrangements. Richard, the provisions in your trust are more restrictive. The agreement your father had in place with RCA and ITT corporations was that you would relinquish control and ownership of the trust assets in return for a one-time lump-sum cash payment."

Richard was overwhelmed by this news, yet relieved to know that in spite of his father's shortcomings and his own neglect of both his parents, his mother would live comfortably for the rest of her life. He thought, *God knows she deserves this.*

Before Richard could ask, Attorney Towers said, "I suppose you would like to know how much money we are talking about."

"Yes, of course," Richard responded. "That was my next question."

"Some of the stock valuations and the execution of the verification of trust forms have not yet been completed. However, I am confident I can accurately tell you the distribution to you will be at least slightly over seven million dollars."

Richard remained silent. He was not experienced in the world of investments and finance, yet he knew that in 1973, seven million dollars made him a very wealthy man.

Towers said, "Major Farnsworth, you are of course free to do what you want with your money. I feel obligated to offer you my advice regarding the next steps. Once the funds are available and ready to be distributed, you will need an account available to receive the money. I am sending you more information, along with the next steps to carry out the transfer of funds. I will include the name of a young man at the Merrill Lynch investment firm in Jacksonville, Florida. His name is William P. Merriam. I have alerted him and he is expecting your call. Don't let his youthful appearance fool you. He is top-notch and well respected for his portfolio management and financial performance."

***

Richard stayed with his mother, and they mutually agreed she would sell the houses and move to an assisted living facility in Provo. She was in fact already frequenting the "old folks' home," as she called it. Every Tuesday and Thursday she visited her friends who were residents there. They had lunch and played bridge all afternoon. Moving in was an easy choice for Eloise Farnsworth.

On the Tuesday morning of April 10, Richard completed the forms that Towers and Merrill Lynch had delivered to his hotel. He left the paperwork with the front desk for pickup by UPS. He flew to Boston, and after retrieving his car from an off-site storage lot, he reported for duty at the ASA's Training

Center Command at Fort Devens. Major Farnsworth was back on duty.

Richard phoned Alyson that evening.

Her answering machine picked up. "Hi, this is Alyson. Leave a message and wait for the beep."

Richard put down the phone without speaking. He thought it was just as well. He didn't feel much like talking anyway and didn't mind staying in.

Chapter 31

Alyson Leaves

Richard's officers' quarters were set up more like a civilian studio apartment. The smallish yet functional kitchen opened to a cozy living room. The two-burner cooktop included a mini oven big enough to heat up a frozen 14-inch pizza. Alyson had expanded and refined his culinary interests and his preference for wine in lieu of Schmidt's beer. He exclaimed to himself, "Tonight, chianti and pizza!"

Saturday, four days later, Alyson was picking up Richard on base. She had previously suggested they drive to Walden Pond for a picnic lunch. They had never been to the historic park together, and the weather was expected to be clear and sunny, with the temperature unusually warming to the upper 60s. Richard hadn't said no, yet in his mind he was thinking Walden Pond was indeed a special place, and not for the reasons Alyson had suggested.

While they relaxed in the sun at the edge of the pond, Alyson talked continuously about nothing of much importance.

Finally, she stopped and sat up. "Richard, are you listening to me?"

He replied, "Yes, of course I am. Your mother's dog will be staying with you for a few days and she always pees on the floor when she is away from the main house."

Alyson shook her head. "Not that part. My future. The army, my life."

From his sitting position, Richard stood up and said, "Let's move to the table. The ground is cold and working its way through the blanket."

They sat at the rustic wooden table. The tree stump sections used as stools were worn smooth from decades of use.

"How about some coffee?" Richard said. "I saw you brought a thermos."

Alyson replied, "Actually, it's peppermint tea. It's good for a cold."

Richard poured the tea into two thick paper cups.

Alyson looked sternly at Richard and said in a serious tone, "I'm getting out. The first of June is my separation date. The war is over, and the Women's Army Corps is offering force reductions with honorary discharges and the full benefits associated with my commission. I feel like I'm stuck in a pattern of going nowhere. So I'm getting out."

Richard dragged a hand over his face and asked, "What will you do? Go back to school? Work?"

"I'm too old to go back to school," she replied. "And frankly, I don't need to make a decision about work right now. I'd like to travel. I want to see the wine country in California and France, and Italy. I want to experience life at a level that's not always so existentially traumatic."

Richard was surprised by his own response; he understood. Alyson had been in a near-death situation. From his experiences in battle and of being injured, Richard felt that life was fragile. Living through a horrific experience opens your eyes to the possibility of not only your own death, but the enormous opportunity you have been given to experience living.

He took Alyson's hand in his and said, "Alyson, I get it. I understand. You are young and beautiful and full of life.

You should do everything in your power to enjoy your life and broaden your experience and appreciation for the beautiful things life has to offer. The army cannot give you that. You've served your country. No one will find fault with your plan to leave the army."

"Thank you, Richard. I sort of knew you'd understand. Of course, my mother is thrilled. She never wanted me to be in the military. My dad … the army is his life. It's funny in a weird sort of way. He wanted me to join the army so I'd be *safe*. What he really meant was so he could protect me. Dad's the one I was most worried about. What about you? I'll stay in Boston. You, on the other hand, could end up in Germany or some other spook station in another hemisphere."

Considering the topic closed, they stood and looked at the sky and the drifting clouds for a few moments.

Richard said, "I'm not very hungry. How about a walk?"

Alyson took his hand and said, "Yes, great idea. You take the lead."

They strolled along the path that followed the shoreline.

Alyson said, "What's wrong with me? All I talk about is myself. Richard, I'm so sorry. You just lost your dad. I know you said the two of you were not close. Still, he was your father. Please forgive me."

"It's okay, Alyson," he said. "The funeral was incredibly well done. The navy treated it like the death of an American hero. My father was strange in several ways. Still, he had good friends, and they came through for my mother and the preparations for the funeral service."

Richard did not say anything about the conversations with the estate attorney or the money. The trusts included confidentiality clauses for the protection of Richard and his mother. The newspapers had only revealed the basic funeral arrangements and a lengthy obituary listing his father's accomplishments.

True to her word, in the weeks that followed, Alyson made travel plans with some of her friends. They'd start with a party week in New York City and, next, travel to Paris. From there they planned to visit the centuries-old vineyards in Bordeaux and Provence. After a mandatory shopping spree in Milan, they'd march through the boot of Italy. First, Lake Como, then Venice and Florence, followed by stops along the Italian Riviera.

Not that it mattered, but Richard thought, *She never asked if I would join her.* It was a stupid thought. He was in the army. Soldiers didn't take luxury jaunts around the world, living like millionaires. She understood that.

Alyson did leave the army and did take her trip around the sun, with stops all over the world. She sent him postcards and telegrams, and they both expected that what they once had was now a memory. A good memory … and that time had passed. Even though Richard was only a few years older than Alyson, it might as well have been many more. She was enjoying her youth, and he was looking back on his.

Chapter 32

Command and General Staff College

A year passed, and Richard anticipated receiving new orders. His position at Devens was always meant to be temporary. When the war ended in 1973, the army and the ASA ranks were overflowing with commissioned officers. The soldiers returning from Vietnam were either honorably discharged or they re-upped and requested duty at the most popular bases in Germany and Thailand.

Richard frequently thought seriously about resigning his commission and leaving the army. He had no desire to move to Germany for three years, and a drinking and screwing tour in Thailand did not appeal to him. He wasn't cut out for his job at the Training Command. If he had any hopes of advancing his career in the army, it would mean taking the army up on the opportunity to return to college for a graduate degree in engineering. As attractive as the thought of being "stuck" at MIT or Berkeley for two years was, it was not motivating him toward an extended commitment to military service. He would be 29 years old that year. It was time for Maj. Richard Thomas Farnsworth to make a decision about his future.

The next day Richard was presented with a note from Col. Thomas Wesley. Richard figured that at some point he'd be hearing from Colonel Wesley or perhaps even General Broughton. Richard and the general had not spoken since Alyson's separation from the army. Richard thought he probably blamed him for not talking Alyson into staying in the army. At any rate, he knew Colonel Wesley was representing the voice and desires of the general. A phone call was scheduled for 1400 hours between Richard and Colonel Wesley.

At the appointed time, Richard's assistant announced, "Colonel Wesley is on line one for you."

"Major, Thomas Wesley here. How the hell are you?"

Richard replied, "I am fine, sir. And you?"

Wesley said, "Major, General Broughton has expressed some interest in your current status. Specifically, he would like you to consider a reassignment to the Deputy Joint Chiefs of Staff. As I am sure you are aware, the general is slated to replace Army Chief of Staff Abrams later this year."

"Thank you, Colonel. With all due respect, the general does not need my interest or approval. He can order my reassignment at any time of his choosing."

"Come on, Farnsworth," Wesley responded, "I know your relationship with the general goes beyond the chain of command. He is aware you are not happy at Devens, and frankly, he needs soldiers like you with recent combat and intelligence operations experience to add some depth and reality to his command. He is swamped with political influences that can easily distort what the reality is for foot soldiers on the ground in enemy territory."

Richard's response was simple. "Colonel, I serve at the pleasure of the president and General Broughton."

Wesley said, "Don't be a smartass, Farnsworth. Be on the lookout for communications from the general's office. He wants to see you."

The next day a telegraph from General Broughton's office included orders for Richard to report to the Pentagon's Joint

Services Command Center at 1600 hours on May 24, 1974. It was common for officers at the rank of major to serve on the staffs of generals in Command Headquarters and at the Pentagon. Richard had the appropriate rank for the general's Joint Command staff, but it was a wartime field promotion. He had the time-in-grade, but had not completed the 10-month Command and General Staff College curriculum at Fort Leavenworth. This was troubling for Richard. If he committed to attending the CGSC, he'd be obligated to extend his commission. This would seriously limit his options and the flexibility to separate from service on his own timeline.

Richard met with General Broughton as planned, and as expected, the general asked him to join his staff.

"General," Richard said, "I am sure you are aware I have not been to Leavenworth and the CGSC."

"Major, I am aware of that, and I do not intend to send you there. We have a satellite program 15 miles down the road at Fort Belvoir. It is an accelerated 90-day program. You will receive the required Intermediate Level Education you need, but unlike the 10-month program, you will not be awarded the Master of Military Art and Science degree. Your classwork will be scheduled in a manner which allows you to work here when you are not in the classroom at Belvoir. Your assignment to Fort McNair will terminate when you start the classes at Belvoir. You will receive the standard Basic Allowance for Housing and live off base. In two years, you will have the time-in-grade for a promotion to the rank of lieutenant colonel. Any questions?"

***

Richard settled into a compact yet comfortable apartment close to the base, and was actually enjoying his time at Fort Belvoir. The classes were interesting and taught by seasoned army officers.

Plus, there was one very interesting sergeant major by the name of Steven "Hoops" Wallace. He spouted out more off-color colloquial expressions than Richard had ever heard. He was also the most decorated soldier Richard had ever encountered. Wallace referred disparagingly to Richard and his classmates as "college boys." Offline, Sergeant Major Wallace privately shared that he had reviewed Richard's background and told him to go with the banter and not take offense. Wallace told Richard he knew that he had been to "the Valley" and respected him for it.

Richard appreciated his sentiments, but not the reminder of the Valley of Death in Vietnam.

The first month of Intermediate Level Education included learning objectives which focused on battalion- and brigade-level leadership in wartime. They studied the history of war and what strategies worked and those that failed. It was like a graduate-level Business Strategy and Policy course, with guns and tanks and soldiers. Wars had to be fought and won on the battlefield, and Richard agreed it was crucial to have a clear overarching objective that could drive the forces to the finish line. As much as he disliked the notion of armchair leadership and wartime directives coming from civilian politicians, it took the entire spectrum working together to prevail in the battle of good versus evil.

The weeks turned into months, and just when Richard felt comfortable in his routine, the game changed again. General Abrams had been the United States Army chief of staff and commanded military operations in the Vietnam War from 1968 to 1972. During World War II he commanded combat operations in the Battle of the Bulge. The army named the Abrams Tank after him. On September 4, 1974, 59-year-old Gen. Creighton W. Abrams Jr. died from lung cancer at Walter Reed General Hospital.

Gen. Thaddeus Broughton was slated to follow Admiral Thomas Moorer as Chairman of the Joint Chiefs of Staff. When the army's Chief of Staff General Abrams died, President Nixon and Secretary of Defense James Schlesinger decided that Gen. Thaddeus Broughton would fill the vacant position for the army. Air Force Gen. George S. Brown then became the Chairman of the Joint Chiefs of Staff. This was a conundrum of great honor and disappointing humiliation for General Broughton. And there was nothing he could do about it.

General Abrams's staff was, as one would expect, fully populated with the required staff. This put Broughton in a tough spot. The army did not work the same as business corporations. He couldn't go in and clean house and start over with newly appointed staff members. Richard understood that his future was about to change one more time. He was nearly finished with ILE training at Fort Belvoir. He might be assigned to the staff for Broughton's replacement, but as a newcomer, his status was not well defined.

Chapter 33

Alyson Returns

Richard had one more week of training at Fort Belvoir when Alyson Broughton called for him. She left a phone number with the CGSC administrator's desk. It was October 3, 1974. After the Bugle Call of Retreat and the lowering of the flag, Richard returned to his off-base apartment and called Alyson's Georgetown number.

"Alyson, it's me, Richard. What are you doing in DC?"

Alyson answered, "Yes, I'm in Georgetown for a few days. Can you get away?"

"I have the weekend free," he responded. "I'm at Fort Belvoir now. Well, I'm actually at my apartment in Springfield."

Alyson said, "Oh, my. A lot has changed. You can fill me in later. Let's spend the weekend at Choptank. No one else will be there. The weather is superb, and I need some downtime."

That sounded good to Richard. He was less intimidated by the enormity of the Broughton family's wealth at Choptank, compared to the family estate in Boston. The natural setting of the Eastern Shore, so close to the world's most powerful city center, was unique. Being on the water was so different from his memories of childhood in Utah.

Alyson said to Richard, "I'll pick you up. Your car is decrepit. Is that okay?"

Richard was driving a high-mileage, 1968 faded blue Ford Fairlane hardtop. Alyson's Mercedes convertible was a far better choice for the trip to the Eastern Shore.

Friday afternoon at 1600 hours, Richard changed out of his uniform and into a more preppy outfit Alyson had prompted him to acquire. Brown corduroy slacks and a plaid Burberry shirt topped with a cashmere wool sweater that cost half of his monthly pay. Garrison shoes were replaced with Weejuns penny loafers without socks. He looked the part, but aside from the clothing, he was still a misplaced Midwesterner.

The weekend at the farm was idyllic by anyone's standards. They sailed the Chesapeake and dined on exquisite seafood preparations presented by the live-in house manager. The wine cellar at Choptank was bottomless. Richard could not spell "sommelier" correctly, yet he was gradually expanding his knowledge of fine wines. The first night at Choptank was both amazing and uneasily strange. When Alyson and Richard first became intimate after her ordeal, it was a soothing, caring engagement of emotions and physical pleasure. It was like a mutual healing process that generated feelings of love and the meeting of mutual needs. That night Alyson transformed into a sexually demanding mode with more aggressive movements and gestures. Richard felt more used than loved. It was such a demonstrative change that his usual ability to easily and eagerly repeat the act of making love was noticeably limited.

The next morning was equally strange. They went sailing, not out of great desire, but because that's what you do on Saturdays at the farm on the Eastern Shore of Maryland.

When they returned to the dock and were walking toward the house, Alyson asked, "Richard, what's wrong? You seem offput about something. Not last night, I hope. That was nothing. All men have their moments."

Richard considered his response and wondered without speaking it. *All men? How many does she know?* He said, "I'm sorry. Things at Belvoir and the Pentagon are consuming my thoughts. I had a plan, but everything was upended when your dad left the Deputy Joint Chief's office. He will be great as the army COS. He was also the better candidate for the Chairman's spot." The job had gone from the navy to the air force, after 10 years of army generals in the position.

They had a late lunch in the expansive kitchen of the main house. Ms. Griggs, the house manager, had previously prepared a tray of lobster rolls on toasted brioche buns and a chilled crab vichyssoise. A bottle of Lafon Montrachet Grand Cru was chilling in a painted porcelain wine vase that could have been a collectible work of art. What seemed like a normal setting to Alyson was considered by Richard as an overdone display of wealth and privilege. It wasn't a big deal to Richard; however, it was another sign that said "You don't belong here."

Alyson and Richard finished their lunch, and Alyson said, "Richard, I have an idea. Screw Choptank. Let's go back to Georgetown and party like college kids. I want to dance and get rip-roaring drunk."

Richard responded, "Alyson, that actually sounds like a great idea."

She added, "You'll have to drive. I'm a little tipsy."

They returned to DC and stopped at Belvoir to retrieve a change of clothes for Richard. It was nearly 6:00 p.m. by the time they got to Alyson's townhouse apartment. They showered in separate bathrooms, and Richard went down to the living room bar for a neat glass of Blanton's barrel-aged bourbon. He was appreciative of the treat, and wondered why she had such a large cache of expensive bottles. She drank only Cosmos and wine drinks. After her routine application of makeup and Coco Chanel perfume, she came downstairs wearing a short and shimmering black sequined dress with a white-gold diamond-encrusted necklace and a matching triple-strand bracelet. Her dark hair was partially pulled up into a messy, sexy-looking bun. Putting the psychological noise aside, she was the most beautiful woman he had ever known.

Richard hailed a cab on the street outside of the apartment while Alyson waited inside the doorway. They were dropped off at the entrance to the club. The plain brick facade and simple entry was not what Richard had expected. He had heard from his friend Bill Dennis that it was a world-premier jazz club. Musical giants like Ella Fitzgerald, Dizzy Gillespie, and Bobby Hackett performed there and recorded live shows at the club. This night featured the iconic jazz pianist Earl Hines. At 70 years old, "Fatha" Hines displayed more energy than Richard could muster on a good day. The pianist pounded out Duke Ellington tunes including "I'm Beginning to See the Light" and "Sophisticated Lady." Alyson and Richard were not really dancing so much as standing and swinging with the music. The entertaining distraction came at the right time.

That night at the Georgetown apartment, Alyson was trying to talk seriously to Richard about their relationship. She made no sense. She was drunk and her sentences were chopped and unintelligible.

Then she said, "Make love to me! Richard, where are you? I want you to fuck me now!"

She was lying in bed, wearing only bikini panties and a lacy bra. Her necklace still sparkled in the semidarkness of the bedroom. She rolled over toward Richard and mumbled something and let out a long sigh and closed her eyes for the night. Richard slipped out of bed to go pee. Then, instead of returning to bed, he put his trousers on and went downstairs for a nightcap.

The next morning Richard was awakened by dogs barking outside. He was still in the soft leather recliner next to a half-empty bourbon bottle. He reflected: *That was one hell of a night!* He walked with baby steps to the kitchen and drank water from the faucet for a full 30 seconds. He found the coffeemaker but no coffee. Rummaging in the refrigerator, he found a diet soft drink called Tab. He drank it and retrieved his clothes and other personal items from the guest bedroom. Alyson would not wake up for at least another two hours.

He walked two blocks up the road to a main roadway and hailed a cab.

Back at his apartment, he made a pot of coffee and read the newspaper he had picked up in Georgetown.

The *New York Times* headlines and feature articles of October 6, 1974, read:

- President Ford appears to be leaning toward proposals to ease the tax burdens of the poor.

- Five thousand people attended a citizens' rally intended to show racial harmony in Atlanta. The one complaint voiced by the Rev. Martin Luther King Sr. at the rally was that "the crowd's too black."

- Leonid Brezhnev, head of the Soviet Communist party, says the Soviet Union is prepared to take additional steps with the United States to curb the arms race. Mr. Brezhnev, the guest of honor in East Berlin at a rally marking East Germany's 25th anniversary, said he favored a ban on underground testing of all nuclear weapons and suggested that the two major powers withdraw from the Mediterranean all their nuclear-armed ships and submarines.

- In Washington, officials have disclosed that the Ford administration, faced with what it sees as almost certain Senate rejection of the treaty limiting the underground testing of nuclear weapons, is seeking to broaden the agreement to include nuclear tests for peaceful purposes. The treaty was signed in Moscow last July by former President Nixon. Negotiations on the treaty will be resumed in Moscow in the next two weeks.

Richard contemplated what the world would be like without wars to fight. Vietnam was still fresh in the minds of US citizens. It was a war that could have been won by the standards applied to past wars. In the Vietnam War, three presidents sent a million and a half soldiers to fight for a cause that quickly faded from noble to distorted surreal chaos. Over 50,000 young men and some women lost their lives for an undefined and unresolved conflict. Generals aspired to be presidents, and presidents sought to be seen as hawkish warriors for a free world. Richard read through the news articles and judged the topics of nuclear proliferation and the false promises to "limit" nuclear testing as foreshadowing for what could be a world war with immeasurable destruction. Feeding those scenarios into his current situation somehow brought clarity to thoughts about his own future. Monday morning, Maj. Richard Farnsworth would begin the process of official resignation and separation from the US Army.

Chapter 34

April 1975 – Big Pine Key

Big Pine Key is located at mile marker 30 in the Florida Keys. The 10-square-mile peninsula extends northwest from US Route 1, 30 miles northeast of Key West. The population of approximately 1,800 keys folks, known as "Conchs," is augmented by 1,500 animals known as "Key deer." The relatively small, 40- to 60-pound white-tailed deer have populated the island since the 1500s. The favorable climate allows for a year-round mating season. Without that increased reproduction, they would have been extinct long ago.

Richard found an old, wooden, two-bedroom Florida Cracker–style home at the end of Geraldine Street on Big Pine Key. The back porch was elevated three feet above the yard, which consisted of sporadically distributed weeds and cabbage palms growing in a ground cover of lifeless bleached white coral. From his rocking chair he could look across a small mangrove-ordered pond. He had a built-in family of great herons, sea ducks, and pelicans. Occasionally a pair of manatees meandered in from the bayside waters. With Richard's invested inheritance he could have chosen to live in any of a thousand luxury homes anywhere in the country. This choice satisfied a side of Richard's psyche which had been ignored for 30 years.

Since Richard's departure from the army and moving to the Florida Keys, Alyson had expressed little interest in visiting him in his new Menorcan lifestyle. His memories of her were still emotional. It was more than her exaggerated physical beauty and unbridled passionate demeanor. A part of him still saw her as the scared, vulnerable girl he'd pulled from a closet in Germany. That memory and image would stay with him, and experience told him she would never completely lose the painful recollections from that traumatic experience.

He made fast friends with his neighbor Mike Gorton. Mike and his wife, Kim, were gracious enough to offer their friendship and introduce him to the neighbors. Mike was a well-known fishing guide in the Keys and had his own fishing lodge in Good News Bay, Alaska. Kim was simply a beautiful person with a face and personality that lit up every room she entered. Mike told Richard about the species of fish and shellfish available in the Big Pine Key waters. A boat would likely be Richard's next big purchase. First he needed some basic training and Captain Mike was the best instructor he could have hoped for. The water was still too cold for some species of fish; however, April and May were approaching fast and would bring the bay and ocean sides of the Keys alive with sea life.

Rising early remained Richard's habit in the Keys. One morning he was taking a walk around the neighborhood, and he ran into Mike Gorton riding a bicycle and carrying a bucket.

Mike called out to Richard, "Hey, white boy! Where are you going?" Mike enjoyed making fun of Richard's midwestern skin tone. He had not been on Big Pine Key long enough to begin tanning from the tropical sun.

Richard replied, "You should watch yourself. Some folks would take offense and think that was a racial slur."

Mike replied, "I am a realist, not a racist, and you, sir, are most definitely white." Mike added, "You come fishing with me a few times, we will get your tan going." Mike said he had grown up in the inner city of Detroit, where he was the only white kid in the neighborhood. On the basketball court in the city park, he was known as "White Boy."

Richard asked, "What's in the bucket, Conch Boy?"

"These little babies," Mike said, smiling, "are solid gold. Silver dollar–sized sand crabs are the very best bait for the giant permit—a challenging fish—that we are going to catch today. I would take you with me, but I have two special anglers on the charter this morning, Mr. and Mrs. Armando Codina. The Codina family owns more real estate in Miami than anyone else. They build warehouses and office buildings. At 33 years old, Mr. Codina is a self-made multimillionaire. When Armando got off a boat from Cuba 25 years ago, he didn't speak a word of English. His relatives in Miami took him in, and with the help of the Cuban community, they educated him and positioned him for great success."

Duly impressed, Richard said, "Good luck today. I'll see you when you get back. Wine will be served on the back porch at 1800 hours—sorry, that's 6:00 p.m. in the land of Conchs."

Richard was really enjoying his unusual lifestyle. Even though life as an army officer in Washington, DC, was not all that regimented, it was nothing like his new laid-back setting in this Florida paradise.

In mid-May, Richard arranged for his mother and a couple of her friends from the nursing home to visit Miami for Easter. He rented them rooms at the Fontainebleau Hotel in Miami Beach. They were thrilled to see Miami. They knew it only from the movies and newscasts. Just seeing the ocean was a larger-than-life experience for the septuagenarians from Provo, Utah. The entourage was accompanied by a young female employee of the nursing home. She kept the ladies on schedule with their medications and arranged transportation to restaurants and other local attractions.

Richard met the group for a festive Easter dinner at the hotel dining room with a grand view of the Atlantic Ocean. He was glad his mother was still physically and mentally able to make the trip. He had always admired her ability to keep a positive attitude and a happy outward appearance. Richard was sure she missed the old life with her husband and family in Utah. However, she kept it stored in her memory. Time had a way of polishing the rough edges of the episodes in life that stay with us. Richard grasped this truism, but his memories still had some sharp points when it came to his dad. Richard also carried around a huge pile of bad memories from Vietnam. They lurked in a box he tried hard to leave unopened. For now, Richard was finally getting his head right and he felt like he might have a chance at living a normal life.

That summer, Mike taught Richard about boating and fishing. They caught the big permit Mike had spoken about. Richard learned to cast a fly rod and it opened up a whole different world of enjoyment. Catching bonefish that swam as fast as a car and giant tarpon that put on unparalleled acrobatic shows brought a refreshing dimension to the world for Richard Farnsworth.

Chapter 35

Bill Dennis's Birthday

Richard's mail was forwarded from his previous apartment address in Springfield. The army occasionally forwarded mail—most of it was V.A. related or DOD announcements, and official notifications about things he was no longer involved with. It was Monday, September 1, 1975, and on that day he opened a letter in a festive envelope that included a personal note and a formal invitation to a birthday party in honor of his old friend, Bill Dennis.

Hear Ye! Hear Ye!
For the Celebration of the Birth of the
Distinguished and Notorious
Sir William George Dennis

You are hereby Commanded to Report to the
Pier House Resort in Key West, Florida
at 1800 hours on October 11, 1975

Bill Dennis was 10 degrees north of energetic and fun-loving. He could turn any conference room into a standup comedy show. His wife Sharon had a lot to tolerate, and Richard knew she was equally amazing in her own way. When they were married, in DC, Richard thought Bill might settle into a more subdued posture. That apparently had not happened. Other than flying into Key West airport, Richard had not spent any time there. He thought—or rather, knew—this would be a birthday party to remember.

Richard decided to book a room in Key West for two nights. He planned to arrive the day before the party and see some of the notable and historic sights. After studying the map and noting everything was within walking distance of Duval Street, he opted to catch the Keys Shuttle and leave his car behind. When he had moved to Big Pine, he was picturing life in the Keys as laid-back: solitary days and long stretches of not much going on. After six months he realized he could not have been more wrong. Every day was packed with new adventures, physical activities, and interaction with interesting friends. At least two days each week he took his skiff out into the canals, winding through the mangroves. At the western end of the canals, he could push his boat with a long fiberglass pole into and across seemingly endless flats of shallow water. Through the gin-clear water, he could see passing sharks and stingrays inches from his boat. On the ocean side of the waterways which cut through the landmass and under US 1, he found more sea life. One of his neighbors had a tourist-style guide boat. She was an attractive young woman by the name of Raquel. She taught Richard how to net lobsters and dip net shrimp in the flowing tide. He now accepted that life on Big Pine Key was anything but laid-back.

On Friday, October 10, Richard caught the Keys Shuttle at Captain Hook's Marina and Dive Center on US 1. The foot of Duval Street and the Pier House Resort measured only 30 miles from Big Pine. With traffic and lower speed limits it could take 45 minutes or more to get there by car or bus.

Richard checked in to the resort and dropped his gear in the room. The modest room had a spectacular view of the Gulf of Mexico and a small island less than one mile from the water's edge at the hotel's beach. First stop: the Hemingway House and Museum.

Ernest Hemingway was born in Oak Park, Illinois, and died in Ketchum, Idaho. Someone once said the birthday and date of one's death are infinitely less important than the dash between the dates. Richard knew that the dash for Hemingway was full of life. His writing was only one component of an incredible history. Since moving to Big Pine, Richard had read Hemingway's most notable works cover to cover: *The Sun Also Rises, A Farewell to Arms, For Whom the Bell Tolls,* and of course, *The Old Man and the Sea*. While Richard did not imagine himself as Hemingway, he did find comfort in knowing that a man can break away from the geographic influences of the midwestern towns of Illinois and Utah and reinvent a new life in the tropics.

Richard spent the day touring the museums and boutiques along Duval Street. He found the most colorful bars and restaurants, including Captain Tony's Saloon, Sloppy Joe's Bar, and Bagatelle Island Restaurant. He decided he'd have to return to Key West for a longer stay. That night, he had dinner at the Pier House Restaurant, which had a panorama of the Key West Harbor and across to the Gulf of Mexico.

The famous Key West sunset was everything he had imagined. He enjoyed spectacular sunsets at Big Pine, but watching the sun slip below the horizon where the Atlantic Ocean and Gulf of Mexico meet was extra special. Hundreds of people assembled along the bulkhead of an old navy pier. Mimes and musicians and people dressed as pirates delighted the crowd. During dinner, Richard was thoroughly entertained by a semi-famous piano player from Miami named Michael

Utley. After an opening solo number, Utley introduced an unfamiliar upstart musician by the name of James Buffett. Together they captured the essence of island life.

Leaving the army and moving to Florida initially seemed like a huge mistake to Richard. Six months later, and especially on this night in Key West, he felt very good about his chosen lifestyle.

The next morning Richard went for a run. He ran all the way to the other end of Duval Street. The round-trip distance was a little over three miles. Duval Street at 7:00 a.m. had magically transformed from "uninhibited" to "uninhabited." Except for an occasional automobile and bicycle, he had the island to himself. At the easternmost point, he found the Southernmost Point of the United States, marked by a bulky concrete structure shaped like a nun-style channel buoy. He had the sense of having arrived. He asked himself, *Is this the end of the journey or the beginning?* As his friend Bill used to say when he caught Richard slipping into a mood of self-reflection, "Too much thinking and not enough drinking." It was party time in Key West, Florida!

Richard met Bill and Sharon at the A&B Lobster House bar at 3:30 p.m.

After the bear hugs and handshakes were done, Bill asked, "Where are you staying?"

Richard told him, "The Pier House next door, where I assume you are as well."

Bill answered, "You assume correctly, Major Farnsworth."

"That's Mr. Farnsworth to you," Richard replied, "and based on your coiffed facial hair, I presume you have also left the army."

"Right again, Farnsworth. After the Paris Peace Accords and the final helicopter ride out of Saigon this year, I was offered the option of an early out, and I took it. Sharon's civilian military service was just a matter of giving notice. Hey, man, I heard about your dad. I'm so sorry. You should have called me."

"Yeah, thanks, Bill, it's okay. You know the truth is, we were not very close."

Bill nodded. "Yeah, but it was your dad, man."

The A&B Lobster House bar, known as the White Tarpon, was on the ground level and open on three sides to a view of the marina.

Bill waved down the bartender and turned toward Richard and Sharon, saying, "It's cocktail time. How about a pitcher of margaritas?"

Sharon and Richard enthusiastically said yes. For the next hour, the threesome laughed and reminisced about their time in Washington. They agreed that they had thought being assigned to Pentagon duty would be more satisfying and more of an elite feeling. They also agreed it was not.

Sharon broke into the banter, saying, "Hey, guys, we have to get going. The party starts in 90 minutes."

As they stood to leave, Bill asked Richard, "You brought your tux, right?"

Richard appeared perplexed and before he could say no, Bill added, "I'm just f-ing with you, man. Pirate wear, fishing shirts, and waders, it's all good."

The party spread itself over the covered and uncovered decks of the Pier House. Bill had invited 10 couples from his hometown in Jacksonville Beach, Florida. Four other couples traveled from Virginia. The decks were decorated in a nautical theme, with crab traps and fish nets and a giant lobster statue. The waitstaff worked through the crowd with hors d'oeuvres, wine bottles, and pitchers of margaritas. The hotel set up games for the party guests. The ring toss matches proved most popular. Dart boards and facemasks for those willing to stand under the target were provided. There was a series of concentric circles floating in the water 30 feet from the shore, and an astroturf miniature tee box on the beach. The water chipping game and other games were there for the guests to bet on. The betting was feverish. The drinking was, in medical terms, "excessive."

As the crowd took their seats for dinner, the glass doors of the adjacent restaurant opened, and the piano and guitar player from the previous night began belting out tunes about Mother Ocean and stepping on pop-tops. The music was very good, the food was great, and everyone was having a fantastic time.

When the musicians took a break, Sharon tapped her glass and said it was time for some birthday toasts to Bill. She opened the floor with a short and moving summary of their life together and their plans. The Miami crowd provided a roast of "Bill, the Man" that was better than most television comedy shows. A few more offered condolences for his aging mind and body. The others followed Richard's lead and simply spoke about how wonderful the evening was and how much they truly appreciated being friends with Bill and Sharon. The balance of the evening and the Duval Crawl was better off being left unwritten.

Chapter 36

Back to Big Pine

Back in Big Pine, Richard was having dinner with neighbors Mike and Kim.

She said to Richard, "You shouldn't be living alone. It's not healthy."

He replied, "Thank you, Kim. I need a little more time before I think about another relationship."

She said, "No, dummy, I'm talking about a dog. Look at Zeke. He's a loving companion full of life and energy and he shares it with us and everyone he meets. That's what I'm talking about."

Richard thought about it and said, "You know, you're right. A black lab like Zeke may be just the ticket. And Zeke would have a playmate. There are not a lot of pet stores here in the Lower Keys, though."

Mike chimed in, "Zeke is a rescue dog. There's an organization in Miami called K9s for Warriors. They bring in abandoned dogs rescued from kennels and donated by families no longer able to care for them. Sometimes the dogs don't take to the training that pairs the dogs with veterans suffering from PTSD or traumatic brain injury, or both. That's where you should look for your dog."

Richard purchased a slightly used Hewes flats boat from a guide in Islamorada who was down on his luck. Mike showed Richard how to safely operate the boat and navigate the shallow waters around Big Pine Key. It was a fast boat, and if the weather was calm he could run up and down the Keys on the bayside or oceanside, and range as far as Marathon to the northeast or southwest, all the way to Key West. He quickly found that the solitude of being on the water at sunrise or sunset was more healing than anything he had experienced. His new friends Mike and Kim had given a fresh start that he felt might work out for Maj. Richard Farnsworth, US Army—status: retired.

***

The Christmas holidays came and went without much hoopla. The theme in Florida's Lower Keys was simply "Every Day Is a Holiday." New Year's Eve was celebrated in the community park on Big Pine Key. At a BYOB and food event, the residents brought a homemade dish which included preparations of beans and rice and creative paella dishes of fish and shellfish. The neighbors pitched in and provided a peel-and-eat shrimp station. A favorite addition was cooked by one of the neighbors whom no one saw much of during the year. On New Year's Eve he brought his own cooking trailer and he'd fry fish and shrimp, and boil vegetables and potatoes. A giant of a fellow named "Big Richard" brought his band down from Islamorada. He played contemporary rock music, and the crowd danced on the park's illuminated basketball court. His scantily-clad backup singers were a big hit with the guys—not so much in the watchful eyes of their wives and girlfriends.

On New Year's Day, some of the survivors caravaned to Key West to gape at the famous Conch parade. Holidays in Key West were marked with colorful Carnival-like processions. Decorated fire trucks playing patriotic music were followed by a troupe of body-painted nudes whimsically dancing down Duval Street. Gay Pride members, dressed in elaborate costumes, danced alongside an assembly of massive rumbling Harleys and black leather-clad bikers. The liquor and beer flowed freely in the crowded bars up and down Duval Street. Captain Tony's and Sloppy Joe's were standing room only by 9:00 a.m. Fortunately for Richard and Mike, Kim did not drink much and provided them with safe transportation home.

Seven weeks later, on February 18, 1976, Richard went to his mailbox and found a letter which had been forwarded from his old DC address. It was postmarked in Provo, Utah, on February 4, from Family Life Assisted Living.

Dear Mr. Farnsworth,

We have tried unsuccessfully to locate you and we sincerely hope this correspondence finds its way to you in a timely manner. We know that you correspond with your mother on a regular basis. With great regret, some of her personal belongings were inadvertently disposed of, along with your letters and your most current address.

The director and staff members wish to convey our sincere condolences on your mother's passing. She died peacefully in her sleep after suffering through a sepsis condition that irreversibly damaged her kidney function and impaired her respiratory system. In accordance with her wishes, she was cremated on January 31, 1976. The St. Francis Catholic Church of Provo presided over a memorial service the following day.

If you would be so kind as to contact our office and provide a shipping address, we will send her belongings to you. Her account has been settled by the executor of her estate named in her trust. Please accept our most sincere apologies for these unfortunate circumstances. Your mother was a shining star for our residents and staff. She will be missed and remembered by all who loved and cared for her.

Sincerely yours,

Mrs. Lori Marvin
Executive Director
Family Life Assisted Living

Richard was stunned. She had been perfectly fine in Miami. Her last letter was upbeat and she talked about how much she enjoyed her friends at the retirement home. She seemed so happy. He did not cry. He felt like his entire body had been desiccated of all tears and emotion. For the first time in his life, he was truly alone.

He went through the motions and the days passed slowly. News of his mother's death spread through his close-knit neighborhood and people wished him well and spoke to him on the street, offering their condolences. He wanted to say "Please don't. Please stop." Being constantly reminded that his mother had died with no family there to hold her hand or say goodbye was punishing to Richard. His guilt was bearable, but unyielding with the daily reminders. Well-meaning friends brought flowers to his house and left them on the front porch with kind notes of sympathy. Others gave him hearty meals which overstuffed his refrigerator. It was a Southern tradition. When someone died, their family would be inundated with generosity expressed through the delivery of daily meals.

Chapter 37

The World-Record Bonefish

Richard was still working through his transition from military to civilian life. He needed a new wardrobe and shoes. Boots and brogans were traded for wading shoes and sandals. His army-issue T-shirts did not fit the fashion standards set by the resident Conchs.

He also needed some money. That afternoon he placed a call to his financial advisor at Merrill Lynch. The receptionist transferred the call, and Bill Merriam answered on the first ring.

"Hello, Richard, how the heck are you? It's good to hear from you. It's also timely that you called. Your first short-term bond has matured and, before we reinvest the funds, I need to know what your cash needs are."

"That's exactly why I'm calling," Richard said. "I'm seriously low on cash. I need your folks to transfer some money into my checking account."

Bill answered, "Not a problem. The funds will be in the account sometime tomorrow—unless you need them sooner."

"No, no. Tomorrow's fine."

"How much? Also, I can set it up for regular deposits if you like."

Richard answered, "No, nothing regular for now. Ten thousand should hold me over until winter."

Merriam said, "Richard, the accounts are performing well. The recession was dwindling last year, and interest rates have come down and the US economy has grown more than 5 percent in the last 12 months. Your overall balance is back to its original value, and you can expect good growth for the next year."

"Thanks, Bill. That's comforting to know. You take care and say hello to your new bride."

"One last thing," Bill said with a chuckle. "If you ever feel the need to do an account review in person, I'm sure I can find my way down to your home in the Keys."

Richard thought, *I should get a job. Living like this is not real life.* At the same time, he was aware that seven million dollars would easily take care of him for the rest of his life. He replied, "Maybe next week."

He was thinking of a trip to Miami. He could go shopping for clothes there and maybe check out the dogs at K9s for Warriors. Mike had suggested that if he went to Miami, Richard should stop at a tackle shop in Islamorada by the name of H.T. Chittum. They stocked the best inventory of fly rods, flies, and other flats fishing gear.

That night Richard met up with Mike and a couple of other guys. They went to what might be the oldest bar in the Florida Keys. The No Name Pub, on Big Pine Key, was a general store back in the early 1930s. When Prohibition ended in 1933, the owner added a small covered outdoor dining area and served food and liquor. Like many establishments of that era, liquor was always available, and during Prohibition it was only sold or consumed in back rooms or sheds out of the sight of any passing revenuers.

Rum was the drink of choice for Richard and his friends. Various concoctions of Jamaican and Cuban rums were made famous by Ernest Hemingway when he frequented Sloppy Joe's Bar in Key West. He built a culture of festive overindulgence that became the normal agenda for any night out with the boys.

This night was no different. Richard, Mike, and their buddies got rip-roaring drunk. Singing songs along with the jukebox and wagering on their own arm-wrestling contests transported them out of the trials and anxiety of their daily Keys life. The surreal setting of the old bar in a mystical tropical paradise brought mental relief that was somehow therapeutic. It cleaned out their troubled thoughts and gave them hope for a better tomorrow. Richard anticipated the deleterious physical ailments known collectively as a hangover. For those enjoyable moments of comradery and laughter, he thought it was well worth it.

Two days later, someone was knocking on Richard's door at 7:00 a.m. "Richard," Mike shouted. "My client canceled on me. Let's go fishing."

Richard had been awake for the last hour. He was lying in bed, thinking about Alyson and wondering what she was doing in the protected haven of her wealthy Boston enclave. He had thought, *She wouldn't last a week here in Big Pine.* Life was so different. His own adjustment had been a shock to his frame of reference. It was unlike anything or anywhere he had experienced. Somehow it seemed to fit. In a twisted way, he did miss the regimented lifestyle of the army. He had experienced trauma and adventure, and near death as a soldier in the war. Still, it had a magnetism that would not go away. He pushed it aside and kept those feelings safely tucked into the box he had built for his memories of Vietnam. He did admit he had never enjoyed the time briefly spent in the company of Alyson's family. The general was okay because even though he was lost in the political ranks of the elite, upper-echelon of the military complex, he was still a soldier at heart and had the credentials to confirm it.

"Good morning, Captain Mike. Come in. Would you like a cup of coffee?"

"No, thanks, buddy, I've had a full thermos already."

"Give me a few minutes," Richard said. "I would love to go fishing with the world's best fishing guide."

Richard dressed and grabbed his 8-weight Sage fly rod and a hip bag of tackle. He slathered on a handful of sunscreen and put on his fishing hat with the oversized front bill and a rear skirt which shaded the back of his neck. He resembled a Moroccan tribesman ready for the Saharan desert.

The day of fishing was epic in proportion to Richard's solo efforts at fishing the flats. Mike was standing on an elevated poling platform over the stern of the boat. He pushed the boat silently across crystal-clear shallow water. Nothing was disturbed by the boat stealthily sliding across the flats. Twenty minutes after shutting down the outboard engine, Mike poled the boat to a ridge of exposed sand and stopped the boat's movement by pushing the point of the 18-foot-long pole into the soft sand.

He whispered to Richard, "Look there, at two o'clock, 40 feet out."

Richard spotted the silvery tail of a bonefish reflecting the light of the morning sun. The fish had dropped its normally skittish behavior and was feeding on a sand crab. When the bonefish tilted its head downward toward its meal, its tail stuck out of the water several inches.

Mike instructed Richard, "Make your cast so the fly gently drops slightly in front of the fish. When I tell you, strip the line."

After a few seconds, the fish returned to a horizontal posture.

Mike urgently whispered, "Strip it, strip now!"

Richard held the rod firmly in his left hand and pulled the fly line with his right, pulling in six inches of line with each strip.

After the second strip, Mike said, "Stop stripping. Wait for it. … Now, long strip."

Richard pulled the line smoothly through the eyes of the fly rod.

The line tightened, and Mike yelled, "You've got him. Hold your rod up. Hold the tip high."

The drag on the fly reel made a hissing sound as the fish swam away at high speed. Bonefish can swim at speeds of over 40 miles per hour. This fish swam speedily across the great white flat of seawater. After nearly 200 yards of line had been stripped from the reel, the fish stopped.

Mike yelled, "Reel. Reel. Keep reeling."

Richard reeled the small golden reel as fast as he could. The line became taut again, and the fish made another run. Richard and the bonefish repeated these maneuvers until at last, the great fish had tired and lay still in the water next to the side of the boat. Mike slipped a net under the fish and lifted it gently to the surface.

Richard was thinking, *Next to firing an M-60 machine gun on full-automatic in a firefight, that's the most exhilarating thing I have ever experienced!*

"Oh my God!" Mike exclaimed. "That is the biggest bonefish I have ever seen!"

Mike asked Richard to retrieve a measuring tape from the console of the skiff. The fish measured 35 inches in length. The girth was equally impressive. Up close the silvery-scaled fish looked like a large, inflated pool toy.

Mike said, "This is a world-record bonefish! You are famous!"

Richard's pulse was still racing. "Thank you, Mike. That was amazing."

Mike said, "To claim it as a record and have your name in the Book of World Records, we will have to take the fish to a certified weigh station in Islamorada or Key West." There was a somber tone to Mike's voice.

Richard asked, "How will we get the fish there? Won't it die?"

Mike answered, "Yes, the fish will die, but your name will go down in history as the only angler landing a 16-pound bonefish on an eight-pound test leader. That record will stand for many years to come."

Richard had never been a star. He was always in the background through high school and at West Point. Being in the limelight was never a motivation for him. He said to Mike, "This fish has given me a gift. I will not kill it. We will return the gift. Let it go, Mike." With a nod, Richard said, "Let it go."

Mike's eyes watered and he shared the emotional relief with Richard as he unhooked the fly from the fish's mouth and gently moved it back and forth in the water. When the fish recovered, it swept its V-shaped tail in blistering movements and sped away from the boat, to its majestic life on the coral flats of Big Pine Key.

Richard and Mike caught more bonefish that day. They even jumped an 80-pound tarpon that took the bonefish fly. It was the same fly that caught the giant bonefish.

Mike told Richard, "That was a Chico Fernandez Bonefish Special fly. I can get more of them. Chico will be disappointed when we tell him about releasing the world's largest bonefish caught on his fly. Though, he will understand why we let it go. These fish are our livelihood. My customers spend thousands of dollars every year chasing these 'gray ghosts' up and down the Florida Keys."

Richard extended a hand to Mike. "Thank you, Captain Mike. This has been an amazing day. I cannot express how enjoyable and healing this has been. Thank you for your friendship and everything you have done for me."

When Mike and Richard returned home, Richard helped Mike wash down the boat and stow the fishing rods. Kim met them at the dock with refreshing glasses of lemonade.

She said, "I made it myself. Our friend Allan was in Homestead this morning and picked up some fresh vegetables. He brought us some beautiful tomatoes, lemons, and some huge pomelos." She laughed and added, "Oh yeah, and your old friend Smirnoff threw in some joy juice for your drinks."

***

That evening Mike and Kim came over to Richard's house. The house was perfect for the setting on Big Pine Key. It was an offgrade, old-Florida shanty-style home. The horizontal wood lap siding was a faded white color with weathered edges of natural wood. The tin roof had just the right amount of rust, and the front and rear covered porches provided the perfect settings for the kind of relaxation you can find only in the Keys.

Kim went over to a brown paper shopping bag Mike had set on a chair. She opened it and pulled out a plank of wood and held it up to the wall by the front door. "This is perfect. Richard, you have officially joined our little village of Big Pine."

It was a hand-carved wooden sign with letters routed out and painted to read "Bay Watch."

"Our houses have life and personality," Kim said, "so we give them names. What do you think of yours?"

Richard stood to hug Kim. He said, "I absolutely love it. Thank you both for being so kind to me."

Mike shook his glass that now contained only ice. "Hey, pal, I can't celebrate with an empty glass." He stood, raised his glass, and announced: "Here's to you and here's to me, you get the rum, sir, while I go pee."

Kim rolled her eyes.

Chapter 38

Duke

Richard was at the hardware store picking up some supplies to repair a couple of loose boards on his back deck. He was chatting with another newfound friend, who owned the store. His name was Alan Woods and he also owned a lumber store in Tavernier, 50 miles up the Keys, just past Islamorada. They were discussing the prospect of Richard acquiring a dog. Alan agreed with Kim Gorton that a dog would bring joy and companionship, and he confirmed that going to Miami and K9s was a great idea. It was settled: Richard would go to Miami, do his shopping, and talk to the folks at K9s for Warriors.

He said to Alan, "I'll go. I will. Maybe next week."

Alan said, "I have a better idea. You know I'm a pilot. That is, I know how to fly planes. I don't do it commercially. I'll ask my daughter to drive us to Miami. We'll do your shopping and pick up my new De Havilland Beaver, and fly back to the strip at Summerland Key."

The following Monday, Paris Woods picked up Richard at his house. Alan was already in the car. The car was a tricked-out yellow four-door Jeep Wrangler. With the roof partially open, they drove 100 miles to the 826 Exit from the turnpike and into the outskirts of Miami. They stopped in Kendall and shopped at the newly opened mall. Richard bought some casual slacks and fishing shorts. Alan told Richard to hold off on the sandals and wading shoes. They would make another trip to H.T. Chittum's for those.

Alan slapped the side of the Jeep from the open window. "Let's find Richard a dog."

The K9s facility resembled a small college campus. There were classrooms and a dormitory building surrounding a courtyard. The obvious difference was that the people milling around the campus were wounded veterans. Some were missing limbs and in wheelchairs. Others walked with walkers and canes. Some sat stoically on a bench at the edge of the courtyard. The dogs were housed in a large kennel next to the buildings, and trainers could be seen issuing verbal and hand commands to the dogs. The dogs that had completed training and been assigned to a warrior sat next to their warrior, waiting for movement or instruction. Richard could see and sense that the dogs were generally happy. They were not being punished or kept against their will. They were fulfilling their mission as guardians and helpers. When approached by a stranger, the dog looked up at his warrior and waited for a command. When the okay sign was given, the dog rolled over in an appeal for a belly rub, or they jumped up and rested their paws on the visitor and begged for attention. They were happy and playful. When the veteran soldiers stood to walk, the dog's demeanor instantly changed to that of a guide and caregiver.

Richard and Alan met with the community relations director and toured the facility. She explained that from time to time they received a dog that was loving and compatible with the warriors, but could not properly adapt to the training regimen. These dogs, like the others, were generally "rescue dogs" that had no future until they were privately adopted or taken in by K9s for Warriors or a similar organization.

The director turned to Richard and said, "Today is your lucky day, Mr. Farnsworth. Our trainers have moved one of the new dogs to the transition facility, and that dog is ready for adoption. He has been checked out by our veterinarian and his shots are up-to-date. Would you like to see him?"

Richard replied, "Yes, of course. What kind of dog is it?"

She replied, "Duke is an 18-month-old black Labrador retriever. Like most Labs, Duke is as friendly as they come."

They walked across the campus to the holding area where Duke was being temporarily housed. The director was right. Richard bent down to entice the dog to come to him. Duke sprang up from his bed and ran over and leaped on Richard. The dog licked Richard's face and put his paws on his chest. He didn't bark, but made a kind of purring, squeaky sound of delight. It was as though they were old friends catching up after a long absence.

Alan said, "I think we have found a match."

"Yes, this looks like a perfect adoption," the director said. "Let's go get some paperwork done and you three can get out of here."

They completed the forms, and Richard pulled an envelope containing a check for the organization. He knew the required processing fee was $150. His check was for $1,500, and they could find that out later, after he was gone.

The director said, "Mr. Woods told me you were flying back to the Keys. You can purchase a crate at our K9s store. Honestly, you won't need it. Duke may not have the full set of commands down, but when you tell him to 'stay,' he will sit or lie down and not move until you release him. Clip his leash to the passenger seat and he will be fine."

Richard and Alan met Paris in the parking lot at the front of the facility. She had run an errand while they were at the K9s Camp.

Alan opened the front passenger door and said, "Hi, honey, we have a fourth passenger."

Paris jumped out of the Jeep and opened the rear compartment. After Duke had given her his standard sloppy wet greeting, he jumped into the open cargo space and lay down with his legs tucked under his sleek black body.

Richard held up his open hand, palm facing Duke, and said, "Stay," and they were off to the Miami General Aviation airport in Homestead.

Richard thanked Paris and offered her some money for gasoline, which she vehemently declined. He took Duke for a short walk in a grassy area next to the FBO. Though Richard was new to dog ownership, he realized he had no poop bag for removing the dog's excrement from the grass. Fortunately, he found a garbage pail containing an empty plastic grocery produce bag. After a bathroom stop, Alan led Richard and Duke to the hangar where Alan's shiny airplane was waiting on the tarmac in front of the hangar.

Richard stopped 20 yards from the plane and stared. Except for the paint job, it was the same U-6 Beaver model he had flown in during his first tour in Vietnam.

Alan yelled over to Richard, "We can board now. She's all fueled up and ready to go. The ground crew will direct us from here."

He showed Richard the airplane and described the various characteristics of the De Havilland Beaver. Only about 1,650 of them were built. Alan said it was powered by a single 450 hp Pratt & Whitney radial engine. The relatively light, dry weight and high wing design made it capable of using shorter runways for takeoff and landing. Richard had learned this from his flights out of Khe Sanh.

Once they were onboard and had Duke settled in the rear seat, Richard sat in the copilot's seat. Alan explained the operation of the headsets they'd wear during the flight. After takeoff, Alan and Richard could communicate normally with each other.

Alan said, "There is nothing you need to do, except do not touch anything. And keep your feet off the pedals." He handed Richard a check-off sheet. "When I tell you, read each of these lines. When I say 'check,' move to the next line."

He flipped a couple of switches and the plane started coming to life. He pointed to Richard and gave him a thumbs-up.

Richard began reading off the items on the checklist. "Altimeter set."

Alan said, "Check."

"Fuel pump on."

"Check."

They moved through the fuel gauges, radios, and landing gear position. Richard read the remaining 15 lines and Alan responded after each one. They taxied away from the hangar and after holding and waiting for clearance, Alan accelerated down the runway and lifted off. They climbed steadily and, after a left banking turn, the plane continued to climb to an altitude of 8,000 feet.

Richard grew pale and began breathing more rapidly. Perspiration covered his forehead.

Alan reached over and put his hand on Richard's arm. "Hey, pal, are you okay?"

Richard answered, "Yes, yes, I'll be fine."

After they landed at Summerland Key and ran through another checklist, Alan shut down the engines and got up from his seat to open the main door and let down a short set of stairs. Richard was unsteady as he carefully stepped from the plane.

Alan opened the cargo door and called out to Duke, "Come." Duke had been unhooked from his seat and walked slowly to the open cargo door. Alan put out his hands and Duke jumped into his arms.

Alan set Duke on the ground and Richard, who had somewhat recovered, walked over and raised a hand, saying, "Stay."

Alan put his arm on Richard's shoulder. "Hey, man, are you sure you're okay? Small planes take some getting used to."

Richard sighed and said, "No, that's not it. I don't have a fear of flying. The thing is, I flew in the U-6 Beavers in Vietnam. Not as a pilot. I sat in the back with …"—Richard paused and took a breath—"I flew in the back with my men. My men … in body bags." Richard's eyes were moist, and he bit down on his lower lip. He willed himself to continue. "We flew the U-6 Beavers from Khe Sanh to Da Nang. It was only 100 miles, but it felt like a thousand. Those were my guys and I was escorting them to Da Nang so they could be flown home to their devastated families."

Alan said, "Ah, man, I'm so sorry. Paris should be here any moment now. We'll be home in time for some serious cocktails. The guys at the Pub are going to love ol' Duke."

Chapter 39

Good News Bay

March and April came and went, and Richard spent his time working on the house and going out fishing or catching lobsters and stone crabs. Friday night was Karaoke Night at the Pub, and it became a mainstay for social engagement in his neighborhood. Also a regular patron, Duke dutifully escorted Richard home after each last call.

May was a big fishing month in the Florida Keys. The water temperature warmed to 80 degrees and the newly spawned baitfish migrations were moving up and down the oceanside waters. Dolphin, blackfin and yellowfin tuna, and blue marlin joined the party. You could easily catch a hundred mahi dolphin any day you ventured out beyond the barrier reef. Dolphin—the fish, not the air-breathing mammals—were served in restaurants throughout the United States. The economy of Monroe County and the cities of Key Largo, Islamorada, and Marathon depended on recreational fishing. Key West did too, while it enjoyed a significant amount of revenue from tourism.

Mike Gorton was making plans for his annual trip to the lodge at Goodnews Bay, Alaska. Kim planned to join him at the end of the season, to help close down the lodge before the harsh winter months. The salmon fishing in the months of July through September was off-the-charts great. Mike told Richard he could catch seven different species of salmon in any given day. The giant king salmon came upriver to spawn and then died on the return trip to the sea. While they were in the Goodnews River, their size exceeded 50 pounds on a regular basis. By adding giant rainbow trout to the mix, you had a fishing expedition that was a lifetime experience for anglers of all skill levels.

Mike told Richard, "It's a two-day trip to Anchorage. The next day we fly charter flights directly to the Eskimo village of Goodnews and take my metal boats with outboard jet-drives to the lodge. It's a long trip and it's expensive. We charge $3,500 per week at the lodge. That includes the charter flight from Anchorage and your food and beverages. The lodge and the village of Goodnews is on the Eskimo Reservation at Goodnews. Alcohol is not permitted on the reservation. You'll need to bring your own fly rods and waders. We'll provide the flies and you can even learn to tie your own at the lodge. Think about it. I still have some single openings you could help fill."

Richard answered quickly. "Okay, I've thought about it. You just tell me when."

On Sunday, August 1, 1976, Richard dropped off Duke at Kim's house. She loved Duke and had no problem looking after him while Richard joined Mike at the lodge. Richard flew from Miami, Florida, to Denver, Colorado, and on to Anchorage.

The next morning he boarded a Spanish-made 20-passenger Casa C-212 turboprop and flew to Goodnews Bay, Alaska. The airstrip at Goodnews Bay was only 2,800 feet in length, so it serviced only smaller aircraft and only in good weather. The airport building doubled as a general store. While waiting for the ground transportation to the river, Richard watched the locals milling around the store and the airstrip. The population of Goodnews Bay, Alaska, was only about 230 people, living in three square miles. He wondered how they survived with such a small population.

More bears and caribou than people lived in the mountains and valleys around Goodnews Bay. Noticing the backyards of the houses near the airport, Richard could see what looked like short clotheslines. The villagers, he learned, cut their freshly caught salmon filets into strips and soaked them in brine. They hung them up to dry on these lines before putting the fish into an outbuilding which served as a walk-in smoker.

A cargo van transported Richard to the river's edge, where a guide from the lodge met him. He boarded a 20-foot flat-bottomed metal boat with a turned-up square bow. The two-cycle outboard was retrofitted with a jet drive rather than a conventional boat propeller. The boat could plane and run fast in shallow water. The metal hull had the durability to withstand regular bumping and scraping of the rocks on the river bottom. The short trip ended at the Goodnews River Lodge. The setting of 12 elevated lodge cabins on either side of the main lodge building was picturesque. The sleeping quarters were a stone's throw from the cold running river. All day and night you could see large chum salmon rolling and swimming into the current. Being so close to the Arctic Circle meant the sun never set. The daylight dimmed in the evening hours, but never to the point of darkness.

Richard fished with three different guides through the week. They caught silver salmon until his arms hurt. After battling two of the 40-pound king salmon on the first day, Richard was ready for a smaller variety of the prized family of salmon species. He loved flyfishing for the aggressive Dolly Varden trout. Every evening the camp chef prepared fresh salmon dishes in more ways than Richard could have imagined. The food and wine and fellowship in the main dining hall was fabulous.

After two days of incredible fishing, some of the anglers opted for a hike to visit an abandoned gold-mining barge. The hike took about two hours each way and was well worth it. Hiking through the tundra was not without some risks. The two guides accompanying the group carried 12-gauge pump shotguns. They said the guns only fired rubber bullets to scare the grizzly bears away. Richard suspected there was also a load of 00 buckshot in the magazines. The old wooden barge measured about 80 feet in length, and it housed a rusty diesel-engine generator which provided power to the dredge boom. The boom looked like a giant chainsaw. Instead of cutting teeth, it had two dozen heavy, five-gallon steel buckets that moved on a chain down the boom and into the river bottom, scooping out rocks and sand and gold nuggets. When the bucket moved to the underside of the boom, it deposited its contents onto a metal mesh screen inside the barge. The sand and water drained through the mesh and the miners sorted through the remaining contents searching for nuggets that contained gold deposits. After the start of World War II, diesel fuel was rationed and the mining operation was shut down. The man-made river that barge had dug filled in over the years. Now the barge was sitting in a field where the river used to flow.

On the last day of fishing, it was Richard's turn to fish with the owner of the lodge. Mike was super excited to show Richard his favorite spots on the Goodnews River. Richard had caught enough salmon for a lifetime of memories.

He told Richard, "We're going upriver today for the Arctic graylings and giant 30-inch rainbow trout."

Richard was familiar with rainbow trout. They were on many menus in Washington, DC. He did not know they got bigger than the 12-inch fish he had seen on his dinner plate.

Mike was a pro when it came to running the river. He sped along the river into the rushing current. When the water got too shallow on a shoal in the river, he raised the engine and the boat glided noisily across the bed of stones on the river bottom. At the first stop, Richard caught more of his favorite Dolly Varden trout. The fish were accomplished fighters. Most of them were 20 to 24 inches, and Mike said they sometimes caught much larger fish, as big as 30 pounds. Mike stopped the boat at the intersection of the main river and smaller tributary. He directed Richard to cast his fly close to a dead tree branch extending from the riverbank into the water.

"This is where we'll find the Arctic graylings," Mike said. "If you look closely, you can see their silver tails and dorsal fins reflecting the sunlight."

Richard made his first cast. The fly slowly drifted by the branches and his line tightened. Richard yelped, "I've got him. I've got my first grayling." He made a fist with his free hand and pulled it down in a show of victory.

After catching two of the beautiful silvery fish, Mike said, "That's enough. It's time to move upriver for some real action."

They motored for 30 minutes, to the base of a mountain range. The headwaters of the Goodnews River originated in the higher elevations of the mountains and snaked down to the basin through endless fields of freshwater marshes. The fishermen were 100 yards below a small island that split the river into two directions. Mike slowed the boat and turned toward the shoreline, gently driving the bow into the soft pebble and sand riverbank. After securing the boat, they walked toward the island. As they approached the bushy area surrounding the island, an enormous male caribou rustled the thin tree branches and turned his gaze on them. The animal stood six feet tall to his nose, and his antlers were massive and wide. After a couple of grunts and foot stomps, the giant reindeer turned and trotted away.

"That was amazing," Richard said. "I was too stunned to reach for my camera."

Mike said, "That beautiful beast will feed several families this winter, back in Goodnews Bay. We keep a good relationship with the Eskimo villagers by sharing our catch and alerting them when we encounter a caribou herd or a grizzly bear. They'll send a hunting party out to harvest the caribou."

At the split in the river, Mike tied a new fly onto Richard's fly line's leader. It wasn't a fly at all. He was gawking at three inches of furry mouse. It was actually rabbit hair tied into the shape of a mouse. Mike described the method of casting the mouse to the muddy bank above the water's edge and then dragging the mouse into the deep running water below. The large rainbow trout would see the bait and aggressively charge upward from the bottom to devour the mouse.

"Walk upriver to the left and cast to the bank where you see the darker water running along the edge. The trout hold near the bottom, waiting for their next meal. When you see the fish strike the mouse fly, hold the line tight and raise your rod tip firmly upward, but don't jerk it. I'll be waiting here and keeping an eye on the island and the other river branch." Like the guides on the hike to the gold dredge, Mike carried a pump shotgun with a shoulder strap.

Richard did as he was instructed, and he successfully hooked the first trout. It was huge and frantically splashed the surface and dove for the bottom. The line peeled from his reel as the fish ran downriver toward Mike. Mike yelled for Richard to walk from the middle of the river to the shoreline. As he did, the fish also veered toward the shore. Mike dipped his net and scooped up the sizeable trout. After taking a few photographs, Mike gently released the 30-inch rainbow trout into the running current.

Richard could only say, "Mike, that was amazing. Simply amazing."

They repeated the process on the other branch of the river and landed another equally amazing trout.

Mike said, "You stay here, Richard, and I'll go get the boat. You can head toward the ledge where you caught the first trout. You may get lucky again."

Walking back toward the boat, Mike was about 30 yards from where Richard was standing in the river, when he heard it—a grunt followed by an exhaled snort. Mike knew it wasn't a caribou. He thought, *Holy crap, holy crap!* He had to get Richard's attention without causing him to panic and run. Mike heard it a second time: grunt, snort. The grizzly was 40 feet from Richard and concealed in the heavy brush at the center of the island. Mike waved his arms over his head in a cautionary signaling pattern. He whistled as loudly as he could. Richard turned toward Mike, and Mike indicated with arm movements that Richard should come to him. Mike started walking toward Richard and the bear.

The sound of the rushing water would drown out normal speech, so Mike was going to have to yell to his friend. "Come to me. Do not run!"

The bear made more noises, and this time Richard heard it, too. He saw Mike holding the shotgun across his chest with both hands. Knowing what that meant, he walked steadily toward Mike and the boat. Mike had the boat pointed downriver and was ready to start the engine as soon as Richard was within reach of the boat. Richard got the message and sprinted the last 10 yards and fell into the boat. His bottom was on the floor of the boat and his legs were sticking up at an awkward angle. Mike started the engine and gunned it. Looking back, he could see the bear running along the bank of the river toward them. Though bears could run fast, this time the jet boat won the race.

On the trip downriver toward the lodge, they rounded a wide bend in the river that passed by a shoal jutting into the water. Standing on the shoal was a 1,500-pound grizzly with its front paws resting on and guarding a dead 600-pound bear. Richard was thinking it could have been him on that shoal. Despite the moisture from his feet and the water leaking into his waders, he wasn't sure, but he may have urinated in his long johns.

The trip home to Big Pine was the reverse of each leg he had traveled getting to Goodnews Bay. He had plenty of time to reflect on the incredible experience Mike Gorton had shared with him. It was the trip of a lifetime … even though he expected to do it again. Maybe next year.

Chapter 40

Bay Watch

After Richard got to his car and headed south on US 1, he had a sinking feeling. He recognized the feeling. It was like the emotion soldiers experienced after a firefight or bombardment from enemy mortar fire. The body goes through some tumultuous chemical and enzyme changes after a sustained surge of adrenaline. He knew firsthand it could lead to a period of debilitating depression. He thought, *This is ridiculous. I've been on a fishing trip in Alaska, not a war zone.* In the back of his mind, he could still see Alan Wood's De Havilland plane. He couldn't get rid of the vision of body bags stacked in the cargo hold of the U-6 Beavers in Vietnam. He told himself, "Put it down, soldier. There is no place for PTS bullshit here."

He arrived at Big Pine at noon and drove straight to Kim's house to pick up Duke. They were not there. He was puzzled, yet was confident in Kim's ability to take good care of Duke. Instead of going home and unpacking, he drove to the Pub for a burger and a beer. It was nearly empty. Most of the guys were out fishing or lobstering. He'd catch up with them soon enough. Mike had remained in Alaska and would not return until the end of September.

Richard was tired from flying all night. He went to Bay Watch to take a nap. At 4:00 p.m. he heard a knock at the door. It was Kim. She had a worried look on her face.

He stepped out onto the porch, and Kim took his hand and said, "Please don't be angry with me. I had to take Duke to the vet in Miami."

Before she could elaborate, Richard interrupted her. "Is he okay? What happened?"

"We were outside, and Duke was playing with the neighborhood kids, who were fishing from the bulkhead. One of them caught a small pinfish, and Duke got excited and tried to eat it. He partially swallowed it. With some effort, we got his mouth open, and I could see the tail deep in his throat. I tried to pull it out carefully, but it was stuck. He was gagging and the sharp dorsal fins were poking at his throat. It wouldn't budge. The fishhook was still in the fish's mouth, and I think it penetrated Duke's throat. I took him to the emergency veterinary clinic in South Dade."

Richard hugged Kim, saying, "It's okay. I'm sure he'll be fine."

She took a deep breath and said, "They sedated him and got the fish and hook out. The vet said she'd keep him overnight and didn't expect any complications. You can pick him up in the morning."

Richard hugged her again. "Kim, thank you. I'm sorry you had to deal with this."

She replied, "I don't mind. I'm just glad he's going to be okay."

The next morning, Richard had an early breakfast at the Florida Keys Café in Big Pine and drove to the Miami Veterinary Specialists hospital in South Miami. He checked in and waited to see the veterinarian who was treating Duke. After 20 minutes had passed, an attractive woman came out and walked over to where Richard was sitting.

He stood, and she put out a hand and said, "Hi, I'm Dr. Genevieve Turner."

"Richard Farnsworth. Thank you for taking care of my dog."

She said, "Come on back. We can talk in my office while the paperwork is being completed."

After checking out, Richard put Duke's collar on and attached a heavy rope leash. While walking down the corridor toward the lobby exit, Richard heard a familiar voice. A woman was alternately speaking Spanish and English. She was interpreting what the veterinarian was saying and repeating it in Spanish. He stopped to listen.

The vet said, "Your puppy has a small growth in her stomach."

The woman repeated this in Spanish: *"Tu cachorro tiene un perqueno creciminto en el estomago."*

Richard recognized that voice. It was Stacie Shatner's voice. He couldn't move.

Another voice said, *"No puedo pagar procedimientos costosos."*—followed by Stacie translating to the doctor, "My friend cannot pay for these procedures."

Richard did not disturb the women in the treatment room. He honestly did not know what he was going to say to Stacie. He thought, *What is she doing in Miami?* Her family lived in Coral Gables. She was supposed to be in California. He couldn't think straight.

He kept walking. With an encouraging "Duke, come. Come, boy," they left the hospital. He lifted Duke into the front seat and connected his collar to a strap in the dog's special car seat. Richard pulled out of the parking lot for the drive home to Big Pine Key. *What is wrong with me? I'm an idiot,* he thought. He considered turning around and going back. He told himself, "No. I have screwed with her life too much already. I do not deserve Stacie Shatner."

As he approached the on ramp to Interstate 826, he went straight and made a U-turn, heading to the animal hospital. He parked the car, lowered a rear window a couple inches, and said, "Duke, stay."

Richard strode past the reception desk and to the double doors leading to the treatment rooms. Ignoring the receptionist calling out to him, he entered the corridor and found the room where he had heard Stacie talking to the doctor. She wasn't there. He said to himself, "Dammit, dammit to hell." He heard someone behind him coming out of the restroom.

"Richard. Is that you?"

He turned to face her.

Stacie said, "Oh my God, it's really you. What in the world are you doing here?"

Stacie wrapped her arms around Richard and held him tight for a full 30 seconds. "Richard, I thought I would never see you again. Oh my God, I have missed you." She let go of him and stepped slightly back. In a more serious tone she asked, "What are you doing here? I heard you resigned. I figured you were living it up in Boston."

Richard said, "I was here with my dog. He swallowed a fishhook. He's outside. I need to get back to him. Stacie, I overheard you talking to the doctor and interpreting for your friend. I left, but thought better of it and came back."

She replied, "Yes, I'm here with a good friend from Coral Gables. Actually, she's a housekeeper for a friend in the Gables. I'm helping her out with her little Yorkie." Stacie moved to the attendant's counter and grabbed a piece of paper and a pen. She turned it over and wrote down her address and phone number. "Here. You'd better call me. I have a thousand questions. I have to get back to Margaurite and the doctor. They went to the annex for an X-ray. Richard, call me. Where are you staying? Hotel?"

Richard answered, "I'm in a house in Big Pine Key. It's a long story."

Stacie appeared shocked. "Okay, make that two thousand questions." She turned to walk away and looked back. "Call me, dammit. I mean it!"

That night he had dinner at the Pub and drank enough beer to float a small boat. He usually preferred wine, but the Pub's idea of fine wine came in a carton.

Back home, Richard sat on the porch, observing the stars. He thought about the nights in Vietnam, at Khe Sanh Combat Base. He thought about being wounded and the guys at Walter Reed. Some of them would never come home. Some of them would never be normal again. He didn't recall much about being wounded. Between the shock and the morphine the medics gave him, he was out of it quickly. His bad memories were about the men he lost in combat. At first he told himself the war made sense, but after Tet and into his second tour, he could not find an acceptable balance between the dead men on both sides and the United States' role in helping the South Vietnamese defend against being taken over by North Vietnam. Duke rested his head on Richard's knee. Dogs had a sixth sense. They could tell when their master was not well. Duke had these penetrating eyes that made you think he was tuned in to exactly what was going on. "Come on, boy, let's go for a walk."

In the dark they strolled up Key Pine Boulevard, toward US 1. It was mid-August and the hottest time of year in the Keys. Richard thought, *It's ten o'clock at night and I'm sweating like a racehorse.* After Duke had done his business, they returned to the house. He was drunk, and thinking, *I'm not calling Stacie tonight. Tomorrow, definitely tomorrow.*

Things were about to change for Richard. He wasn't smiling, yet he knew things were going to get better. At least he hoped that was true. He slept off and on that night. When the booze wore off, he got an adrenaline rush and could not fall asleep. It was too late to take a sleeping pill. And he didn't like the grogginess the next day as the drugs wore off. He looked at his watch: 0400 hours. In the army he'd fall in for PT at 0500. Not today. He had to figure out his life and where he was going to take it. He closed his eyes. "Stacie, Stacie, I'm coming for you." He smiled for the first time in days.

Chapter 41

Falling in Love Again

Stacie and Richard made plans for a date night. Richard was going to drive to Miami and take Stacie to Joe's Stone Crab restaurant. Since Richard had never been there and it was her idea, it was more like Stacie taking Richard. Stacie tutored Richard on the covert procedures for getting a table. Joe's was always sold out, with a waiting list. She told him to give the valet $20 and ask the maître d' if he knew who killed Jimmy Hoffa.

Richard found the maître d' and extended the hand which contained the second 20-dollar bill.

The maître d' asked, "Do you have a reservation?"

Richard replied, "Yes, we do. It's Richard Farnsworth." He squeezed the maître d's hand and added, "With a dash."

The tuxedoed man replied, "Yes, of course, Mr. Farnsworth. If you would be so kind as to wait over there, the hostess will seat you right away."

During dinner, Richard and Stacie talked about their time at Fort Devens. He gave Stacie a summary of everything that had happened and how he came to his decision to resign his commission and leave the army. She did the same. After Stacie's ordeal in Turkey, she realized that military intelligence and world travel were not for her. Her life had been much simpler when growing up in South Florida. Her proficiency in foreign languages was the only reason she had been recruited by the Army Security Agency. Life at Devens was pretty good and she had enjoyed being in California. Not because of the work. California weather and the proximity to Santa Barbara, Pebble Beach, and Carmel made life on the Central Coast interesting. She clearly assessed it would have been more desirable if she had been there as a civilian.

Stacie was direct, and asked Richard, "What about your girl back in Boston? I heard from my friends that you two were a serious item."

Before Richard could respond, she went on to say, "I guess it's really none of my business. Still, I need to know where you and I stand."

Richard took her hand in his and looked into her eyes. "Stacie, a lot has happened so quickly in my life this year, and yours. You are the closest thing I have to a relationship with anyone. Both of my parents have passed away. Alyson, the general's daughter, is entrenched in a wealthy lifestyle that just isn't, as they say in Boston, my cup of tea."

He told Stacie about his move to the Keys and the little house on Big Pine Key. "You said you were living at your parents' house," he said. "How is that working out?"

She replied, "It's tolerable. They love having me there, but I need to get a place of my own. Hell, for that matter, I need a job."

"What do you want to do?" Richard asked.

"I could try the State Department. They always need interpreters. That's not much different from my military assignments. I could teach language courses at the University of Miami or Florida International University. The pay wouldn't be so hot. The benefits are very good, though. What about you, Major Farnsworth? What kind of big-shot job do you have?"

Richard chuckled. "I'm an unemployed radio man. I guess I could be a private eye and track down cheating spouses."

Stacie laughed. "No, really. What are you doing?"

"The unemployed part is true," Richard said. "I'm taking my time and getting settled into life in the Lower Keys. I made some good friends there, and they seem to have life pretty well figured out. You should come back with me and see for yourself."

This time Stacie took Richard's hand in hers and said, "If that is a serious invitation, soldier, the answer is yes."

Their meal was as delicious as Richard had ever tasted. He had eaten some stone crabs at the Pub in Big Pine. These were better. The waiter explained that they came from the restaurant's own traps in the gulf waters off the southwest coast of Florida. The coleslaw and collard greens were exceptionally tasty. Richard had impressed Stacie with his knowledge of wines when he ordered a Montrachet from the Côte de Beaune region of Burgundy. He was about to order a second bottle.

Stacie abruptly said, "No. I have big plans for dessert, but not here."

Following Stacie's earlier recommendation, Richard was booked into an oceanfront room at the Fontainebleau Hotel. They joined the guest list with notable past guests which included John F. Kennedy and the Beatles.

Stacie and Richard drove north on the coastal highway to the hotel. He turned the car over to the valet, and they went upstairs to Richard's room.

Entering the room, Stacie spread her arms out, taking in the room and the ocean view. "Richard, this is amazing. The army must have given you a pretty good separation package."

"Yeah, right," he said. "I got the same thing you did. A final monthly check, some cash for accrued leave time, and a free airline ticket home. Since I didn't have a home, I picked Miami."

The coffee table held a complimentary fruit tray and a bottle of champagne chilling in an ice bucket. He was thinking this was awkward for both of them and maybe a glass of champagne would help. He gently popped open the bottle and poured them each a glass.

Stacie dropped a fresh strawberry in hers and showed Richard the glass. "See, it makes more bubbles."

Richard fumbled with a portable cassette player and managed to get it to play Patsy Cline's greatest hits. While not his favorite track, it helped smooth out the sterility of the room.

Stacie opened the glass doors to the balcony and the sheer white draperies billowed into the room. She walked out onto the balcony and turned around. "Join me, Richard. It's so nice out here."

They embraced on the balcony and kissed lightly at first, and then the passion escalated, and they kissed more deeply.

When they paused, Stacie said, "I missed you so much. Don't leave me again. Please."

Richard kissed her, held her close, and whispered, "I'm here now. I'm not going anywhere."

They drank most of the champagne and turned the bed down. Stacie went to the bathroom and came out in one of the hotel's satin-lined terrycloth bathrobes. Richard was standing next to the bed with only his trousers on. She stepped toward him and let the robe drop to the floor.

Richard instantly reminded himself she was one of the most beautiful women he had ever seen. He thought, *I've been such a fool. Why did I ever let her go?*

Stacie loosened Richard's belt and pushed his pants toward the floor. He stepped out of them and pulled his boxer shorts off. The couple fell onto the king-size bed and held each other close. Richard was fully aroused and positioned himself on his side, facing Stacie. He kissed her warm mounds of flesh.

When he put his mouth on her nipples, she took in an audible breath. There was more to their relationship than pure physical attraction. It had been that way from the beginning, at Fort Devens. They connected in the way soulmates do when their minds meshed in an unbreakable bond. He guided Stacie onto her back and slipped into her. She groaned with pleasure. He kissed her, and their bodies moved synchronously in the throes of passion. Patsy Cline played softly in the background, singing "Sweet Dreams of You." They made love two more times before falling asleep in each other's arms.

The next morning, Richard had coffee delivered to the room. They sat on the balcony and watched the terns and seagulls dancing on the beach. The soft sounds of the waves breaking on the sand was the best way to wake up and face the day. They enjoyed a full hour of the serene setting before the brightness of the sun forced them inside to shower and dress for the day.

Stacie said, "I'm such a dope. I don't have any clothes except for the skirt and blouse I wore last night."

Fortunately, there were some travel-style toiletries in the bathroom.

Richard said, "The gift shop downstairs has some casual beachwear. I can run down and get you something fresh to wear."

"That would be great," she replied. "And some flip-flops or cheap sandals too."

After they were dressed, Stacie said, "I have to go home from here. How do you feel about meeting my mom and stepdad?"

"Oh boy," Richard replied. "I guessed that was coming."

She said, "Don't worry, Richard. They already know what a scoundrel you are. Besides, they're really just a couple of aging beatniks. They get the seventies lifestyle and aren't hung up on the same social mores a lot of folks adhere to."

Richard asked, "So, Tom is your stepfather?"

"Tom is my real-life dad. I never really knew much about my biological father. He left when I was a toddler. Tom adopted me right after they got hitched. I think you'll like them. Pick up a bottle of that special Barbados rum you like, as a gift, and he will love you."

Richard responded, "Okay. And afterward, you come to the Keys with me for the weekend. Okay?"

"You got it, soldier. I want to see this little love shack you've been talking about."

Chapter 42

Stacie's Parents

Stacie and Richard drove to Coral Gables to meet Stacie's parents and for Stacie to pack for a weekend in Big Pine Key. Stacie's stepfather, Tom Shatner, was an interesting fellow. He had served on a submarine in World War II. His navy memorabilia was proudly displayed in his home, along with posters of every band he liked in the fifties. Bill Haley and the Comets, Elvis Presley, and the Kingston Trio adorned the walls throughout their modest Campina Court home, two blocks off West Flagler Street. Stacie's mother was a 70-year-old hippie who danced barefoot through the house in a tie-dyed muumuu.

Tom told Richard he'd bought the house in 1960, for $49,000. Today it was worth more than $350,000. He said he might have to sell it if the taxes kept going up.

Richard asked, "What did you do after the war, Mr. Shatner?"

Shatner said, "Please call me Tom. I stayed in the navy for another hitch and went to college on the G.I. Bill. I was a pharmacist for 20 years. I had a small store in Homestead and sold it in 1972." He asked, "What are your plans, Richard?

Stacie tells me you resigned your commission. Man, if I had your rank, I would have stayed in for life."

Richard responded, "I don't know, Mr. Shatner—sorry, Tom. I'm 32 years old and I feel like there is something more for me than what I was doing. A lot of things changed when the Vietnam War ended."

Tom said, "Yeah, my daughter sings the same song. You kids follow your heart. You're young and healthy and educated. You'll find your place. Whatever you do, choose something that makes you happy. Both of you."

Stacie's mother, Pam, said to everyone, "Let's eat. I made some fresh conch salad."

After lunch, Stacie came out of her bedroom carrying a duffle bag and a dry-cleaning sleeve with a couple of outfits for evening wear. She called out, "Okay, Major Farnsworth, I'm ready for some action. Let's get to it. I want to see the Keys while the sun is still shining."

"Don't worry," Richard replied. "It's Sunday and all the traffic will be headed north."

Stacie's mom hugged them.

Richard thought, *I bet ol' Mom was quite a looker in her prime.* He could see where Stacie got her looks and her spunky attitude.

Giving Richard a full-on hug, Pam said, "Be kind to my little girl."

It wasn't lost on Richard that Stacie's well-endowed mom wasn't wearing a bra under her muumuu. They said their goodbyes and Tom thanked Richard for the Mount Gay Barbados Rum.

Chapter 43

Home, Sweet Home

ig Pine Key was a straight shot down US 1. The 100-mile drive would take about 2 hours and 45 minutes. As Richard predicted, the Sunday afternoon traffic was heavy in the northbound lanes and wide open heading south. They rolled in to Big Pine Key at 4:30 p.m. He stopped at the driveway to Mike Gorton's house. Kim saw him pull in and came out with Duke in tow. Richard and Stacie stepped out of the car.

"Hi, Richard, welcome home. As you can see, Duke is ready to go."

Duke barked and jumped up on Richard, tail wagging and tongue trying to reach Richard's face.

Richard said, "Easy, boy. I'm home."

Stacie knelt down, and Duke came over and let her hold his head in her hands. Duke raised a paw and put it on her knee. They were fast friends. She jumped up and put out her hand. "Hi, I'm Stacie."

Kim ignored the hand and wrapped her arms around Stacie. "I'm so glad to meet you. Richard has been keeping you a secret."

Duke wiggled past the open car door and jumped into the back seat.

Kim said, "Richard, I thought you might be a bit tired from your trip, so I made dinner for the three of us. I hope that's all right. It's paella with fresh lobster, your favorite. There's no rush. It's all made. I only have to warm it up in the oven. You bring the wine."

Richard unlocked the front door to Bay Watch and pushed the door open. "Make yourself at home, Stacie. The bathroom is to the left. I'll unload the car."

Duke squeezed by Stacie and headed straight for the kitchen.

Richard said, "Sorry about that. It's past time for his dinner."

From the living room, Richard watched Stacie stand at the rear porch, staring out at the water. He left her there and went to the kitchen to feed Duke. He made two rum and cola cocktails and joined Stacie on the porch.

Stacie smiled as she took the glass. "Thank you. That's perfect. Richard, how in the world did you find this place? It's paradise. I am never leaving."

He raised his glass, saying, "Cheers. I'm okay with that plan."

They clinked glasses.

"Stacie, we're very informal here on Big Pine. You can wear whatever you want, but don't make it too fancy. This is a shorts and jeans kind of place. You may want a long-sleeved top. The no-see-ums are bad this time of year."

That evening in Kim's living room, Richard told Stacie and Kim about his amazing trip to the Goodnews River Lodge.

Kim graciously listened as though she was hearing it for the first time. Then she said, "Next year I'll join you, and you can bring Stacie."

Richard was thinking that he had been living his life on a day-to-day and week-to-week basis for so long, the idea of planning something a year ahead was foreign to him.

Kim took a sip of her wine and said to him, "You need to help Mike with the wine selections for the lodge. You obviously have a more sophisticated taste in fine wines."

"He was a Schmidt's beer connoisseur when I was with him at Fort Devens," Stacie said. "Duty in DC seems to have given him a bit more polish."

Richard said, "Thank you, Kim. The meal was absolutely wonderful."

Stacie added her accolades.

"So," Kim said, "are you two lovebirds going to the Pub tonight?"

Richard said, "No, absolutely not. After one night in Miami, I need some rest."

***

At Bay Watch, Richard and Stacie sat on the porch, gazing at the water and the mangroves. It was a moonless night and the clouds hid the usual canvas of stars.

Stacie said, "I can see why you like it here. It's so peaceful."

"Hopefully not too laid-back for you," Richard said. "When I take you out on the water, you'll see another dimension to life in the Keys. Tomorrow morning we can go by boat to the Conch Hut Café and have breakfast. I'll give you a tour of the oceanside reefs and the amazing white sand flats on the bay."

In bed that night, Richard was overcome with emotion. His troubled mind was hard at work. Nevertheless, his feelings—amplified by the wine—and having Stacie Shatner lying there next to him helped put everything in the past few years behind him. He felt like an immense blanket of pressure had been removed. He could breathe.

Stacie sensed what he was feeling and made a comforting effort to make him feel at ease. She held him tightly to her body and kissed him in a way that conveyed the intensity of the love she felt for him. Without speaking, she pushed Richard onto his back and straddled him. She put her hands on his shoulders and rubbed her body against his until he was fully erect. He arched his hips, and she guided him into her luscious womanhood. She slowly rose up and down and her large breasts danced in Richard's face. He was taken to a place that only the most fortunate of men ever go. One act of love simply connected to the next until they were both physically and mentally spent.

The next morning, Richard was up and dressed before sunrise. He made coffee and mashed fresh avocados into a topping for toasted English muffins. One of his neighbors had a landscape maintenance company that worked for wealthy homeowners up and down the Keys. The vacation homes were unoccupied for months at a time in the summer. Instead of allowing the produce to rot in the trees, the landscape workers picked the ripened fruit and avocados. His neighbor brought the harvest back to Big Pine Key. In the evenings after work, he put out orchard-size baskets of avocados and mangos at the end of his driveway, to share with his neighbors in Big Pine.

An hour later, Stacie was awake and standing in the doorway to the kitchen. She said, "I smell coffee. Oh, I'm sorry. I must look a mess—and in men's pajamas. I hope you don't mind."

Richard gave her an admiring look, thinking, *How did I get so lucky?* He replied, *"Todo lo mio es tuto, mi hermosa mujer."* ("What's mine is yours, my beautiful girl.")

She was astonished. "So you do know some Spanish. *Gracias, amable señor."* ("Thank you, kind sir.")

Richard responded, "You're correct. I know a little, as in very little Spanish. I'm trying to learn more. It's a common second language in the Keys."

Stacie laughed and said, "Richard, did you forget I am from Miami?"

Later that morning, Richard took Stacie for a boat tour of the Lower Keys. They snaked their way through the mangrove canals between the beautiful bayside flats to the endless expanse of the Atlantic oceanside. They ran the boat toward Key West and stopped at the Little Munson Island Resort. The tiny island was accessible only by water and had a dozen thatched huts for overnight guests. A fortunate few knew the island enclave existed. The reception hut displayed a portrait of their most famous and frequent guest, President Harry S. Truman. The owner did not advertise for or allow public access. Richard had access because Mike Gorton had taken him there on his tour of the Lower Keys.

Stacie returned to Miami and worked toward settling her affairs there. She helped her parents sell their house and move to an assisted living compound with like-minded folks who enjoyed their remaining days with frivolity, rum, and an occasional cannabis bong party. They were happy to make the move. With the money from the sale of their home, they could live out their days in peace and be free of the taxes her dad always complained about.

Every weekend through August and into September, Stacie visited Richard in Big Pine. Since she was officially homeless, Richard pressed her to come live with him full-time. He had to tell her about his steady income from the money he had inherited from his father. It was truly enough for both of them to live on for the rest of their lives.

They realized that as relaxing and enjoyable as the laid-back Keys lifestyle was, it wasn't going to endlessly satisfy their need for travel and adventure. Fortunately, they were still young. The era of one's "thirties being middle-aged" had passed long ago.

Chapter 44

The Holidays, 1976

Richard had no family to travel to for the Thanksgiving holidays. His family consisted of the Gortons, Duke, a few other neighbors, and a manatee named Oleg. Lobsters and conch took the place of stuffed turkey for the holiday. Most of the residents of Big Pine Key celebrated Thanksgiving Day at the No Name Pub. Well into this Thanksgiving drink-a-thon, the locals decided it was "time for Big Pine and Key West to secede from the United States and declare the region to be forever and from this day forward known as the micronation of the Conch Republic."

The Christmas holidays in Key West were as festive as Richard and Stacie had ever experienced. The parades of exotic costumes and body-painted nudes created a surreal lifestyle that would be hard to explain to people living outside of this cultural island microcosm. Days turned into weeks and months on Big Pine Key. After the New Year, the festive lifestyle in the Lower Keys slowed to a doldrum state of quiet solitude.

Stacie had talked Richard into subscribing to the *New York Times* newspaper. The news was several days old by the time they received the paper deliveries, if they came at all.

While enjoying her morning coffee, Stacie asked Richard, "What's in the *Times* today? Read it to me, please."

Richard rustled the pages and began reading: "James Earl Carter Jr. is sworn in as the 39th president of the United States. Jimmy Carter was born in 1924 in Plains, Georgia. His father was a farmer and his mother was a nurse."

"He sounds like a hick to me," Stacie said.

Richard skimmed the article. "Not so fast! President Carter was educated at the Georgia Institute of Technology and received his degree from the United States Naval Academy. You will be further comforted to know that this hick was also a nuclear submariner and served as an officer in the Atlantic and Pacific fleets."

"Okay," she said. "He'll do for now. What else have you got for me?"

"The Soviet Union has successfully launched Soyuz 24 and docked in space with the Salyut 5 space station." Richard added, "Stacie, except for our new Space Shuttle program, the Russians seem to be staying one step ahead of us. ... Whoa, get this. The Russians are blaming the Armenians for three bombs that exploded in Moscow. Seven government officials were killed in the blasts. Sounds like an inside job to me."

Stacie said, "You know, it's so sad. Not just that people are killed. It's sad that 4,000 miles away, we read about the deaths and simply move on with our lives like it was somehow normal."

Richard did not reply, except to say, "Okay, last article. Our North Vietnamese friends want more war and have started another one with Cambodia."

"That's horrible!" she said. "I hope we stay the hell out of it. Is anything in there about the plane crash in Cuba last week? Everyone here is talking about it."

Richard skimmed the second-page headlines. "Here it is. Aeroflot's Ilyushin IL-62 airplane crashed in Havana, killing 69 people."

"Aeroflot!" she exclaimed. "That's a Russian airline. Do you think we had anything to do with it?"

"It would not surprise me. The CIA has been entrenched in Cuba since the Cuban Missile Crisis in '62."

They were well aware of the threat the Soviet Union posed to Europe and the United States. A war with the Russians was not out of the question, and they knew it could quickly lead to a worldwide nuclear disaster.

Richard stood up and said, "I've ruined your life enough for one day. I'm going for a run, and then you and I are going to the A&B Lobster House for lunch."

***

The water in the Keys was chilly in February and March. Boating was shut down for a while. Richard and Stacie were bored. They began making plans to visit Stacie's parents in Miami and look up some of Stacie's old friends.

The television news talked a lot about President Carter and life in the state of Georgia. It got Richard and Stacie thinking about extending their Miami trip and driving up to Savannah to see some of the historic sites along the Georgia coastline. And maybe stop in Florida's Ancient City of St. Augustine along the way.

It was Friday, April 1, 1977, April Fool's Day. Richard and Stacie were packing the car for the drive to Miami. A black sedan pulled up to their driveway and parked on the street. A woman in a dark-gray business suit and a muscular Black guy wearing a narrow-lapeled blue suit a size too small got out of the car and walked up the driveway. Richard immediately recognized the woman. It was Anna Valent, from the DOD Secretary's office.

She walked briskly up to Richard and stuck out a hand. "Good morning, Major Farnsworth. It is good to see you. I'm glad we were able to find you. This is my associate from the agency, Mr. Clark Burton."

Richard surmised this guy was a CIA shooter, not a desk jockey.

Ms. Valent said, "We were hoping we could talk with you in private about an important matter of national security."

Hesitantly, Richard said, "Okay." He directed them to the front door, and Stacie came out as they approached.

After Richard's introductions, Stacie said, "I'm going to run up to the market and buy some things for our trip. It's very nice to meet you both. I'll take my car." And she left.

Richard led his visitors to the chairs on the back porch of Bay Watch. He offered drinks, which they declined.

Ms. Valent said, "Major, I'll get right to the point."

Richard stopped her and said, "Ms. Valent, to be clear, you do know I'm no longer in the army, right?"

She responded, "Yes, I am aware that you resigned your commission. I am also sure you are aware that your Inactive Reserve status allows the Department of the Army to recall you to active duty in times of war and national emergencies. Which is precisely why we are here. We have a serious problem with the Iranian Ayatollah Sayyed Khomeini. The lives of seven American CIA operatives are at stake, and we need your help to locate and rescue them before things escalate to a declaration of war with Iran."

End of Book 1

US Army Terms

AIT: advanced individual training

ARVN: Army of the Republic of Vietnam

ASAFS: Army Security Agency field station

BAH: Basic Allowance for Housing

BAS: Basic Allowance for Subsistence

BISN: Bureau of International Security and Nonproliferation

BOQ: bachelor officers' quarters

CENTCOM: Central Command

CGSC: Command and General Staff College

CGSS: Command and General Staff School

CIA: Central Intelligence Agency

CID: Criminal Investigation Department

CO: commanding officer

COMINT: communications intelligence

COMNET: communications network

CWO: chief warrant officer

DLI: Defense Language Institute

DOD: Department of Defense

ELINT: electronic intelligence

EOB: electronic order of battle

EW/SIGINT IMC: electronic warfare signals intelligence using international Morse code

FBO: fixed-base operator; an organization granted the right by an airport to operate at the airport and provide aeronautical services such as fueling, hangaring, tie-down and parking, aircraft rental, aircraft maintenance, flight instruction, and similar services.

hooah: a battle cry used by members of the United States Army

HUMINT: human intelligence

ILE: Intermediate Level Education

IMC: international Morse code

INS: inertial navigation system

INSCOM: US Army Intelligence and Security Command

Ka-Bar: 12-inch combat knife

KSCB: Khe Sanh Combat Base

LANDCOM: Land Command

MACV: Military Assistance Command, Vietnam

MACV-SOG: Military Assistance Command, Vietnam, Studies and Observations Group

MASINT: a measurement and signature intelligence system

MICC: US Army Mission and Installation Contracting Command (MICC-Fort Belvoir)

MMAS: Master of Military Art and Science degree

MOS: military occupational specialty

NSSC: Natick Soldier Systems Center

NCO: noncommissioned officer

NSA: National Security Agency

NSSC: Natick Soldier Systems Center

OIC: Officer-in-Charge

OMPF: official military personnel files

PAVN: People's Army of Vietnam; officially the Vietnam People's Army (VPA)

PSYOPs: Psychological Operations

PX: post exchange

RDF: Rapid Deployment Force

RRU: Radio Research Unit

SAM: surface-to-air missile

SDAP: Special Duty Assignment Pay

SDS: Socialist German Student Union (*Sozialistische Deutsche Studentenbund*)

Semper Vigilis: Vigilant Always

SF: Special Forces

SFC: sergeant first class

SIGINT: signals intelligence

SOAR: Special Operations Aviation Regiment

SOCNORTH: Special Operations Command North

SOCOM: Special Operations Command

TIG: time-in-grade

TOT: time-over-target

TRR: Test Readiness Review

TUSLOG (troops): Turkish US Logistics Group

USACC: United States Army Chaplain Corps

USARCENT: US Army Central Command

USASA: United States Army Security Agency

USEUCOM: US European Army Command

VC: Viet Cong

WAC: Women's Army Corps

XO: executive officer